What Lies Within

S.D. Tooley

Full Moon Publishing

Library of Congress Catalog Number: 2010921148

ISBN 978-0-9820352-3-8

Published March 2010

Printed in the United States of America

Logo Design by Lesley Staples

Full Moon Publishing LLC
P.O. Box 408
Schererville, IN 46375

www.fullmoonpub.com

PRAISE FOR THE SAM CASEY SERIES

When the Dead Speak

"A promising first mystery of particular interest to readers of Native American mysteries."
— *Booklist*

"…an action-packed mystery that will garner much attention from fans who enjoy a police procedural with a twist."
— *Midwest Book Review*

"For those readers with an interest in the religion of Native Americans and specifically the Sioux, they will find tantalizing hints of these practices within the pages of When the Dead Speak. It looks like Tooley has a winner on her first novel and I look forward to her next, Nothing Else Matters."
— Leslie Doran, *Mystery News*

Nothing Else Matters

"Entertaining reading in what looks to be a solid series."
— *Booklist*

"The author, who spent six years as a casino dealer, effectively blends Native American lore with the world of riverboat gambling."
— *Publishers Weekly*

Restless Spirit

"An exciting mix of police procedure, spiritual 'intuition,' creeping suspense, and page-turning narrative."
— *Library Journal*

"Sam Casey is amazing—a beautifully described and magically interesting character…the plot, characters and pacing are all excellent."
— 4 Star Review, *Romantic Times*

Echoes from the Grave

"Author S. D. Tooley delivers this fourth installment in the exciting Sam Casey series with suavity and grace in a writing style which will rivet the reader to the roller-coaster plotting."
— *EuroReviews*

Also by S.D. Tooley

Sam Casey Series

Echoes from the Grave

Restless Spirit

Nothing Else Matters

When the Dead Speak

Remy and Roadkill Series

The Skull

Written as Lee Driver

Chase Dagger Series

Chasing Ghosts

The Unseen

Full Moon-Bloody Moon

The Good Die Twice

Short Stories

Sara Morningsky, *Mystery in Mind Anthology*

The Thirteenth Hole, *Mystery in Mind Anthology*

Solving Life's Riddle, Amazon Shorts

1

Unincorporated areas were like worts and scars, hard to ignore and impossible to hide. They clung to the outer edges of developed towns trying their best to remain hidden, but like bratty kids they had a tendency to draw attention to themselves. Some people liked to put out a shingle or back up a doublewide onto a chunk of land and call it their own, thankful they were avoiding the taxes and other fees associated with belonging to a real city. And sometimes these obscure chunks of landscape attracted the wrong people.

On the outskirts of such a section of land in Chasen Heights, Illinois, a man maneuvered his pick-up truck onto the shoulder of a gravel road. He kept the headlights off as he used the moon's meager light to keep from steering into a ditch. He put the gear in park and climbed out of the truck. Young trees sprouted next to its larger parents. Overgrown brush crowded the ditch and made the perfect hiding place.

He spent several minutes standing in front of the truck watching and listening. The warm earth collided with cool air producing an eerie mist which rose up like steam from a hot spring. Branches moved overhead while something stirred in the brush. Nature was fighting for a front row seat to whatever the visitor had brought her. His eyes slowly skimmed the shadows looking for human movements. A crunch of dried leaves brought his head around. Something small had just scurried across the road behind his truck.

Satisfied he was alone, he opened the back seat door and pulled on a set of legs as pale and thin as the moon overhead. All she had wanted in exchange for her silence was a ride to a large Amish flea market in Indiana. Just one time, she had promised. Right, he thought. Nosy bitch. And how many people had she already told about the disguise he wore? Who else might be suspicious of his true identity?

He dragged her toward the drainage ditch and rolled her in. The mist swallowed her up, welcoming the new addition. Weather forecasts called for rain which he hoped would erase any trace of tire tracks and footprints. With any luck, animals would get to her first but luck had rarely been his friend. He stood for several minutes as though waiting to see if she got up and walk out of the ditch or if the mist would find her unworthy and roll her back out.

The thought that he should return in daylight to make sure the body was hidden crossed his mind but he quickly decided against that idea. Twigs crunched close by, and he paused to listen closely. He had adapted to the dark over the years so his hearing was acute. Satisfied he had gone unseen, he climbed into the truck, and drove away.

2

Two men waited patiently in an expansive hallway of worn carpeting and chipped wainscoting. The dank and musty smell had met them at the door and quickly saturated their clothes and filled their heads. They stood across from each other leaning against marred walls. A chase up three flights of stairs had their uniforms clinging and their pulses pounding. Now it was just a matter of catching their breaths and waiting for their quarry's next move.

Their eyes drifted, each listening to the groans and creaks of the aged building, reluctant to express verbally how appallingly creepy the boarded up hotel felt. It used to be easy for Jake to dismiss any such reactions, at least before he had met his wife. His partner, however, was showing signs of folding, backing out on his agreement not to engage in any further banter. Frank had started with comments about how much the Embers Hotel reminded him of the hotel in Stephen King's book, *The Shining*. Then he had started guessing how many people had died over the years and how many were still roaming the halls. Jake's death ray stare had squelched Frank's lips, at least for a short time.

Frank's fingers were tapping out a tune on his thigh. His head bobbed to an imaginary beat while his eyes continued to dance with each sigh and groan from the decrepit building. The only way Frank knew to drown out the sounds was to fill it with his voice. "How long are we going to wait her out?" He glanced down the length of the hall where she rested, challenging their patience.

"As long as it takes."

"Should have shot her when we had the chance." Frank squatted down and opened the door to the pet cage. "Although it should be Chief Murphy in our crosshairs. Assigning us for a month with the animal control officers. Bet he's laughing his ass off."

Jake wasn't happy about it either. Their exile was the result of their last case where the suspect had been deposited into a hospital room with a window that opened. Neither he nor Frank had been aware of what rooms were available. They had been too busy helping to dig up the bodies of twenty-three victims. How were they to know the murder suspect would jump to her death? Chief Murphy hadn't seen it that way. He pulled them off Homicide and tossed them to the Animal Control Department for four weeks. They had thought of filing a complaint with the Board of Police and Fire Commissioners but Murphy threatened to revoke Frank's recent promotion.

"Did you know a cat barely waits for your body to cool before it begins eating you?"

"I take it Claudia still has the cat," Jake said.

"Yeah, and now my son has become attached to the beast. Damn thing sleeps in my bed and when I roll over all I see are these slitted eyes staring at me, its pink tongue smacking its lips. One time it tapped my neck ever so gently, right on the carotid artery as though checking to see if I still had a pulse." A flash of black darted toward a table at the end of the hall. "Do you know how many times this black cat has crossed our paths today? This is not a good sign." They took off at a trot, the cage knocking against Frank's thigh.

"We do have our guns," Jake reminded him.

This brought a devilish smile from Frank. "That we do." They paused several feet from the feline as it cowered under a narrow table, inching itself against the baseboard. Amber eyes blinked slowly and the cat yawned as though tiring of the game. "Heh, heh, heh," Frank taunted. "Nowhere to go now." The feline's eyes shifted from Frank to Jake then inched back on its haunches and licked one white paw. Frank set the cage down and moved with the caution of a hunter sneaking up on a cobra. "Come here, kitty kitty kitty."

The cat stopped licking and stared at Frank, not blinking but its eyes seemed to say, "Come here, piggy piggy piggy."

"You see what I see?" Jake nodded at a chunk of missing plaster near the baseboard several feet to the right of the table, which could provide another narrow escape for the feline. "You don't think…" The words no sooner tumbled from his lips when the cat lurched toward the baseboard, appeared to magically shrink in size before poking its head through the opening.

"NO!" Frank ran toward the wall as the cat disappeared. He pounded both fists repeatedly on the wall in frustration. The force of the blows collapsed the wall sending Frank, arms flailing, riding the wallboard like a surfer. He landed on a narrow stairway leading up to another floor.

"What the hell?" Jake studied the debris. Two eyes smiled back at him from eight stairs up, then disappeared into the dark. He found a light switch on the wall and flipped it.

Frank scrambled to his feet and brushed dirt and drywall dust from his clothes. "There wasn't a fourth floor in this place, was there?" The stairwell was less than four feet wide, a far cry from the ten-foot wide marble staircases and hallways on the previous floors. They lifted the wallboard, dragged it out of the way, and leaned it against a wall.

"Leave it up to you, Frank. We have a simple job of chasing down the cat that dug up the mayor's garden and all hell breaks loose." Jake swiped at cobwebs hanging from the ceiling, their cottony fingers sticking to his clothes. Tiny paw prints disturbed the film of dust that coated the wooden stairs. A loud whelp and screech erupted from the floor above them.

They pounded up the stairs and down the hallway. The cat was hissing at a closed door, its back arched and fangs showing. As the detectives approached, the cat gave one last hiss before darting around a corner. Instinct kicked in. The detectives slowly pulled their weapons even though common sense told them this floor had been closed up for sometime. But that didn't mean there wasn't another entrance somewhere. Jake gave a nod to Frank who grabbed the doorknob, turned it, and pushed the door open with one fluid motion. Jake stepped through, gun in his right hand, flashlight in his left.

Sunlight streamed through the top half of shuttered windows revealing a room cluttered with mismatched furniture. Newspapers were stacked on the floor next to an old time box television set. A couch was centered on an Oriental rug. In front of the couch was a wooden coffee table white with dust. Next to the couch was a recliner where a body sat, facing the television set as though waiting for someone to turn it on. The body was fully clothed leaning back in the recliner, its legs extended by the foot rest.

"Oh god," Frank groaned. "Please tell me that's a very ugly mannequin."

"Shit!"

"See?" Frank motioned toward the room. "That damn black cat brought us bad luck."

They spent several seconds taking it all in from a stationary position, letting their eyes survey the room from the doorway, storing the details, looking for signs of a dispute, a discarded weapon. From their angle they couldn't see blood on the clothes or an entrance wound from a knife or gun. The person may as well have sat down to watch television and died in his sleep. The fact that there was an ancient television set in the room gave them a clear indication it wasn't in this decade. Then in unison they holstered their guns and stepped back into the hallway.

Jake pulled the door shut and stood staring at the floor for several seconds.

"What do you think? Should we call Homicide or work it ourselves?" Frank asked. "After all, we are still Homicide."

"Not for another two weeks." Jake pulled out his phone, flipped it open, and punched several buttons. When the phone was answered, he said, "Hi, hon. What are you doing?"

3

Sam moved swiftly through the parking lot behind the hotel and through the courtyard to the back door where Jake and Frank were waiting. Jake was checking his watch as she approached. "How many speeding laws did you break?"

"I wasn't caught," Sam said breathlessly. "Hi, Frank." She immediately turned her attention back to Jake. "Where is it?"

"Third floor."

"Congrats on the promotion, Frank," she yelled over her shoulder as she raced through the doorway.

"That's Sergeant Travis to you," Frank yelled back.

Sam didn't take time to admire the woodwork and moulding as she hustled through the lobby and up the marble staircase, her tote bag slung over one shoulder. She hadn't taken the time to change out of her jeans after Jake called. Just shoved her feet into gym shoes and grabbed a tote bag she kept stocked should occasions such as this arise.

She rounded the corner and raced up the next flight, hearing the clamoring of shoes on the stairs behind her. When she reached the third floor she stopped and checked both directions, not sure which room to enter. At the end of the hallway she noticed a large gap in the wall and a partial sheet of drywall propped on its side. Plaster and paper littered the floor. Sam waited for the men to catch up.

Frank slapped Jake on the back. "Not even a kiss hello. It's a sorry day when you play second fiddle to a dead body."

"You haven't been paying attention, Frank. I have always played second fiddle to a dead body."

Sam wasn't listening. She was focusing on a wisp of frosty fingers motioning her closer to the narrow stairwell. Jake had said the third floor but he obviously meant one floor up. It wasn't until Jake's arm moved around her and said "this way," did her feet finally move.

"We think this might have been an attic apartment for the manager or maintenance," he explained. "There's one apartment on the right and a storage closet further down the hall. Can't really see this floor from the ground."

"Did you find a door out onto the roof?"

"Didn't look yet," Frank replied. "We got a bit sidelined."

Sam studied the debris on the stairs. If apartment doors had been hanging on one hinge and holes knocked in the walls along the hallways, she wouldn't have given a second thought to the broken wallboard. Other than peeling paint and worn carpeting, the interior hadn't suffered major damage from its previous residents.

"And how did this wall come down?" Sam asked no one in particular.

Frank explained their morning chase and how they had cornered a cat in the alley which ended up slipping into the building.

"Chasing a cat?" Sam's attempt to hide her amusement was unsuccessful.

"It was huge," Frank argued. "And a black cat to boot."

They started climbing the stairs single file with Jake in the lead. Rank and moldy air pressed down as they climbed. The wisp of frosty air appeared to gather in front of the apartment door and then dissipate near the floor as though sucked into the room.

Sam shook the chill from her body as she grabbed latex gloves and booties from the tote bag. As she slipped into the gear Jake checked his watch and said, "Let's make it quick, Sam. I'm going to have to call this in but I don't want you anywhere near when the crime scene unit shows up."

Sam turned the door knob and entered the room. It creaked like an arthritic knee. It felt as though the temperature had dropped fifty degrees. A stream of sunlight moved across the floor and centered itself over the body as though it were opening night at Zany's and the body were the main attraction. The two detectives remained in the hallway as

Sam took several steps toward the body. She paid little attention to the surroundings, focusing only on the body. "Definitely died here. Signs of slight decomp on the chair and the floor. Dressed in what looks like corduroy so could have died in the fall or winter, although I'd have to guess a frigid winter. The body doesn't look ravaged by insects."

"Cause of death?" Jake asked.

Sam realized she had been holding her breath when it wasn't necessary. There wasn't the typical odor of decay. The body was beyond that point. "No rope around the neck, no indication of knife wounds or a bullet hole. Can't even tell if the victim was strangled."

Frank pulled out a notepad and started writing. "Male or female?"

"Can't tell. Clothes are sort of unisex. Hair is short. No earrings or nail polish." Sam saw a matching corduroy jacket draped over the arm of the couch. "Jacket is a size seven so the deceased could be either female or a teenage boy but I'd go with female." She tried not to look at the body but it was difficult. The skin, or what was left of it, was like dried parchment. The eyes were non-existent, the empty sockets appearing to stare at her. "How does a body mummify in the Midwest?" she asked no one in particular.

"Good question," Jake replied.

"You mean like Boris Karloff-type mummy?" Frank had an unmistakable edge to his voice.

Sam knew better than to go through the pockets of the victim. That was Benny's job. But that didn't mean she couldn't search the jacket pockets. The right pocket was empty but the left pocket had a slight bulge in it. She pulled out what looked like a locket on a chain. The moment she touched it Sam saw a house in the woods, a log cabin with a wrap-around porch. A petite blonde with a model's face smiled as someone climbed the porch. She held a bouquet of lilacs. *Hey, Slick.* Sam heard the words distinctly. The voice was sultry; the crystal blue eyes flashed with intimate knowledge of Slick. This was followed quickly by a sense of profound loss in one wisp of aura but Sam couldn't detect the source of the loss nor could she see the man climbing the stairs, just the back of his head, brown hair cut short. Military? A medley of images filled her head—a bank teller window, a truck of some type, a leather couch with a bright-colored wool blanket thrown across the back. It sported a rustic scene of bears and evergreen trees. Suddenly the room filled with an overwhelming aroma of lilacs.

"What's that smell?" Frank snapped. "Why does it smell like flowers?"

"Lilacs." Sam told them what she had seen, but she was surprised they could smell the lilacs. Usually all of the auras associated with a deceased were sensed only by her.

"Oh shit oh shit oh shit," Frank mumbled.

"Just write." Jake tried to appear calm and reserved, but he was as antsy as Frank to get out of there. His eyes surveyed the room taking visual snapshots.

Sam checked to see if the men were watching. Frank was too intent on writing and Jake was leaning against the doorjamb making sure Frank had all the details correct. Slowly she slipped the locket into her pocket. Highly irregular but it was her only link to the deceased once the body was removed.

Frank looked up from his notepad. "Does your crystal ball tell us when she died?"

Sam picked up a newspaper from the floor next to the television set. "The newspaper is dated September 4, 1976, but..."

"But what?" Jake asked.

Sam shrugged. Like in the past, the aura started strong then faded, visions were clear then opaque. She received pieces of evidence like a jigsaw puzzle. Eventually she would put the pieces into their proper place. "Any idea how long this building has been empty?" Sam asked.

"We'll find out." Frank said but then stopped. "No, the detectives assigned to the case will find out."

"They can't turn this over to another team. You are still detectives even if Murphy has temporarily assigned you to Animal Control."

"Right, tell that to Murphy," Frank replied.

Sam stepped back into the hallway and removed the booties and latex gloves. She dropped them into the tote bag just as a black shadow rounded the corner and stopped. It looked directly at Sam and meowed.

"Look at you." Sam squatted down and held out her hand. "Come here. I won't hurt you."

"There's that damn cat," Frank growled.

The cat ignored Frank and pranced up to Sam. When she picked it up it continued to meow as though telling her how terrible her morning had been. The cat appeared to stab accusing glares at the two men while lightly tapping Sam's chest with its white paws.

"Aren't you a beautiful kitty." Sam stood and cuddled the cat in her arms.

"No, Sam." Jake folded his arms in defiance. "You are not taking it home. We have to take it to the Humane Society. It doesn't have a collar."

"But look at that sweet face."

"It's a black cat, Sam." Frank stressed the word *black*.

"Poco will eat it for lunch," Jake reminded her. "Just place it in the cage at the bottom of the stairs. We've been chasing the damn thing all morning. She won't let us near her."

Sam turned on her heel and stomped down the stairs. "Meanies."

4

Since they were probably going to be there awhile, Frank called one of the animal control officers to retrieve the cat while Jake notified Dispatch of the dead body. "Glad it won't be us having to go through these rooms," Frank said after ending his call. "Who do you think the captain will assign to the case?"

"Probably the baby dicks." Jake lit a cigarette, the first of two he allowed himself each day. They were sitting on the front bumper of the ACO van which was parked in the back lot.

"Should be interesting how close they come to Sam's assessment. How do you think she does it?"

Jake shrugged. "Ours is not to question why."

"Yes, ours IS to question why. That's our job. We detect. We question. We seek answers."

"I would think after we dug up those twenty-three bodies Sam deduced from her methods that you would realize there aren't any logical answers," Jake reminded him.

"Good point." Frank shielded his eyes from the sun as he looked at the roof. "No wonder no one can see a fourth floor. There's a brick wall all the way around concealing that small apartment on the roof."

They studied the hotel in silence. It was one of the last vestiges of a bygone era. A three-story structure of rot and decay left over from the days when this part of downtown had been the focal point of Chasen Heights, a town clinging to the southern shores of Lake Michigan far south of Chicago. Over the years the hotel had teetered between renovation and demolition. The building claimed two square city blocks yet remained relatively unblemished by vandals. What had helped was that it was caged within a black wrought iron fence which fought the overgrowth of trees and bushes. The lobby was raised one floor above the ground so there wasn't easy access to the first floor windows should anyone scale the fencing. Sidewalks branching from the building were riddled and bled weeds between the cracks, as did the parking lots.

At one time downtown had been the host to big name stores as well as condos and apartment buildings. It was close to the rail station which transported thousands to Chicago for even better paying jobs. But the shopping center changed all that. Customers preferred the indoor mall and restaurants. Downtown stores started closing and investors were unwilling to keep the buildings presentable. The only businesses that survived were the bars, package liquor stores, and drug trades made in the darkened alleys and street corners. An investment banker had dumped millions into the restoration of some of the buildings but downtown could never be resuscitated.

"How pissed do you think Captain Robinson will be that we didn't get the owner's permission before entering?" Frank said. Jake slid his eyes toward him with a look that said, *Do you really need to ask?* "Then again, one of Chasen Heights was in danger," Frank added. "That's why I had to use my pick gun."

"Robinson won't have a problem with it. The chief shouldn't either considering we were doing the bidding of the mayor."

"I'm curious," Frank said. "You usually discourage Sam from sticking her nose into our cases yet today she's the first person you called. What gives?"

"Sam has been miserable since Abby and Alex left with Dillon for the reservation. She tries to hide it but I can tell. A wadded up crib blanket, her puffy eyes. Abby was hoping Cora, her friend, might have a video cam on her computer so Sam could see Dillon but she doesn't. There might be one in the local high school but Abby hasn't had a chance to check into it yet."

Three black vehicles slowly made their way into the parking lot. The first was the crime scene van followed by two medical examiner vans, one carrying Benny Lau, the second reserved for the deceased. Two men clad in white overalls emerged from the van. They each grabbed a case from the back. Benny gave a wave to the detectives as he climbed out of his van, his colorful Hawaiian shirt flapping in the mild breeze. The driver of the last van opened the door but remained seated, drinking something steaming and opening up a newspaper.

Benny nodded. "Should have known it would be you two." He let his gaze run down their mode of dress, brown uniforms that made them look more like UPS drivers. "Thought you two were relegated to animal control."

"Yeah, well, you know us," Frank said. "Crime comes to us, we don't go to it."

"In other words, you attract trouble." Benny started toward the building then stopped and turned to Jake. "Did she tell you anything?" When Jake raised his eyebrows to question who *she* was, Benny replied, "It's subtle but I can smell the perfume she wears."

5

Sam hated handing over the cat to the ACO. Once it was neutered it would be put up for adoption. If it wasn't adopted, the cat would be euthanized. Jake was right. Poco, Alex's Irish Setter, would be a little put out. Sam had no doubt Poco would play nice but Sam couldn't saddle Abby with a baby, a dog and a cat. And how could anyone stop at one cat? Their one hundred acres of land already was home to a number of wild animals who instinctively knew of Alex's healing abilities. Jake still doubted his eyes when he would witness Alex tending to an injured animal. The last place Sam needed to enter was the Humane Society because she knew she would be walking out with a yard full of animals. She pushed the hands free button on the console and dialed.

"What's up, girlfriend?" came the familiar reply.

"I need a friend."

It was a short drive to Mimi's Café. Sam found Jackie seated at a booth by the window looking intensely at the cars in the parking lot. Jackie jerked like a startled bird when Sam approached and slid onto the seat across from her.

"Been waiting long?"

"Not at all." Jackie reached across the table and patted Sam's hand but just as quickly her eyes returned to the parking lot.

"You okay?" Sam noticed Jackie wasn't her usual bubbly self. She hadn't jumped up and rushed to greet her when she walked in.

"Fine. I just…" Jackie took a long sip of water sending lemon wedges floating to the bottom of the glass.

"Just what?"

Jackie shook her full head of Donna Summers hair and set the glass down. "I have the feeling someone is watching me." Her attention swung back to the parking lot.

Sam followed her gaze, checking for movement, cars with occupants sitting and watching, men lingering by vehicles, but she didn't see anything. "When did this start?"

"Couple days ago, I think. Probably shouldn't have gone to see that zombie movie with Lamon. Now I see shadows behind trees, cars trailing me, eyes watching me when I don't see anyone around." She picked up the glass of water and stared at the contents, set the glass down again. "Maybe I need to drink something stronger."

"Do you think it was a man or a woman?"

Jackie shrugged. "That's the strange thing. Sometimes I glimpse a woman, other times a man, but when I try to give it my full attention, there isn't anyone there. They either move quickly or I'm really letting my imagination run wild."

"Have you told Lamon?"

Jackie disregarded her question with a flip of her wrist. "I am not going to bother him with my silly goose bumps. He has criminals to catch. Besides, he warned me three times that I shouldn't see that movie, but all I said was, "Who you'all calling a sissy?""

A waiter who didn't look old enough to drive came over to take their order. His eyes lingered on Jackie for a few seconds too long and he almost dropped the menus when he left the table.

"You have to admit it, Jackie," Sam said with a nod toward Jackie's yellow knit keyhole dress which did little to contain her cleavage, "you do draw attention. Even if you wore a sack dress, you'd still garner stares."

The waiter brought two iced teas and a basket of bread. Jackie smiled at the young man. "Thank you, sugar." Once the waiter left Jackie said, "I know I am a little too friendly at times. It's my nature."

"You just have to be sure men take it as friendly and not as an invitation."

"Now you sound like my mama. Don't lecture me." Jackie's gaze drifted back to the windows.

Sam winced. It wasn't like Jackie to snap at her. If ever she needed confirmation that Jackie was unnerved, it was her loss of patience. She and Jackie had never had a disagreement. They may have differed over certain plans Sam had instigated in the past where she had coerced Jackie's assistance, but nothing that would have angered her friend.

"I'm sorry. I didn't mean for it to sound like a lecture. You can take care of yourself. You've always been able to take care of yourself."

Jackie waved her off again. "No, I'm sorry. I shouldn't be taking all this out on you. Especially with Dillon gone and all." She reached across the table and patted Sam's hand again. "Forgive me?"

"No problem. But you will let me know if you find proof that someone is following you, won't you? Slip into a store, snap some pictures with your phone in the area where you might have seen someone. You never know. It might pick up something."

Their waiter deposited their Caesar salads in front of them. "Can I get you more bread? Iced tea?"

Jackie studied the salad for a few seconds. "Do you have some anchovies, sweetie?"

"Sure."

Sam waited until he left to say, "Would you believe Jake called me out on a case today?"

"Jake Mitchell? You sure you got the right guy?" Jackie thanked the waiter as he set a plate of anchovies in front of her. She placed several strips on her salad, then pushed the plate toward Sam.

"I know. I couldn't believe my ears when he called. Just out of the blue." Sam scraped the remaining anchovies on her salad.

"I doubt it was out of the blue. You carry your emotions on your sleeve, girlfriend. Ain't nothing gets by your husband. He knows you are suffering being apart from Dillon."

"The puzzling question is, why isn't he?"

"You should know by now that your husband doesn't show emotion. He is as wooden as a Buckingham palace guard. But there ain't nothing that gets by him." They finished their salads in silence with each glancing occasionally toward the parking lot. Jackie picked up the dessert menu and studied it for several seconds. "Want to split something?"

"I shouldn't."

Jackie smiled slowly. "That means you can be tempted." When the waiter came over to remove their plates, Jackie ordered a brownie delight. "Extra scoop of vanilla and two spoons, sweetie."

Sam could swear she saw the waiter blush.

"So, tell me about the case."

Sam explained how Frank and Jake had spent their morning chasing a cat, how it led them to the shuttered building and the hidden staircase to a fourth floor apartment. Jackie howled with laughter at the vision of the two tough cops tramping around downtown streets and alleys in pursuit of a kitten. Her amusement ended at the graphic description of the remains they had found.

"Good thing I didn't ask for blood red strawberry syrup on this brownie."

Sam pulled the chain from her pocket and set it on the table. "This was in the victim's jacket pocket."

"Eeyuuu." Jackie backed away from the table. "That still have her remains on it?"

"You think I'd be touching it?"

Jackie gingerly picked up the locket and studied it. "Not cheap. Fourteen carat gold." She turned it sideways. "Hmmm, I wonder." She pried one of her long talons into a split on the side and the locket popped open."

"You broke it?" Sam leaned across the table. "What is that?"

"A locket-type thingie with a picture in it. Looks like it was taken in one of those old time photo booths. *Love Always, Slick* engraved on the other side." Jackie handed the locket to Sam.

"I heard her say that name...Slick." The picture showed a man and a woman, young, possibly in their early twenties. "Picture is pretty clear. It's the same woman I saw when I first held the locket."

"If she was a homeless woman, she could have stolen it."

"I don't know. It all depends on Benny's examination, the estimate of age at time of death. But I only saw the young blonde in my vision, not an older woman."

"These days, sweetie, even the young can be homeless. Are your boys working the case?"

Sam reminded her friend that Murphy was playing hardball. "He'd leave Jake in Animal Control for the rest of the year if he had his way."

Jackie did a slow smile, then broke out in raucous laughter. She leaned across the table and whispered, "You stole this from the crime scene, didn't you? Afraid you wouldn't have an in if Jake wasn't on the case."

Sam just hoped the locket wasn't an intricate part of the case, something that would prove the person who bought it was the killer, if it was murder. Then it would be inadmissible in court. Just like in the past, Sam had a habit of acting first, consequences be damned.

6

"Anything?" Benny asked as he climbed down the staircase to the lobby. Andy Brainard and Maury Jackson stood like obedient altar boys in their Sunday school best. They moved in tandem to meet the medical examiner in the middle of the lobby.

"We still have a couple guys going through the rest of the rooms but it doesn't look like anyone has been here for years." Jackson's bright Miami Vice colors were stark against his dark skin.

Andy Brainard flipped through his notepad. Wisps of baby-fine red hair dotted the tops of his freckled hands. "There are twenty-four apartments on the second and third floors. The first floor has eight apartments, four offices, and miscellaneous rooms which might have been a utility room, gym, and laundry facilities. There's a huge banquet room which might have been turned into a recreation room. We found empty bookshelves and markings on the floor that could have been made by pool table legs. The former hotel kitchen has been stripped of all equipment so it's hard to tell what the apartment renters used it for.

"No sign of a break-in," Maury added.

"Or vandalism," Andy finished.

"The crime scene guys are just finishing up their scavenger hunt. So far they haven't seen any signs of foul play. No injuries I can see to the skeletal remains but I'll know more once I get her back to the lab. Weird case. Did you find an access to the roof?" Benny said.

"There's a ladder in the third floor stairwell and a hatch leading out to the roof of the third floor but there isn't any access to the fourth floor from there. The only way in was through that stairwell. Somehow she found a way into the hotel that none of the homeless have been able to find." Andy folded his notepad and shoved it in his pocket.

Benny nodded his thanks. "I'll head back to my office and wait for the lady to arrive."

* * *

Jackie checked her watch. It was nine o'clock but she still had one shopper left in the store. The woman was attractive, maybe in her early twenties, petite with curves in the right places. Her skin was a shade darker than caramel, as Jackie's mother used to call it. The hair needed help though. Whatever straightening product the woman was using on her shoulder length hair was doing more harm than good.

"Is there anything I can help you with, sugar?" Jackie asked. "We're about to close up."

The young woman held up a black lace teddy in one hand and a white bra with matching thong bikini undies in the other. "Which do you like?"

Jackie took a step back and studied the woman, not the garments. The young woman looked more like a seminary student who would blush at the thought of wearing anything that didn't go up to her neck. "Is this a present for someone or is it for you?"

A sudden flush rose in the woman's cheeks. "I just thought I'd be a little daring."

"Are you wearing it for yourself or for the man in your life?" Jackie could see more color rush to the woman's face. "No need to blush, sugar. I have a lot of customers who just want to feel feminine." Jackie took the garments from the woman and hung them up. She led her over to another rack. "Some customers just want to feel sexy. They pour themselves a glass of wine, light a couple mood candles, put on a Michael Buble CD and just sit and relax. Ain't nothing wrong with that." Jackie pulled a lime colored spaghetti strap two-piece silk lounging set from a rack and handed it to the woman. "Perhaps you should take baby steps. This color looks perfect on you." She held it up to the woman and watched her reflection in the mirror.

"That is so pretty." Her eyes widened like a school girl's.

Jackie touched the tips of the coarse straight hair. "You need a better relaxer, sugar. And you should leave some curl in your hair. The shape of your face calls for more fullness." When she saw the look of shock on the girl's face, Jackie added, "You have beautiful features. You should really play them up."

"Thank you," she stammered.

Jackie held out a hand. "I'm Jackie Delaney. I own this shop. Hope you didn't think I was criticizing your appearance." The young woman's hand was soft and warm to the touch.

"I think you've sold me on the outfit."

"You've made a wonderful choice."

* * *

The young woman walked to the corner then turned down a side street. The black Nissan rental car started up as she climbed into the passenger seat. She glared at the driver and tossed the package into the back seat. "You owe me eighty dollars," she snapped. "I had to buy the damn outfit or she would have gotten suspicious."

7

Captain Robinson groaned inwardly when he stepped off the elevator onto the fourth floor of Precinct Six. Not only was a bookworm with a press badge clipped to his lapel waiting at the front desk but the reporter also had the full attention of Chief Dennis Murphy. It was the start of Robinson's day and already it was headed downhill at a fast clip.

"What are your top priorities if elected mayor?" the reporter asked Chief Murphy, his pen hovering over a spiral-ringed notepad.

Robinson stepped closer to the front desk. The name on the press badge was Rafe Bennett. Brown hair was spiked and had that just stepped out of the shower look, all wet and glossy. Black square-framed glasses appeared too large for his narrow face but served to enhance the penetrating eyes. To Robinson the reporter looked like the president of a college debate team. With a notepad filled with what could have been the man's grocery list, Bennett fired off questions barely giving Murphy time enough to respond.

"Since you have been with the police department for thirty-three years, are there any changes that are on your list of top priorities for the department?"

Murphy held up a hand and leveled his own patented stare at the young reporter. "I haven't seen you before. What newspaper do you work for?"

"*Post Tribune*. I'm one of their on line correspondents. Just got into town."

Murphy glared at him with a cop's eye. "You must be a fast learner." Murphy appeared to let that slide as he added, "I will be holding a press conference this afternoon so you are more than welcome to pose your questions then, Rafe." The beady stare told Rafe to watch his step. The warm handshake and pat on the back said he could be the chief's best friend if he played ball. The elevator door opened and the chief, with his entourage in tow, stepped on.

Rafe wasn't deterred. "Your main opponent is former councilman and trucking company owner Jeffery Schuler. He says crime has gone up in the city since you took over as chief. Any comments?"

Murphy's smile was camera-ready as the doors closed.

Rafe turned to Robinson, but before he could open his mouth the captain said, "I'd sure like to hear what his planned changes are, too. Do fill me in after the news conference."

"What about the body found yesterday morning in the vacant building?"

"Still sifting through the evidence. When I know something firm, we'll notify the press."

"I'd like to hear first. Would be great to impress my new bosses at the *Post Tribune*."

So if Murphy wasn't going to play ball with him, Rafe wanted to make sure he had a backup. Robinson wrapped a mitt-sized hand around his coffee mug as he studied the reporter. "Where did you work at before?" Rafe appeared youthful but now that Robinson stood closer, he could see the looks were deceiving. The tie which hung askew, the hair which looked more punk than preppy, the puppy enthusiasm which was peppered throughout his questions, were all a smokescreen. He was a seasoned reporter which meant he had previous gigs.

"All over. I freelance, selling stories to a number of newspapers. I'm not getting rich but I get by. Had my own on line news site for a while which caught the attention of the Associated Press."

"Any specialty? Sports? Entertainment?"

Rafe gave a smile that almost made him look dangerously sinister. "Corrupt politicians. If there's dirt anywhere, I find it. Wasn't given the nickname *the gardener* for nothing."

Robinson slowly smiled. "Well, you've come to the right state."

"From what I've read about Chasen Heights, you have one heck of an exciting town. It may not be New York City or Chicago but it sounds like it might keep me busy for sometime." Rafe saluted with his notepad and stepped onto the elevator. He slammed his hand against the door to hold it open. "Captain, is it possible to get a ride-along? And I don't want to be with traffic cops. I want a night ride. I want to be where the action is."

"See the desk sergeant on the first floor. He'll have to set something up with the night patrol shift." Robinson watched the elevator door close then turned to Sergeant Scofield who was peering over his bifocals, eyebrows raised. Robinson chuckled. "This town is going to eat him alive."

* * *

The office was a fury of moving bodies stacking yard signs in one corner, window signs in another, barking orders on phones, shoving leaflets into outstretched hands, and wishing the man in the crisp white shirt would go hit the gym or the links at the country club. Jeff Schuler's campaign headquarters was in a strip mall in the heart of the city.

Jeff Schuler - A tough man for tough times

"I'm still not sold on that slogan, Tom. Makes me sound like a boxer." Schuler stared at the glossy red, white and blue bumper sticker in his hand. The moving bodies stopped in sync, a collective gasp catching in their throats. They had just spent months of frantic work getting campaign materials printed after Schuler made numerous changes.

"Not at all, Jeff." Tom's voice was calm and soothing, a lyrical backrub that workers joked could hypnotize listeners rather than put them to sleep. Behind his back they called him the magician. Just when the councilman was on the verge of changing strategies or scrapping an ad campaign, Tom would magically turn him around.

"These are tough economic times and who better to handle it than a successful businessman," Tom continued. "It says it all in simple terms people can understand." He opened up one of the pamphlets and pointed to bright red bullet points. "These are the tough issues facing voters and below each point is your solution. We aren't criticizing Mayor Jenkins, after all that would be interpreted as heartless by the voters seeing that the man's health is deteriorating. You aren't running against Jenkins. You are running against Murphy who hasn't been tough on criminals. We point out the waste in spending, lack of oversight on casino revenues. We stress how your frustration to buck the system is why you wouldn't run for another term on the council, but now you have a chance to make a difference as mayor."

"I don't know."

Tom Lukavich pulled out a chair and patted it, indicating for Jeff to sit down. The young crew behind him started to relax, feeling somewhat confident that they wouldn't have a repeat of the last forty-eight-hour all-nighter. Tom did more than put out fires. If one needed a go-to guy to dig up dirt, manipulate the media, finesse a campaign strategy, there was no one better. Just as some people say pet owners start to look like their pets, people in politics start to look like how they operate. One look at Tom's beady eyes and pointed features, the first word that came to mind was weasel. He moved as though he mainlined caffeine and loved the dirty side of politics more than the politician. Some like Schuler had to be coddled, cajoled, their feathers unruffled, and delicate psyches soothed. But Tom didn't doubt for a minute that Jeff could go for the jugular. He just had to make sure it wasn't his.

Tom looked at his team of workers and nodded at the door. "Let's get those items distributed. You've got your names and addresses. And don't come back until all your signs and literature are gone." As they moved en masse toward the door, he barked out, "And I don't want to hear about campaign literature being dumped into the garbage because you're too lazy to go door to door." Then he remembered their psyches also had to be soothed. "I know you can do it."

Once the door closed, Tom pulled out a seat and sat across from Jeff. He did a quick assessment of his boss from the threads of hair which failed to hide the shiny pate to the starched white shirt and alligator loafers. The executive health club obviously helped to keep him in shape. "First, that comb over has to go. People don't trust someone who isn't authentic, who doesn't accept who he is. Second, tone down the smell of money. I have been studying Murphy. He dresses like a millionaire when he isn't one. He's got the gold cufflinks, the two hundred dollar shoes, and Armani suits. When you are a millionaire and dress like Trump, people feel you are flaunting it. You aren't feeling their pain. You want to wear a white shirt and tie? Fine, but make it short sleeved or roll up the sleeves. Rolled up sleeves shows the voter you are ready to do tough work. Loosen the tie. Find some comfortable shoes and for god sake, don't make them alligator. The more flashy Murphy looks, the more he'll look like he's on the take. It plants the idea in the voters' minds without you having to open up your mouth."

"This isn't the first time I'm running for an office, Tom."

The tone of Jeff's voice bordered on irritation but Tom didn't get where he was by not being forthright and honest. "But it's the reason you didn't run for councilman again. You knew your poll numbers were slipping. People didn't feel you could relate to them. You couldn't get down to their level. That is what my post election focus group proved."

Jeff dismissed him with a wave of his hand. "Fine, now what are you doing to discredit the competition? With Jenkins throwing his support at Murphy, I'm going to need a hell of a lot more ammunition."

"I'm working on it," Tom said as he rubbed his hands together, anticipating a down and dirty fight. "I have your speech ready for the press conference this afternoon. We're going to touch on the current murder rate and increase in drug gangs in the city."

"Murphy will say he has increased the number of police on the street."

Tom never doubted for a minute that Jeff did his homework. "And you will be out in front reminding people you led the push for more police when Murphy's predecessor was police chief. You were the one to introduce the bill and sway the rest of the councilmen that the protection and safety of the citizens of Chasen Heights was a top priority. It was because of your willingness to spend money when it was needed that had the other council members blacklisting you. They wanted to tighten the purse strings and the hell with the citizens." Tom could almost quote the speech verbatim since he helped to write it. Now the touchy questions. Tom knew Murphy had more resources at his disposal to shake Schuler's family tree. "Anything out there Murphy could use?"

"I've covered my bases. I have been audited, turned up one side and down the other. I've paid my taxes, paid off the girlfriends…"

"Oh Christ," Tom moaned. "They will be crawling out of the woodwork for more money to keep their mouths shut."

"Doesn't matter. Extra marital affairs are no big deal these days. If a former president of the United States can use the Oval Office as his harem, the subject is no longer taboo. Besides, my wife and I are solid, we did the marriage counseling bit, talked to our pastor. People respect a man who owns up to his faults. Besides, *it's a private matter* is the buzz phrase of the decade."

He was good, Tom reminded himself. "Any disgruntled employees ready to picket your speeches?"

"I made sure they all received yearend bonuses last year. I worked from the ground up when my dad owned Schuler Trucking. Swept floors, drove the trucks, was a dispatcher." He looked at the paper in Tom's hand. "Did you mention that in my speech?"

"Yes, and it's in great detail in the flyer."

There was a steely glint in Jeff's eyes. Tom was no fool. Jeff didn't get where he was today without knowing his opponents' weaknesses, whether in the boardroom or the courtroom.

"What about Murphy?" Jeff asked. "I need better ammo than crime statistics. He's a cop for crissake. Aren't they all on the take? There are skeletons and I want you to shake the trees until you find them."

"There's a new reporter in town. He's young and hungry for a big story."

"And to make a name for himself. Good. Cultivate him. Feed him whatever you dig up on Murphy."

Tom jotted notes on a notepad. "On the downside, he's probably hungry enough to take whatever Murphy's people feed him, too."

"Murphy is lazy. He's banking on Jenkins' support and putting very little money or effort into his campaign. Do you see a campaign headquarters for him? No. He hired a PR firm to do ads and get the word out. That's it. But I don't doubt that he isn't using his own resources at his disposal to try to find every fight I picked in school all the way back to my kindergarten days."

Tom looked up from his note writing. "I want them all. Every nose bleed, every pigtail you pulled. I don't want to be blindsided at a press conference."

Schuler opened his briefcase and tossed Tom a book. "I wrote it eight years ago. *Cultivating Success the Schuler Way*. I'm surprised at you, Tom. Thought you researched me thoroughly. I spell out every nose bleed, pigtail, marital indiscretion, handling problem employees, living with a demanding father, you name it. I smoked pot in college, had to file Chapter 13 for the first company I tried to grow. Spelled out every wort on my ass. The good, the bad and the ugly. It's the latest thing. Get out front with a book on your life story and no one can say you are hiding anything."

Tom's eyes narrowed as a spark of creativity hit him. "Here. Hold the book up." Tom grabbed his camera and motioned for Jeff to stand. "Roll those shirt sleeves up, lean against the bookshelves holding your book and give me a smile."

"Need I remind you the book is eight years old?"

"And there's a possibility there are voters who also forgot or are unaware of your book. Sales will go through the roof."

At the thought of royalties, Jeff gave a broad smile.

8

"I have a great deal more respect for our AC Department." Frank held the screen in front of the fireplace. Trapped behind the screen were two ducks. It was difficult to tell if they were male or female since they were covered in soot from the chimney. "Can't believe the shit they have to deal with. Alligators, pythons, ocelots and all the other exotic pets people purchase on the black market."

Jake opened an animal crate and set it aside. "If Alex were in town he'd have them walking right into the crate."

"Well, Alex isn't here so how do you think we should handle it?"

"You need bread. They like bread." A man in a crisp white shirt and bow tie leaned over Frank. One gnarled finger pointed at the duck. "She's scared. Look at how she's shivering."

"You need a big pan with Palmolive liquid dish soap. That works best for washing birds," a woman wearing layers of wool chimed in. Her hair was cut so short they could see pink scalp between blades of white hair. "They do that for the birds caught in an oil slick. I seen it on the *Discovery* channel."

Frank looked over his shoulder at the crowd assembled behind them. They had pulled up chairs in a half circle. It was probably the most entertainment they would see this month. The Shoreline Shelter was located two blocks from the Embers Hotel. The downward spiral of the economy had forced more residents into the shelter than it could handle. The local churches had stepped in to help find foster families for those without relatives.

One couple in their thirties was holding back their two curious children. "Don't hurt them," the young girl around age five yelled. She refused to sit down so her father had to force her onto his lap.

An elderly woman teetered over and stood next to Mister Bow Tie.

She spoke to the entire room. "Anyone seen Eleanor? We were supposed to go to lunch today." She searched the faces in the room but no one replied. She was decked out in a hat and gloves as though going to Sunday services. "Anyone seen Eleanor? She never misses lunch at her favorite restaurant."

"What? McDonald's has one buck burgers again?" Bowtie said.

The two ducks edged further away from the screen.

"Quiet. You're scaring the birds," the little girl shouted.

"Amy, shhhh." Her father tried to keep her quiet.

"Can we step back a little and let these men do their job?" A woman in a suit who appeared to have some authority clapped her hands as though standing in a room of third graders. She turned to Jake. "I am so glad you were able to make it here so quickly. I'm Marie Bakowski, the director here at Shoreline. I have my maintenance guy up on the roof putting a screen on the chimney. It must have blown off. That's how the birds got in."

The church lady tugged on Marie's sleeve. "Have you seen Eleanor? She never misses lunch."

Jake turned toward the church lady. He couldn't help it. His cop senses were twitching. "When was the last time you saw her?"

"Did you see her at dinner last night, Lucille?" Marie asked.

"No, come to think of it she missed dinner. She never misses dinner."

The ducks started squawking and jumping onto the gas logs. Someone yelled to turn the fireplace on which had the children whimpering. Jake had to keep Lucille busy until he had a chance to question her more. He stood and directed his words to Lucille. "Could you find us a large pot and fill it with warm soapy water."

"Fill the large sink in the kitchen," Marie suggested. "Then we can place a large rack over the top so they can't fly out. They can wash one bird at a time."

"How do we handle this so they don't fly the coop?" Frank held on tight to the screen as the ducks flapped their wings in an attempt to fly up the chimney.

A young boy handed Jake a piece of bread. "They won't come unless you feed them."

Jake shrugged. What did he know? "Worth a try." He placed the bread close to the back of the cage and told Frank, "Remove the screen just from one side until I can get the front of the cage in the opening."

It didn't take long. It was unknown how long the ducks were in the chimney or how long it had been since they had something to eat and drink. They looked briefly at the cage, then waddled in. Frank dropped the cage door, closing off the exit.

"All done. Now we just need to set the cage in the sink and wash them," Frank said.

"Maybe you should fill the sink to the top," Bowtie chuckled.

"You'll drown them," the young girl cried.

As Frank left with the cage, Jake waited for Lucille to return, then took a seat next to her. "Tell me more about Eleanor. Did she usually go off without telling anyone where she was going?" The majority of their audience trailed after Frank to the kitchen.

"Sometimes. I'm not sure, or at least she doesn't tell me. But today is the day we go to Red Lobster. It's SS day. We receive our Social Security checks on the same day. We always split a meal so it's cheaper and today is their shrimp special."

"What was she wearing the last time you saw her?"

"Doesn't matter. She changes for every meal."

"She doesn't change that damn hat," Bowtie chided. "Looks like some pheasant made a nest in her hair."

"Her necklace," Marie added. "Doesn't she wear the pearl necklace her husband gave her?"

"Yes. She even sleeps in it." Lucille opened her purse which by the looks of it Jake was sure weighed ten pounds. She hauled out a packet of coupons, an eyeglass case, a sewing kit, and two tins of mints until she finally found an envelope of pictures. "This was me and Eleanor at the Labor Day carnival at Memorial Park. You can have it as long as you return it."

Bowtie wasn't kidding about the hat. In the photo Eleanor was eyeing the camera as though she was suspicious of the gadget or the person holding it. She wore little makeup but did have the string of pearls and a hat that was an explosion of feathers.

"Did she get along with everyone?" Jake spoke to the picture not wanting the questions to be directed to Lucille alone.

"No one got along with her," Bowtie chimed in. "Everyone grated on her nerves and the feeling was mutual. Kids were too loud, television blared, food was cold, rooms were cold. You name it."

"Anyone more so than the rest?" This time Jake did zero in on Bowtie.

Marie had stayed behind, either because of curiosity or out of responsibility for one of the home's residents. "Eleanor was harmless. You could just about describe everyone in this house as losing patience. How could they not given their circumstances? Some have lost their jobs, their savings, their cars. They have no place to go and are embarrassed that they have to live one step away from being on the street. She was good-hearted, though. Went through a rough spell after her husband died."

"How long has she lived here?"

"Oh, several years. When her husband died his insurance couldn't even cover his medical expenses. Eleanor lost her house, all of her savings, and only has a meager Social Security to live on."

Jake tapped the picture and asked Lucille, "Can I keep this?"

"Do you have to?"

"Here, I'll make a copy on my color printer," Marie offered. "Then Lucille doesn't have to give it up."

* * *

Benny motioned from a darkened booth in the Stirred Not Shaken martini bar near the expressway. Jake and Sam wove their way between aisles of chrome and glass and slid into the booth across from him.

"Could you pick a more expensive place to meet?" Sam admired the old movie posters of *Casablanca, The Maltese Falcon, Rear Window*, including posters of actors such as Humphrey Bogart and Jimmy Stewart. It was so dark in the bar it was difficult to see the faces of those seated across the room. The booths were high backed. The black leather was complimented by the black and white tiled floor and black marble bar. The only contrasting colors were in the bartender's red dress and the vases of red roses on the bar.

"Can't meet you at Izzy's. Every cop in town goes there," Benny said. "And it's not like you can't afford the seven dollar drinks." Benny fingered the salt clinging to the rim of the glass.

A waitress wrapped in red sidled up to the booth.

"I'll have what he's having," Sam said, pointing to Benny.

"One Virgin Mary," the waitress said.

"Oh, no. I want the good stuff in there," Sam corrected her.

"One Bloody Mary."

Jake ordered a Miller Lite. As the waitress rushed off Jake pulled a twenty from his wallet and set it on the table.

"What did the baby dicks find?" Sam asked.

"What? No, 'how was your day'?" Benny said.

"How was your day? Now what did the baby dicks find?"

Benny looked to Jake who shrugged. "They did find an access to the roof from the third floor stairwell but no access into the fourth floor apartment other than up the stairs, which were drywalled shut." Benny waited as the waitress deposited their drinks and took the twenty. "Anyway," he continued, "maybe the victim hid while the new owners had the renovations made. She died of exposure, starved to death, a host of possibilities."

"Any identification?" Jake asked.

"Nothing on the woman, no purse in the room, no personal belongings, no food, no garbage. The baby dicks are leaning toward the woman being homeless or a hooker who brought her clients there."

Sam slid the olive into her mouth, then passed the stalk of celery to Jake. "I doubt she brought johns there. That would have compromised her hiding place."

"Probably just used it for sleeping, a place to get in from the cold." Benny said. "Could have died of natural causes, maybe drug overdose. Certainly didn't die of old age. She was between twenty and thirty. Not much older. Might have died from the elements, maybe winter, no heat."

"What about the body itself?" Jake asked.

"No wounds, no sign of blunt force trauma, no bullets or knife marks. Could have had health issues, maybe anorexic, AIDS, pneumonia, alcoholism. Won't know til I get tox reports back. Nothing in the stomach or digestive tract. Techs say surface fingerprints are degraded. And I can't get fingerprints from the vic. Techs are still analyzing fibers on the couch, stains in the bed, and hair and teeth for DNA. When it has been that long all we can go on are the dates on the newspapers, type of clothing she wore. Christ, the television set is at least forty years old."

"The body was partially mummified," Sam commented. "How is that possible in this part of the country?"

"Takes two environmental conditions—hot and dry, or freezing cold. Since we have high humidity in the summer I would say she died in the winter. But once the spring thaw started, the organs and other soft tissue started to break down." Benny leaned across the table and stared into Sam's face. "Now you tell me what you gleaned from the victim." Where Frank usually backed away from Sam's eerie assessments, Benny found them fascinating.

"She was blonde, pretty, in her mid-twenties, I think. She lived or I saw her in a log cabin that is surrounded by lilac bushes." Sam wondered if she should mention the locket but thought better of it. "I heard her call someone Slick."

"Well, that describes about half the guys in the country," Benny said.

9

The headlines in the *Post Tribune* the next morning screamed *Do You Feel Safe?* Murphy slapped the newspaper onto Robinson's desk. "Can you believe those bastards? Not one word from my speech yesterday, nothing about my gang task force or the convention center project. Just the crime statistics. I swear the editors are in bed with Schuler."

Murphy paced while a redness seeped through his suntanned cheeks. "From this point on we focus only on major crimes. Forget the purse snatchers, drivers on their cell phones, even speeding tickets. Damn paper would only ask why the police aren't out catching real criminals rather than writing tickets. Make sure every detective is out on the street. I want their presence known. Pull them off dead end cases."

"The baby dicks are working on that body found at that abandoned hotel."

"Some homeless lady, no signs of foul play. I don't want them wasting their time."

Robinson shifted in his leather rocker causing the chair to groan in protest. Part of him hoped Murphy would win the election just to get him out of his hair. Another part of him feared the unknown. The chief's replacement could be worse than Murphy, if that were at all possible.

"Could use our two best detectives who are out chasing stray pets."

Murphy stopped his pacing. "They are lucky I only gave them four weeks. Had half a mind to bump them both down to beat cops."

Robinson ran his hands through his close-cropped Afro. "They have two weeks to go and all the public sees are two of our finest chasing down Snookums and Pookey while shop owners are being robbed, young girls are being snatched off streets and raped in alleyways, satellite banks are being held up at gun point. It all gives fodder to your opponent."

"Don't try my patience. Four weeks, not a day less." He moved toward the door, signaling his stay was finally ending but something he saw in the outer office stopped him in his alligator tracks. Murphy surveyed the desks, his eyes squinting in disbelief. "What kind of pigs work here? Their desks look like landfills." If one were to walk into Murphy's office, they would be hard-pressed to find one useless scrap of paper gracing his desk, one folder out of place. Even the appointments in his desk calendar were color-coded. "Re-post my memo on organizing and efficiency and get me your updated monthly crime stats by lunchtime."

Robinson wanted to tell Murphy he didn't do campaign work but bit back the snide remark as Murphy headed toward the elevator. Robinson took bad press personally. He would go above and beyond Murphy's request. After all, it was September and crime rates always spiked in the summer months. He would do a comparison of crime stats this summer with previous summers and also remind Murphy that Councilman Schuler introduced the bill that would pay people to turn in their guns. The crime rate didn't go down after that stunt because the criminals weren't the people turning in the guns.

He hefted his linebacker-sized bulk from behind his desk, hearing the hiss of relief from the special-order chair. Now he had to break the news to the baby dicks that their Jane Doe was to be shelved until further notice.

* * *

Jackie struggled with a box as she barreled up from the basement. "Jenny, we need an exterminator. Could swear I saw a mouse down there." She pushed the door closed with her hip.

"Mouse?" The young girl's eyes widened. "Are you sure?" Her pale skin appeared paler as she instinctively hopped onto the stool behind the cash register, her feet propped safely on the foot rail.

"Let me get that for you." A young man pulled the box from Jackie's arms.

Jackie's breath caught in her throat. The stranger was one of the most delicious looking men she had ever seen. "Why thank you, sugar."

He set the box on the counter. His broad smile revealed perfect white teeth. He wore a shirt that was contoured to his broad shoulders. Jackie had to look up to see his full height.

"You must be a basketball player, sugar. Do you play for the Bulls?"

His laugh was full throated, rich and deep. His skin was a deep tan and his eyes twinkled with mischief. "Don't I wish. And I'm not quite tall enough, just six foot two."

"Well, if you are a salesman, I'll buy ten of everything you're selling." Jackie gave her own full throated laugh while Jenny kept checking the floor around her chair for anything that moved.

"I wish I were selling mouse traps. Sounds like you can use a few." He stuck a mitt-sized hand at her. "Armando."

"Armando. That just rolls off the tongue, doesn't it?" Jackie laughed, wondering if he were a pool boy for an elite country club. She guessed him to be in his mid-twenties.

"Maybe we do need some mouse traps or those glue traps," Jenny suggested.

"Oh no." Jackie clawed at the air with one inch talons. "I couldn't stand to have to touch those dead bodies." She studied the well-dressed man. He looked more like a lawyer than a pool boy or a bodybuilder. "We didn't mean to ignore you, sugar. Was there something we could help you with?"

"Well." He looked around the shop as though just realizing he might have stumbled into the wrong building. "I, um, have to admit I wasn't sure what type of store this was. My auntie's birthday is coming up and I thought if I just browsed some women's shops I might get a clue."

"Can you call your mama for some hints?" Jackie asked.

The broad smile faded. "Mama died years ago. My auntie raised me so she's really dear to my heart."

Jackie placed a hand on his arm, feeling solid muscle under the knit sleeve. "I'm so sorry, sugar. Let me see if I can give you some help. How old is your auntie?"

"Old." He laughed again, lighting up his eyes and filling up the room with his deep voice. "Why don't you let me browse a bit and you ..." A scratching came from the box Jackie had set on the counter.

Jenny's eyes widened. Jackie took several steps back. "Oh dear god I hope that isn't what I think it is please please," Jackie rambled in a hushed tone.

Armando sprang into action. He ripped off a piece of mailing tape from the dispenser on the counter then slapped it over a small hole he saw at the corner of the box. "Another piece," he instructed Jenny. She quickly ripped off a piece and handed it to him. He found another small hole and covered it with the tape. "They don't need too big of an entryway." He carefully picked up the box. "Do you have a back door? I saw a drainage ditch at the end of the strip mall. As long as you aren't squeamish about it, I'll hold the box under water and drown the little buggers. You'll lose all of your product but they have probably already been using the fabric as nesting material."

Bracelets jangled as Jackie waved her hand in the air. "Go, please. Do whatever you need to do." She led him to the back door and held it open. "I hate to think what else they destroyed downstairs."

She stood by the backdoor and watched as he gingerly carried the box around the building next door. Jackie felt the warmth of the sun and welcomed the heat as visions of tiny feet scampering around the basement sent a chill through her body. Usually the basement held new fixtures for seasonal displays plus empty boxes and packing material. She had just recently started storing stock downstairs. Now she'd have to see if she could get someone to add a few more shelves in the storage room.

Armando returned holding a piece of paper dripping water. "I was able to retrieve the packing slip so you know what product was damaged."

"Thank you, Armando. I didn't even think of that. Just wanted to get the little rodents out of the store."

"Unfortunately, where there's one there may be more. I noticed a hardware store down the block. I'm going to go pick up some mouse traps for you."

Jackie wanted to tell him he didn't have to do that but the thought of going back downstairs was the farthest thing from her mind. "Let me get you some money."

"I'll bring back a receipt." He was gone before she could even thank him.

"Isn't he a cutie," Jenny said.

"He certainly is. Those muscles. Nice tush. Very nice tush."

"Wonder what he does for a living. Do you think he was really here to buy something for his aunt or a girlfriend?" Jenny took a tentative step onto the floor, her eyes searching under the counter. She was college age and worked around her school schedule. Her marketing skills came in handy as Jackie let her get creative with sale flyers and ads for the local newspaper.

Armando returned fifteen minutes later with a bag from the hardware store. "I'm sure you ladies don't want to set these traps so just point me in the direction of the basement."

Jackie turned on the basement light. "I'll let you lead the way."

"I think with those four inch heels you should be able to do considerable damage to any critter down here." His deep voice echoed off the ceiling. The basement floor was concrete, the walls cinderblock. Fluorescent bulbs lit up a room stored neatly with chrome display cases, shelving, and cardboard boxes.

Jackie took cautious steps as she followed Armando. "I really shouldn't store anything down here. This is one of the few businesses on the block that has a basement. With the way neighborhoods have been flooding, I shouldn't take the chance that I could lose equipment in a flood."

"At least put things up on a platform so they aren't ruined."

"I have another room upstairs I can turn into a storage room. Then nothing will be kept down here that I can't afford to have destroyed."

"So far I haven't seen or heard anything moving. I'll put one in the furnace room and one at each of the four corners of the basement. Oops."

"Oops? Oops what?" Jackie's voice quivered. "I don't like oops."

"Something scurried. Maybe it was a dust ball. All I know is it was gray."

Jackie didn't wait. She hustled up the stairs as fast as her tight dress would allow. "How on earth did we get mice in this building? I don't remember mice being in the basement before."

"Why? What did he see?" Jenny perched back on the stool. "Are there more?" She picked up her book bag from the floor and set it on the counter.

"He saw something moving. That was good enough for me. I don't need to know anything more other than how to get rid of them."

The basement door opened and Armando emerged. "If there are more than six then I'll have to set more traps."

"I really appreciate your help. All you did was walk in here to buy a gift and I feel like I'm taking advantage of you. Jenny, refund his money for those mouse traps."

"No problem. I'm always eager to help a beautiful woman."

Jackie flashed her Whitney Houston smile. "You have gone through a lot of trouble for a woman you don't know. You must let me repay you somehow. Can I buy you lunch? There is a wonderful café down the street. It's such a nice day we can eat outside on the deck."

Armando smiled back. "That sounds like a wonderful idea."

10

Sam checked the alley behind the hotel building. The newspapers had reported that the victim possibly died from exposure years ago. There wasn't any speculation as to how long ago the stairwell was walled up or quotes from any prior hotel owner as to whether they had noticed the hotel had a fourth floor. After spending one day on page one, the story had been buried on page twenty and probably would never be mentioned again. Jake wasn't happy about that. Robinson wasn't too happy either but he had no control over Chief Murphy. Benny didn't have anything conclusive to rule it a homicide.

On the other hand, Sam's suspicions and curiosity were on high alert. She knew the victim wasn't a homeless person, nor had she been a drug addict. The only thing Sam was missing was proof. One place to pick up more auras was where the body was found.

She pulled a lock pick from her pocket, checked behind her to make sure she wasn't being watched, then quickly inserted the tension wrench and jiggled the pick. How simple. Her shoes clicked along the tile floor. The emptiness of the building felt heavy, as though silence had a weight to it. She took her time going through the lobby, imagining earlier days where travelers filled upholstered couches and cozy chair groupings. But the former owners had emptied the building of all furnishings. Walls were bare. The only thing in the lobby was the front desk which had been built into the floor. The mosaic tiles appeared to be the original flooring. Some were chipped, the colors faded, but with the wear and tear the building had gone through, it was a wonder the tiles were still intact.

Grime and haze coated the tall windows. Sam was surprised sunlight was able to filter through. The second and third floors were mezzanines which looked out onto the lobby. The wide staircase emptied out onto a ten foot wide hallway. Sam hadn't taken time to study the décor when she had first visited. Now that she had a chance to see the details, Frank was right. The hallway reminded her of the hotel in Stephen King's *The Shining*. She half expected a torrent of blood to gush from an opened elevator. Sam shook that thought from her head as she passed apartments. All of the doors had been left open, probably by the crime scene investigators checking for signs of a break in. But the rooms were all identical, empty of furniture and looking worse for wear. There was a lot of history in these walls and Sam couldn't wait to visit the Historical Society to check on the building's past.

Once on the fourth floor she stood in the doorway of the apartment. The chair where Jane Doe had sat along with the couch and rug had been removed as had the newspapers and anything else that had been dated. The wood under the area where the recliner and rug had sat was stained. Fingerprint powder could be seen on the windows and windowsills as well as the countertop. There was only one large framed picture on the wall above the television set and a wooden coffee table abandoned near the center of the room.

Sam moved down the hall to the bedroom. There was a claw foot tub in the corner of the bathroom with a shower rod but no shower curtain. The piping under the sink was exposed and there was a mirrored cabinet above the sink. The bedroom was just as antiquated. A four-poster bed was against one wall and a dark mahogany dresser sat with drawers gaping open. From what Sam could tell, the baby dicks had gone over this place thoroughly. She turned from the bed and gasped. The hallway was strewn with lilacs: pink, light lavender, dark lavender. The aroma was breathtaking. Sam gingerly stepped around the lilacs and entered the living room. A woman was sitting on a non-existent couch, but it wasn't the couch removed from the apartment. It was a leather couch with a bright-colored wool blanket laying across the back. Sam imagined the woman had a basket of flowers in her lap, but when she walked around the couch she saw that the woman was counting money. The couch was filled with cash in all denominations. Then Sam remembered she had seen a bank teller window the first time she saw the woman. Had the deceased been a bank employee? How long ago? How many banks were in Chasen Heights years ago?

"What is so significant about that year?" Sam asked. But the woman just looked up at Sam, smiled, then faded as quickly as she had appeared.

* * *

"It seems like I've been doing all the talking," Armando said. He reached for the bill but Jackie slapped his hand away.

"You know about all there is to know about me, sugar. I own a business and I have mice. You, on the other hand, are leading such an exciting life. You have a law degree from Indiana University. You are staying here for the summer, doing odd jobs to make extra money before leaving to build Habitat Homes in Haiti. I will certainly do all I can to help you out." Jackie pulled out her checkbook and pen. "When we get back to the store you can measure the wall for the shelving units. And do pick up more mouse traps. If there are any bodies down there I would appreciate not seeing them." She ripped off the check and handed it to him. "Now don't forget that gift for your auntie. I assume she's the one you are staying with for the summer."

Armando looked confused then smiled. "Oh, yes. Auntie Mookie. I need a gift that says, 'Thanks for putting me through college but I don't want to be a lawyer. I want to work for the FBI.' Do you have something like that?"

"You want to work for the Bureau?"

Armando's gaze breezed through the various tables in the outdoor cafe. He lowered his voice as he said, "My uncle was a cop and was killed in the line of duty. She wanted me to work in anything but law enforcement. But it's in my blood, you know?"

"She would have reason to worry. It's a tough line of work." Jackie saw his face collapse, as if he were counting on her to be the one person to support his decision. "Armando, what do you think your mom would have said if she were still alive?"

He leaned back in the chair, arms crossed, as though giving the question considerable thought. If Jackie didn't know better, she would have said Armando was trying to summon his mother's spirit right at the table. "My mom was a wonderful lady. She believed in working in a field where you could make a difference, where you thought you could utilize your God-given talents."

"You've already applied, haven't you?"

Armando shrugged, a sheepish grin crossed his lips. "Only problem is, I know they are going to be contacting auntie and I need to head it off at the pass, kind of soften her up a little. I saw some perfume in your store. Did you have it specially made for you?"

"Yes. *Jackie* is a subtle fragrance. Not too flowery so the more mature women love it. It should make a perfect gift for your auntie. Not sure if it would soften her up much, though. You may need to send her on a cruise."

* * *

"Is that all there is?" Robinson thumbed through the file folder on the Jane Doe found in the Embers Hotel.

Andy leaned over the captain's desk while his partner, Maury, stood by the door. "We haven't had time to do anything but speak with Adam Folker, the Property Assessor at First State Bank."

"There have been a number of owners over the years but unless the chief gives us the time we need," Maury added, "we won't be able to thoroughly investigate the hotel ownership much less make any headway in identifying the deceased."

The captain spent several minutes skimming through Adam Folker's brief statement. His eyes flicked to the two baby dicks in their slick Miami Vice clothes. Where were they when Murphy was assessing the tidiness of the office? Just looking at these two GQ candidates would have dragged Murphy's attention from the cluttered desks.

"He did provide photos of the interior of the hotel when they foreclosed on the property in 2004," Maury added.

Robinson pulled the photo from the file. These two practically alphabetized the contents of the folder. "Huh. No stairway to the fourth floor in these photos."

"Reed Management was the owners foreclosed on," Andy continued. "Mr. Folker has pictures from 1994 when Reed purchased the hotel and turned it into an apartment building. That stairway was wallboarded over then, too."

"I would like nothing better than to have you follow up on Jane Doe but the chief considers it low priority. It's an election year and he doesn't want us wasting valuable hours on a cold case. It's bullshit if you ask me. Sorry to do this to you guys."

"According to Mr. Folker, the bank donated the hotel to the city...," Andy started.

"Yeah, I know. Newspapers have been filled with the eminent domain case and the pissed off residents and the new youth center."

"The city is going to tear down the hotel in a couple weeks. We'll lose whatever evidence we might find." Maury continued his pleading as though anything the baby dicks said would change the outcome.

"Whatever the crime tech boys found will have to do. The election will be over soon and we can get back to a normal routine." *Hopefully*, Robinson prayed silently. "For now we have to go along with the chief's wishes. I'll keep this file. I want to read through it in more detail. Thanks for a great job."

* * *

He scoured the newspaper for any reports of a body discovered in the unincorporated area. So far the old lady had remained undiscovered. With feet propped on the windowsill, he sipped a cup of lukewarm coffee and reread the article on the body found at the Embers Hotel. It had been found a little later than he had expected. Having the wrecking ball expose the remains would have been far more dramatic. The timing may work to his advantage.

His room was on the second floor of the Shoreline Shelter and had all the reminders of what his life had become. He should be living in a mansion with servants to wait on him, a driver to take him where he wanted to go, his own private plane to jet off to Paris for dinner, and a garage of classic cars. Instead, he was camouflaged as a homeless war vet with signs of post traumatic stress disorder. What little money he had left was stuffed in hiding places.

The ring bit at his finger. He pulled it off and stared at the dried blood clinging to the surface, remnants of the old lady. If she would only have shut up he wouldn't have had to hit her. The incessant chatter had driven him crazy. Someone that chatty had to have run off at the mouth. Women always do. So far, not one curious eye had stared at him at the shelter. He wasn't sure how much more of this place he could take. A tiny voice in his head kept tempting him to try one more score. Stealing wallets out of purses at the grocery store reaped few results. People shopped with credit cards these days so the chances of finding hundreds of dollars in wallets was about as likely as finding a gold bar lying in a gutter.

If only he had a computer, but that would be useless. He didn't have the high tech knowledge to do the kind of credit card theft geeks do these days. And he was running low on cash.

The throw-away danced on the window sill. He picked up the cell phone and checked the screen. Looked like the bank just opened for business.

11

Frank stood in the doorway to his office amid the muffled laughter and giggles from the officers and clerical staff behind him. On the desk was a stuffed beagle and kitten. A sign propped in front of the desk read, *Property of the Fearless Pooch and Pussy Chaser*. It was taped to a piece of wallboard. He turned to glare at the hecklers. Heads immediately bowed toward paperwork. The women busied themselves at the copy machine or in front of file drawers.

"All right. Who's the wiseass?" Frank yelled.

"Hey, Frank," Sergeant Scofield yelled from the front desk. "How come you didn't have to wear those cute brown safari outfits with the shorts like the rest of the dog catchers? I hear you got some great looking legs."

"You been peeking in the shower room again, Sarge?" Frank's rolling laughter was infectious.

Jake's office was next to Frank's. He unlocked the door and swore under his breath to shoot anyone who had placed a similar display on his desk. Everything was as it should be. Murphy may be neat and tidy but Jake's FBI training gave new meaning to the word sanitized. The glass covering the polished wood desk gleamed under harsh lighting. A pecking on the window drew his attention to two mourning doves. They waddled aside as he cranked open the window and tossed a handful of sunflower seeds onto the windowsill. Tonto and Cochise were regular visitors ever since Sam had been the previous occupant of this office. There didn't appear to be stuffed animals anywhere. It paid to look threatening and to leave the door locked.

Frank strolled in and appeared disappointed at the appearance of Jake's office. "How come you got off easy?"

"I lock my door. You should try it sometime."

A large fist assaulted the door jamb. "Got a second, boys?" The door jamb breathed a sigh of relief as Robinson pulled his hand away. He tossed a folder on Jake's desk and sat down.

"What's up?" Frank hefted one cheek on the side of the desk.

"I'm sure you heard the chief shelved the Jane Doe case."

Jake gave a casual glance at the folder. "What was his reason?"

"The campaign, crime statistics, voters' perception, pick one. The baby dicks barely started digging so there isn't much to go on."

The two detectives exchanged curious stares, then looked at the green folder on the desk. "Uh, are we done chasing animals?" Frank asked with a hint of hope in his voice.

"Well, I know you have that easy job of helping little ducks and abandoned baby squirrels," Robinson said with a deep chuckle. "Unfortunately, no. I tried back flips but Murphy won't cut your penance."

"Sooooo," Frank dragged out the word as though it contained multiple syllables.

"The chief can tie any pretty colored ribbon he wants on this case but one thing is glaringly obvious." Robinson nudged the folder closer to Jake. "Someone boarded that stairway up, then took time to paint and wallpaper the alcove. We can kid ourselves that renovations were completed without checking the fourth floor but you and I know that is highly unlikely." He rose to his full six foot six inch height and sighed heavily. "I will be filing that folder away. Course, I can't control it if someone makes a copy of it first to give to a certain someone who's been crawling all over this case like an ant on a sugar cube." Robinson checked his watch. "Think I'll go to dinner before I do my filing."

The captain lumbered out and headed for the elevator.

* * *

Sam was fingering the locket when she heard the back door open. She quickly slipped it under dish towels in the second drawer, then moved to the stove to stir the simmering pasta noodles. "My fearless animal hunter is home. I trust you shot some possum or squirrel for dinner."

Jake growled something unintelligible as he retrieved a beer from the refrigerator. "Remind me to check the laws regarding owning exotic pets."

"Why? Did you get bit by a cobra?"

"No, I want to go on patrol with a cobra."

Sam poured the pasta noodles into a colander and turned the water on to rinse them. She lifted the lid on another pot on the stove and stirred the simmering spaghetti sauce.

"Smells good." Jake planted a kiss on her cheek. "Another of Abby's meals from the freezer, I take it."

Sam elbowed him aside but failed to come up with a retort. After all, she would be the first to admit her culinary skills were as good as her talent for keeping plants alive. "You could make yourself useful by bringing out the salad and pouring me a glass of wine."

The kitchen table was set for two. Sam preferred the formal dining room where they usually ate dinner but that was when they had five people at the table, or at least four adults and one baby. Now it was just a vacant fifteen-foot-long table with unlit candles and a driftwood floral arrangement guarding the center.

Once they were settled and plates filled, Sam asked, "Corner any more rabid cats?"

Jake searched her face with suspicion, then let his eyes sweep the corners of the kitchen and down the hall to the back door. "Swear to me that you didn't bring that cat home."

"It is still at the shelter as you had ordered." Sam stressed the word *ordered.*

"If it's as cute as you think, I'm sure it will be adopted soon."

Sam wanted to tell him there were at least ten identical cats at the shelter so the chances of that particular one being adopted were slim. She looked up to find Jake glaring at her from across the table. "Honest. I didn't bring it home. I only have a few days to find it a home." She stabbed at her salad, her mind going through names of family friends who might need a pet but she came up with zilch. All family friends were on the reservation and she wasn't sure when Alex was planning another trip. "Maybe Frank would like a cat?"

"Frank almost shot the damn thing because it was making him chase it. Besides, Claudia has a cat which Frank loathes."

"What about someone at the precinct? Maybe Sergeant Scofield or Captain Robinson. It's in good health, no fleas. And it is friendly. At least it was with me."

Jake was shaking his head even before she finished the sentence. "Forget it."

"Doesn't Animal Control have a list of foster homes like they show on *Animal Planet*? People take in strays until a permanent home can be found." She watched him scoop more salad into a bowl, his silence confirming Jake lacked one sensitive bone in his body. "Didn't you ever own a pet?"

"Sure, a beagle. His name was Roger but it was more my mom's dog. My dad kicked it down the stairs and it died from a broken neck."

Sam had to remind herself that Jake revealed only slivers of his childhood and so far she hadn't heard anything that painted a pretty picture. He had purchased Poco for Alex so he did have a sensitive side. Of course, it was also a bribery gift so maybe that didn't count.

"I did bring you something to play with." Jake left the table, disappeared into the study, and returned with a folder which he placed at her elbow. He returned to his chair and continued eating.

Her curiosity piqued, Sam moved her plate aside and opened the folder. "This is the Jane Doe case. Aren't the baby dicks working it?"

"Murphy wants the public to see the police focusing only on serious crimes. He wants them to show a presence out on the street, not working dead end cases so he told them to shelve it."

"Until after the election, I take it."

"Unless miraculous evidence shows that Jane Doe is a prominent socialite, Murphy considers it a waste of time. So far Murphy hasn't dictated what cases Benny can work."

Sam flipped through the baby dicks' notes. "How did you get the file?"

"Robinson feels what Murphy doesn't know won't kill him. One thing is for certain: Someone took time to not only close off that stairway but paint and wallpaper the alcove. Course, if Murphy finds out we let you onto the crime scene we'll probably be permanent dog catchers."

"He's the one that approved the department hiring an investigative consultant."

"With a little arm twisting."

"Well, we'll just have to see how long we can keep it a secret." She felt a stirring in her chest, an excitement she always felt during a hunt, a case to puzzle over, something to occupy her mind while Dillon was gone. Sam suddenly realized why Jake was doing it. She looked across the table at her fabulous husband and whispered, "Have I told you lately how much I love you?"

A smile tugged at the corner of his mouth. "You can show me later."

12

The Chasen Heights Historical Society was one block from City Hall in a two-story brick house donated by Hester Schrumn, the founder of the Historical Society. Hester had been the city's first librarian and a stickler for facts. Deceased for over twenty years, her staff carried on in the same vein.

The woman behind the counter stood barely five feet tall but Sam didn't doubt for a minute that she ruled the office with the proverbial iron fist. She placed a large scrapbook on the counter next to a book titled, *The History of The Embers.* Her eyes narrowed behind red framed glasses as she said, "No eating or drinking anywhere near these treasures, no licking of your fingers, no bending of pages, no marking on the pages with pen or pencil." She handed Sam a pair of latex gloves.

Sam instinctively straightened, feeling scolded for gross errors she had yet to make. "I will guard them with my life." Her eyes caught the name on the name tag. "Lucy. What a wonderful name."

Lucy wasn't impressed. Not one eyelash twitched. She passed a clipboard across the counter. "Sign your name and time next to each of the items you will be reviewing. You have one hour."

One hour? What can I accomplish in one hour? Sam thought as she signed the clipboard. "That's a lot to go through in one hour."

"Then you better get started."

Sam narrowed her own eyes. "You didn't happen to be a drill sergeant in a previous life, did you?" She snatched the items off the counter before Lucy banished her from the building.

The scrapbook was more an overview of the historical buildings in Chasen Heights. There were snapshots of The Embers in various stages of completion but no mention of when it had changed hands. The Historical Society also steered away from scandal. There weren't any pictures of the police raiding the hotel during the raucus early 1900s or the first owners being frog marched into the police station. The history of the hotel had been sanitized.

The book, on the other hand, had been published in 1978. It had pictures of the Sobieski Brothers and did document their arrest. It showed the hotel boarded up in 1945 before the Sutton Company purchased it in 1949. Sam scribbled pages of notes while keeping her eye on the clock. She had hoped to squeeze a few more minutes out of her time slot but at fifty-nine minutes and fifty-five seconds, Lucy appeared at her elbow, arms folded, one gnarled finger tapping her watch.

Sam left the Historical Society and headed to the County Clerk's office. The parking lot was full since the county building also housed the courthouse. She pulled around to a side lot and had to hoof it to the main entrance on ankle wrap espadrilles. Gym shoes would have been a better choice for comfort.

There were four people in line with one woman at the counter. Ten women seated at desks appeared to ignore the growing line. Sam took the opportunity to write out her request listing just the hotel's name and address.

The man in front of her was shifting from foot to foot, wearing his plaid shirt outside of his pants, a red bandana tied biker-style around his head. "Can you believe this?" he moaned. "I've been in line for fifteen minutes and not one of those women has moved off their ass. My tax dollars at work."

"It's her ass," Sam corrected him.

He shot her a look of annoyance, his gaze riveted on her third earring of beads and feathers.

"One is the subject and it's singular so *one of those women has moved off her ass* is the correct way to say it." Sam flashed him a smile.

"Are you being a smart ass?"

"Am I?" Sam could smell smoke and liquor fumes drifting from the man.

"Listen, little lady…"

A security guard walked up to Sam. "Everything okay, Sergeant?"

Sam didn't recognize him but with as many times as her picture had been in the news over the years she wasn't surprised that he knew her. She also didn't have to be addressed as sergeant but knew he was using her old rank as a way to hopefully diffuse the situation. And it worked. The impatient customer snapped his jaws shut and turned around.

Two of the women abandoned their desks and approached the counter, opening up their registers.

Sam obviously made friends because when it was her turn, the clerk was more than pleasant and eager to help. She had a list of names and addresses of all the owners within twenty minutes. The sky had hazed over by the time she walked out. Her spidey senses were triggered on the walk back to her Jeep. She stopped, then pivoted. The troublemaker was following her. Sam slipped the copies into her tote bag but kept her hand inside. Although she wasn't armed, the troublemaker didn't know that.

He held up his hands. His eyes reflected a man in need of sleep or at least three aspirin. "Just wanted to apologize, that's all."

Sam kept her right hand in the tote. "What set you off? I know long waits can be irritating but it's only ten o'clock in the morning."

"Lucas Rucker." He held out a hand to Sam but she ignored it. "I found out yesterday I'm losing my house. Guess I'm not in the best of moods these days." He sank onto the bumper of a truck as if the sheer weight of whatever he was carrying was too much for his legs to bear.

"The bank foreclosed on it?" Sam wasn't sure she wanted to get involved but as far as she knew he could be there to rob her so her right hand stayed buried in the tote bag.

"Nah. House has been paid off for years. Only place I've ever owned. Wife died last year from cancer so just about all my money goes to pay her hospital bills."

Where Abby would have sat down with the man and listened to his story, Sam wanted to run to her Jeep and get the hell out of there. Maybe she had been a cop for too long, even if it was five short years. She had seen and listened to her share of sob stories, most of them pity fests, and she wasn't in the mood for another one. Sam just wanted to say, "good luck with that" and move on but his next sentence stopped her.

"City's tearing down that Embers Hotel to put in a youth center. They want the surrounding property for a parking lot. The house and business are all I have. They are condemning the property within three blocks of the area, claiming eminent domain. Guess I drowned my sorrows a little too much last night. Little hungover this morning and wasn't in the mood to have the city make me wait in line to get a copy of my tax bill. Just adds salt to the wound, you know?"

"I didn't know there were any inhabited buildings in that part of town."

"There are a few residents and businesses still there. Even if the city were to buy it from me, that wouldn't be enough to buy something else, not at today's prices. I just…" He ran a calloused hand across his chest. Sam saw dirt under his nails and cuts on the tops of his hand.

"What do you do for a living?" Sam asked.

"I repair bikes, motorcycles, four wheelers. Do all my work in the garage next to my house so I'd be losing my house and the garage where my business is." Lucas stood with a shake of his head. Instead of looking like a man in search of a fight, Lucas had tears in his eyes and the look of a man beaten.

"Isn't Councilman Schuler the one pushing for this youth center?"

"Yeah, he's the one."

"You know, he's running for mayor. You and the other homeowners who are being displaced should see that new reporter who is covering the mayoral campaigns. Publicity about residents being screwed is not something Schuler is going to want in the news. I think Bennett is the reporter's name. He seems like the kind of guy who likes to stir things up. He isn't going to play nice with either candidate. He wants to make a name for himself, get noticed by the bigger newspapers and this is one way to do it."

Lucas dug around in his shirt pocket and pulled out a piece of paper. "Bennett is the guy's name?" When Sam nodded he wrote it on the paper and shoved it back into his shirt pocket.

"How far away from The Embers do you live?"

"Three blocks."

"It's changed hands over the years. Have you seen any work being done in the hotel? Maybe a workman carrying wood, wallboard, anyone suspicious?"

"That about that body being found?"

"Yes."

"There's always been work going on over the years. Since it was donated to the city though, I haven't seen anyone around except for some homeless people who seemed to always be looking for a way in out of the cold. Some stay at the homeless shelter over on First Street."

Sam handed him a business card. "If you remember anything else or any of your neighbors remember seeing anything suspicious since it has been closed, give me a call."

Lucas studied the card. "I thought you were a cop."

Sam smiled as she turned to walk away. "I was."

13

It took awhile but Sam finally located the white board in the basement. She remembered drawing on it as her father wrote notes when he worked on a criminal case. No more than four years old at the time, Sam could barely reach the board with her erasable marker. Samuel Casey had built a stand for the white board. It was a simple railing which flipped out from under the fourth shelf on one of the bookcases. Four feet of railing was enough to support the board.

There were two groups of seatings in the study. One was by the corner fireplace and consisted of a couch, two chairs, and a coffee table. Sam's computer was against the wall by the fireplace. The other grouping was by the two walls of bookcases, a haven with a couch and love seat. A wet bar was against the wall straddling the two seatings. A television set and entertainment center were built into one bookcase.

Once the board was in place, Sam cleaned it off, noticing with amusement the row of circles running along the bottom, a four-year-old's attempt to draw flowers. Her father didn't even get upset when she had accidentally used a permanent marker. Even now, after all these years, she could smell his aftershave, feel the warmth of his arms. But those memories brought back the bad ones…her father being blown to pieces in a car bomb, a scene no five-year-old should have to watch.

Sam clenched her trembling hands into fists. "Work," she told herself. That always got the kinks out. She laid out her notes on the table by the bar, more memories flooding back of friendly poker games, her father and other reporters gathering on a Friday night while she was shooed off to bed. She would sneak back down and sit on the bottom stair, the pocket door not quite closed all the way. There weren't that many memories a daughter could have of a father she only knew for five years but what little time she had she learned a lot. When working on a story her father never stopped working, even during those friendly poker games. She would watch through the opening in the door as an idea would strike and he would get up from the table and go to the whiteboard. He would bounce things off of his fellow reporters and the night would briefly turn to business.

Tears sneaked from the corners of her eyes. She wiped them away wishing Abby were here for a quick hug. It was amazing how seeing scribbled markings from over twenty years ago could still have an effect on her.

Sam opened a box of markers, reading the box first to make sure they were erasable, then set to work.

* * *

He trained the binoculars on the hotel two blocks away. His room on the second floor gave him a good view of the building. The yellow crime scene tape had been removed so the police were no longer scouring for clues. It was as though the body were low priority. It was a former front page story reduced to a blurb on page twenty. At least there weren't any articles about the old biddy in the ditch...the ditch witch. Who says he doesn't have a sense of humor?

Now all he had to worry about was the woman who showed up prior to the medical examiner and crime scene investigators. Then she had returned later. Why? Who was she and what did she have to do with the case? Was she going to put a roadblock in his plans?

He tossed the binoculars down and returned to the task he had started earlier. The gun lay in parts on the table where the morning newspaper was spread out to protect the finish. Time to clean the gun. It had a job to do, then he would do a little more investigating on his own.

14

The next morning Sam made a stop before heading over to Jackie's boutique. Once she obtained her present, she was at the boutique's door when it opened at ten o'clock.

"What have you done to the place? It looks wonderful." Sam did a slow three-sixty of Jackie's store hoping her over enthusiasm wasn't too transparent. "I swear every time I come in here the place is different."

"Jenny put up new displays in the windows. Other than that, not much." Jackie's eyes narrowed much the same way Jake's did when his bullshit meter was flashing. "What's in the box, sugar?"

"It must be the colors," Sam rambled on. "You color coordinate the racks so well. And your perfume display is new, isn't it?"

Jackie folded her arms and tapped one long talon on her chin. "What's in the box, Sam?"

Sam placed the box on the counter. "You were the first person I thought of when I found this little…gem."

A scratching came from inside the box. Jackie took a step back. "Whatever you have I don't want. I've had enough of scratching boxes to last me a lifetime."

"You've never refused a gift from me." She opened the box and a meow erupted. She watched Jackie's eyes widen and she expected her friend to jab a finger toward the door and yell, "OUT!" But what Jackie did next surprised her.

"Oh, Sam. How did you know?" Jackie gathered the cat in her arms. "Look at you."

Huh?

Jenny emerged from behind the counter. "Someone must have told you we have mice in the basement."

"Actually, no. This is the cat Jake and Frank were chasing into the

Embers Hotel when they found the mummified remains."

"Well then, we need to call you Cleopatra, right? And we have just the spot for you, Cleo." Jackie opened the basement door and set the cat on the floor. Cleo took several tentative steps, sniffed the air, then charged down the stairs.

"I'll go to the store and pick up some cat food, litter box and all the other essentials," Jenny said.

"Don't forget a cat bed," Jackie called out as Jenny rushed out of the store.

"Hey, Jackie." A black Adonis walked out of one of the side rooms carrying a hammer. "Oh, hi."

Sam's eyes shifted to Jackie.

"This is Armando. Armando, this is my closest friend, Samantha Casey. She used to be one of the best cops in the Heights. Now she's the best P.I."

"P.I., huh? Guess that's good to know if I ever need help."

"Sam brought me a cat. We've named her Cleopatra because she was found in that old hotel where they found the body yesterday. You know, tomb, mummies."

Sam watched the two walk into a side room and wondered where Jackie had met him. Did Lamon know about him? He looked at least a decade or more younger than Jackie. Sam tried to ignore the suspicious voice in her head and reminded herself it wasn't any of her business. But giggling erupted from the back office and Jackie soon emerged all smiles.

"Isn't he just gorgeous," Jackie said. Sam said nothing. "He has been so helpful around here. I would have never known we had mice if it wasn't for Armando."

"Armando. Sounds like a stage name. How did you meet him?"

"He came in looking for a present for his auntie."

"His aunt? Right." Sam leaned in close, checked to make sure Armando wasn't near, and whispered, "How do you know he wasn't the one who was following you?"

"Does he look like a stalker to you? You aren't the only one who can read people, sugar."

* * *

Councilman Schuler checked his watch then pointed a finger at Rafe Bennett. "Next question."

Rafe stood amid the residents and campaign workers at city hall. Schuler had picked one of the smaller rooms so there was standing room only. It looked better on the front page of the *Post Tribune*. Rafe gave his notes a brief glance. "The city plans to have a youth center built on the property where the Embers Hotel currently stands. Does the City Council really plan to condemn the surrounding property and displace six homes and businesses to build a parking lot and baseball field?"

Schuler had been ready for this question and eyed Lucas Rucker standing in the back of the room. "A youth center is something that this town needs, and especially that part of town. Many of the residents can't afford to move during these economic times so we have to try to bring the parks and shops to them. The prime location for the center and park is the five square block area where the Embers Hotel and, unfortunately, a few residences and businesses now stand. We have to look at what is best for the majority. We can certainly help relocate these people."

"Who's going to pay for it?" Lucas yelled from the back of the room. "I don't have the down payment for another house much less another business."

"Yeah, I don't see the city chipping in," another resident yelled.

"Bettye Williams is a single mother working two jobs to support her boys."

"And is that my problem?" Someone else yelled.

If Schuler was ruffled it didn't show, Rafe thought. He remained calm but a steely glare was aimed at the most vocal of the residents in the back of the room. Seemingly unaffected, Schuler made a motion to the young woman planted in the front row with her two sons.

"We can't have our young people playing in back alleys with broken beer bottles and discarded needles. My job as your new mayor is to clean up the downtown area and make it a safe place to live and play. There are more than one hundred and thirty low income families living near downtown. What we do affects the lives of almost five hundred people versus the displacement of six houses and several businesses."

Rafe wasn't sure if there was prompting from a campaign worker but the audience broke out in applause.

Lucas didn't waver. "And what kind of kickback are you and the Council getting from the developer, huh? You can't fool us. We know how the city works. A crooked councilman will make the perfect crooked mayor."

Schuler held up both hands. "I understand your frustration."

"You feel our pain?" another man mimicked which brought laughter from the crowd.

"Like hell you do," a female voice yelled.

"My office is calling banks to find out the best loan rates for those displaced. Please get in touch with my people tomorrow." Schuler drowned out responses by holding up a hand and yelling, "Thank you all for coming. Please remember to vote." He motioned for several families in the front row to join him for a photo op.

Rafe weaved his way through the crowd to get to the back of the room where Lucas Rucker glared at the councilman as if his stare alone could cause considerable harm. But Lucas and his group stormed out of the room. It was just as well. Rafe actually wanted to first corner Chief Murphy and get his opinion on the eminent domain issue. He knew where Lucas lived and worked and Rafe could readily see a picture of the area the city planned to condemn. It would make a great story for the on line edition.

15

Sam's next stop was the Little Sisters of Mary assisted living facility in South Bend, Indiana. While reviewing the list of previous owners she obtained from the books at the Historical Society, she remembered the newspapers left in the hotel were dated 1976. Deciding that was a significant date, Sam checked to see who had owned the hotel back then. A little sleuthing and some owed favors gave her a current address for John and Ann Kendall. They had comprised MK Enterprises and had owned the hotel for almost twenty years.

Sam had called ahead to verify that they still resided there. She learned that Ann passed away a decade ago. However, John was still a resident, in relatively good health, and, hopefully, had a good memory. The nurse was kind enough to share John's fondness for chocolate malt balls so Sam stopped off at a store and bought several bags of candy as a bribe.

The Little Sisters of Mary was a short mile off of Interstate 80, not far from Notre Dame University. Sam planned her visit around lunch time to assure that John would be awake. Sister Angela met Sam in the doorway and pointed out John. He not only was awake, but he was also engaged in a lively chess match with a male nurse. Sam would have never guessed John's age. His hair still had streaks of brown, his eyes alert. His back wasn't stooped nor did his hands tremble. Not bad for seventy-seven. Now her only hope was that his memory was still good.

"I'm sure you don't want me to give him all five bags of malt balls," Sam said. "Maybe the nurses and other sisters can share these. "

The young woman smiled. "Oh, I'm sure we can put these to good use. They will be serving lunch soon. John would love to have company. He usually eats his lunch on the patio. Come." Sister Angela led Sam down a hall through the cafeteria and to a patio door. "Someone will bring your lunches out." She nodded toward a doorway. "John usually likes the table by the fountain. It's out of the sunlight and has a great view. Please have a seat."

Sam thanked her and made her way to the patio. It was a nice facility, just one floor but spread over thirty acres. There was a decorative brick walk through the gardens, a bocce ball set, even a putting green. A rock garden with a waterfall played host to floating lilies. Weeping willows swayed in the distance, their long tendrils kissing the ground. The facilities look more like a resort. John's favorite table was on the opposite side of an urn filled with one large hibiscus tree. It overlooked a spouting fountain.

Ten minutes later John was wheeled out by the male nurse. Sam didn't remember John sitting in a wheelchair when he was playing chess. And she didn't see any noticeable injuries.

"So you are my lunch date. And what a lovely thing you are. I'd get up but it would be a little difficult. Got a bum hip that bothers me from time to time."

"Now you behave yourself, John," the male nurse said. Adam was in large letters on his name tag, probably so those with poor eyesight could see. "Just press your buzzer when you are ready."

A wait staff in bright floral outfits rolled out carts and distributed beverages. Other residents were starting to shuffle into the building or search for tables on the patio. Twin sisters held onto each other in what looked like a talon grip as they hobbled past.

John nodded toward a menu in the middle of the table propped between the salt-free Mrs. Dash and pepper shakers. "I'd stay away from the meatloaf if I were you." When a young woman in a floral uniform walked up to the table and set two glasses in front of them, John said, "I took the liberty of ordering our drinks. Hope you don't mind."

Sam took a sip. "Tonic?" She didn't mean for it to sound like a question.

John pulled something from the inside pocket of his jacket, unscrewed the cap, then poured a healthy dose into one of the glasses. "Here you go.

Nothing like a vodka tonic to wash down lunch." He handed the glass to Sam then did the same to the next glass.

"I take it they don't have an open bar on the premises."

"Saturday afternoon wine party. Limit of two glasses per person. Half of the people enjoy their own happy hour in their rooms. It's a wonder they haven't searched our rooms for secret stashes."

Sam studied the sparse lunch menu and when the waitress came back they each ordered a tuna salad on a croissant with fruit.

"So, what brings you to my humble abode, Miss Casey?"

Sam showed him her business card and asked if he had heard about the body found at the Embers Hotel. When his face reflected the shock of the uninformed, she unfolded the *Post Tribune* newspaper and showed it to him.

"Well, I'll be damned." He slipped on a pair of glasses and read the article while Sam sipped her drink. John didn't even stop to inspect his lunch when the waitress set two plates on the table. "Unbelievable," he said with a shake of his head as he handed the newspaper back to Sam. He removed the reading glasses and slipped them back into his shirt pocket.

"What made you want to own a hotel?"

John had half of his sandwich eaten before he replied. "Wasn't just owning A hotel. It was owning THAT hotel. What an era. Even *Life* magazine featured Chasen Heights. It reported that in the early 1940s it had 14,000 residents, no churches, no traffic lights, no central telephone system, 308 nightclubs and seven policemen."

Sam remained silent, preferring to eat to keep the vodka buzz away and to also let him revel in his memories. She was too young to know about the wild Sin Strip era of Chasen Heights but made a mental note to check back further in the archives.

"Chasen Heights was known as the Las Vegas of the Midwest," John reminisced. "I was just a boy in the '40s but remember my mother yelling for us kids to get down on the floor of the car as my dad drove down State Street. She didn't want us to see the silhouettes of the topless dancers in the nightclub windows. But you know boys," he added with a wink to Sam. "We just had to take a peek. Sidewalks were so crammed people walked shoulder to shoulder. When train tracks finally opened up I heard even Capone and his boys made weekend trips here. There were headline acts in the hotel—Tommy Dorsey, Louis Armstrong, Lottie Devine did her feather dance at the Cabaret Nightclub. My buddies and I would pass the bouncer a saw bill to let us in when we were teens. We looked twenty and the bouncer didn't care as long as it looked like we were old enough to shave."

John finished his drink then waved the waitress over for another. Sam declined a second tonic and instead ordered an iced tea. Behind the safety of the potted plant, John added a shot of vodka to his tonic.

"How did seven policemen handle all the crime?"

"State Street was the safest street in town. Day time, night time, didn't matter. Women could shop downtown without fear. And even if there was a complaint about one of the establishments, the chief would send a couple boys down to belly up to the bar, have a beer and a talk with the owner, and everything was settled. We were not that big a town. Everybody knew each other, looked out for each other, took care of their own."

"What about the hotel itself? Was there gambling? Prostitution?"

"Gambling, sure. But what else the Strip had to contribute I can't say. Topless dancing, of course. If there was any prostitution, it wasn't going on in our hotel. Ann wouldn't have it. Sin Strip was only three blocks long and the hotel was a block off the Strip. My wife didn't care if there were a few poker games going on in the rooms but she wouldn't put up with prostitution. No way. Course the convention guys were always looking for a good time. We provided some good nightclub acts but if they wanted topless dancing, they'd have to go down the street. We offered good food, upscale accommodations and great nightclub entertainment."

"So you owned the Embers from 1964 to 1982."

"Did pretty good, too, until the East Coast boys muscled their way in.

Brought in the drugs and prostitution. Now there's nothing wrong with a girl making a little extra money in a darkened room but these guys had their girls standing on the corners half dressed, all coked up, trying to score just about anything. Things changed. People started looking at the Strip as an eyesore, an embarrassment. It was no longer safe to walk the streets at night or even shop during the daytime. With a drop in visitors, businesses started to lose money. So town officials started to clean it up in the nineties. Claimed some kind of eminent domain so they could demolish the establishments."

The waitress and a busboy came by to gather up the empty plates. Another waitress came by with a dessert cart.

"Stay away from the rice pudding," John cautioned.

Sam reached into her tote bag and brought out two bags of malted milk balls. A wide grin spread across John's face and he waved the dessert cart on.

"Why you sweet thing, you."

"Vodka and malt balls. I am a terrible influence on you."

"Nah, just sheer bribery is all it is. So why don't you tell me what brought you to my doorstep? There were lots of owners of the Embers." John grabbed a handful of malt balls and popped them in his mouth like mints.

"There was a newspaper next to the body. It was kept out of the article you read. The newspaper was dated September 4, 1976. Since you owned the hotel during that time, I thought I'd start with you."

"Plus most of the previous owners I'm sure are dead."

"That too, except for investors who couldn't make a go of it but I still believe 1976 is a significant date."

"Wish I could help you. I can't recall what I was doing last year let alone what might have happened in 1976. Did you gaggle it?"

Sam laughed. "You mean Google? No. Other than possibly being the year the victim died, I'm not sure if that specific date has any significance." Not that she would tell him. How could she explain to any stranger how lilacs appear out of nowhere or the newspaper dangles in front of her eyes as though suspended by some invisible puppet maker? She pulled a photo from her tote bag and placed it on the table in front of him. "Do you remember when you walled up this staircase on the third floor? If one of the detectives hadn't accidentally hit the wall, he would have never known there was a fourth floor."

"What?" John shook his head as he studied the picture. "It was never walled up when we owned it. Our maintenance man lived there. When we started using an outside maintenance company, we let our nephew use it. He did odd jobs during the summers and we let him live there. Made enough money plus tips to help put himself through college."

A scenario played out in Sam's head. Did the nephew know the woman who died? But someone would have found the body if the staircase wasn't walled up. "Did your nephew also work for the people who purchased the hotel after you?"

"Nah. He was out of college by then and working."

Sam pulled the locket out of her purse, opened it and passed it to John. He slipped his glasses back on and studied the picture.

"Have you ever seen either of these people?"

"Why, yes. That's my nephew and I think a girl he was quite taken with. Hard to be sure, the picture is so small. This isn't the girl that died, is it?"

"I'm assuming it is because she had it on her. Do you know her name?"

John took his glasses off and handed the locket back to Sam. He waved a staff member over and ordered another tonic. He waited until he received his drink, doctored it, and took a long sip before talking.

"Alice, I think, or something like it. She did something fancy with her name."

Sam couldn't think of how fancy you could get with the name Alice. "Alicia?"

"Yeah, I think that's it. Boy, did he fall hard. They were inseparable for weeks and then poof. She disappeared." He looked at the opened locket on the table. "But my nephew had nothing to do with her not returning."

"Why do you say that?"

"We spent a lot of time with him. He was cocky like most guys at that age, but he was good hearted. He went from college to the police academy. He wouldn't have done anything to jeopardize his career."

"He's a cop?" Sam made no effort to hide the shock from her face. "Where at?"

"Why, in Chasen Heights. Haven't seen him in a long time. Would be nice if he would come visit once in ..."

"What precinct does he work at? I don't recognize the name Kendall." It would be just Sam's luck that he was no longer a cop or was killed in the line of duty.

"He wasn't a Kendall. He was from my wife's side of the family... Murphy."

16

Dennis Murphy? Sam gathered her thoughts as she waited for the waitress to bring her another tonic. Once the waitress walked away, Sam handed her drink to John. "Put a healthy dose in there. I think I need it."

"I take it you know my nephew."

She grabbed her glass from John and took a long swallow. "You can say that. He's the reason I'm no longer a cop. And he's now the chief of police."

"Chief? You don't say," he replied with a little more pride than Sam had expected. "Had a feeling he'd be much better at kissing political ass than chasing criminals."

"You have that right. He's running for mayor now."

"Really?" John threw back his head and laughed. "Ass kisser and a camera hog. I can see it. He had a way with the ladies in his youth. Could charm them right up to his apartment. Course, didn't want to let his aunt catch him with a different girl each night so he'd bring them through that old delivery door in the back. We found it by accident. When the cops would raid the place in the forties the gamblers would head down the stairs and out the passageway. They'd be standing in the gardens having a drink claiming they had no idea what was happening inside. Worked every time, so I hear."

Sam wondered if Murphy wasn't all that innocent. After all, he had told the department to put the case on the backburner, that the victim was nothing more than a homeless woman.

"Did Dennis keep working for you while he attended the police academy?"

"Off and on but he still had that part time security job at the bank. That's where he met Alicia, I think. She was cashing a check or something. Alicia." John looked up as though answers were written on the clouds dotting the sky. And they obviously were. "PRINCE! Yes, that was her last name. I just love it when the memory cells connect. Too bad I couldn't remember all this when that reporter fella was here."

"Reporter? Here?" *Oh shit*, Sam thought, but again had to squelch the glee at all of this information being blasted on tomorrow's front pages.

"He beat you by about two hours." John reached into his pocket and pulled out a business card. It was Rafe Bennett's.

"I bet he asked you to call him if you remembered anything else."

"Why yes, he did."

"Could you do me a huge favor and not tell him about Murphy or Alicia just yet? I think it's only fair I find a way to break it to Murphy first."

John frowned and for a moment Sam wondered if Rafe promised to pay for the information. But money wasn't on John's mind. "As I said before, Dennis may have been a cad and an opportunist, but he's no killer. Please remember that."

17

Sam paced the study while waiting for the two aspirin she had taken to kick in. She wasn't used to drinking before six o'clock at night. She stopped her pacing and stood in front of the whiteboard. The image she had drawn looked like a family tree with THE EMBERS HOTEL written at the top. Lines branched out from under the name representing each of the owners and the dates they owned the hotel starting in the 1920s when the hotel was built by the Sobieski Brothers. Back then it was believed that the Embers was a front for the local syndicate which ran the gambling and liquor in Chasen Heights. Just like Al Capone, the authorities could only nail the Sobieskis for income tax evasion.

The hotel was closed from 1945 to 1949 when it was purchased by the Sutton Company. Mega bucks had been spent on renovations. This was the period when a fourth floor was added and called the Lighthouse Bar. It didn't look like a lighthouse. It was centered in the middle of the hotel and had a flat roof so there wasn't a peak that could be seen from the ground. The Lighthouse Bar was reserved for gamblers in search of high stakes poker games. Cops looked the other way for several years until pressure from local newspapers and the public forced the police to clamp down. Once citations, violations, and repeated raids started to hurt business, Sutton Company filed for bankruptcy.

It sat empty for two years when MK Enterprises purchased it in 1964. Under Murphy's aunt and uncle the hotel thrived. They ran a successful business until the area started deteriorating. With the declining downtown area and people moving to the newer sections of town, the hotel was closed in 1982.

It wasn't purchased again until 1994 by Reed Management which renovated it for apartment dwellings. Although never 100% filled, the business limped along until the bank had to foreclose in 2004. The property was donated to the city in 2008.

It was the period between 1982 and 1994 that was critical. According to John Kendall, the fourth floor was accessible when he closed the hotel. But according to photos in the Reed Management file, there wasn't a fourth floor when they purchased it.

Sam had written down the years Murphy had worked at the hotel and an estimate of the date he had known Alicia Prince. What if the deceased wasn't Alicia Prince? Maybe she really was a homeless person or drug addict who stole the locket. She couldn't check the name with the DMV. That was something Jake would have to do.

She had called Jake on her way back but had to leave a message. She thought of calling Captain Robinson but this was news Jake should probably break to him.

There was a part of her leaping for joy at Murphy's just desserts. She could almost picture newspaper headlines:

> *Murphy a possible suspect in hotel death.*
> *What did Murphy know and when did he know it?*
> *From chief to candidate to convict.*

"Stop it," Sam scolded herself. She was already happily convicting her ex-boss. Mentally she was even justifying her suspicions and silencing her doubts. One doubt was that the fourth floor had been closed off after the Kendalls sold the building. But that could be explained by saying Murphy still had a key to the hotel and returned before the hotel was sold in order to board up the fourth floor after killing Alicia.

She heard the back door open, keys jingle as they were hung up on the rack in the hallway, footsteps down the hallway, then pausing at the doorway to the study.

"Whatever it is, can it wait until I take a shower?"

"I don't think so."

Muffled footsteps sounded on the carpeting as Jake pulled up next to her. "What the hell?"

She gave him time to absorb all of her notes, then explained her lunch with Murphy's uncle and all she had learned, although she was careful not to mention the picture in the locket. "John said Murphy lived in that fourth floor apartment and remembered one of the girls his nephew dated. That's probably why Murphy wanted the case placed on the backburner," Sam said. "He knew if the detectives dug deep enough, they'd find out he knew the deceased. Remember, he has an election coming up. Murphy was probably counting on the victim being written off as a homeless woman."

Jake sank onto the couch and studied the board for several minutes. All he emitted were heavy sighs before rubbing his temples. "There are a lot of suppositions here. Just because Murphy worked at the hotel and dated a girl doesn't make him guilty. Had this uncle ever heard them arguing?"

"Well, no." Sam didn't want to admit to taking the locket and hoped his logical brain wouldn't pick apart her findings too quickly. "But it's worth the captain asking Murphy to stop in for a little sit down to find out what he knows about Alicia. Maybe he knows her history, whether she broke a leg or arm in her youth. Something that could help Benny verify her identity." She studied Jake's clothes, the dirt and grass stains, a dried piece of leaf that clung to his hair. The best detective the department had, one of the top FBI agents during his term, and he had been relegated to climbing through brush and crawling through alleys chasing animals. The fact that Murphy did this to him made her even more angry. "Murphy may not have personally owned the hotel but he should certainly, at best, be interviewed as someone knowledgeable of the hotel and the years his relatives did own it." She sat down next to him on the couch and picked the leaf from his hair.

"I see a certain amount of glee in your eyes, Sam. Are you sure you aren't hoping Murphy is in deep shit?"

"Hey, toss the karma dice in the air and see where they land. I'm just looking at the evidence."

"Evidence should be conclusive."

"Before arresting said person but certainly not before hauling his ass in and questioning him."

"Shit." Jake pulled out his phone and flipped it open.

"Who are you calling?"

"The captain."

"There's one more thing."

Jake rolled his eyes. "Do I really want to know?"

"Kendall told me Rafe Bennett also dropped by and questioned him. Murphy's name never came up but if Bennett starts checking out Kendall and his wife, the wife's maiden name is sure to come up."

Jake made his call, doing most of the talking. Then he fell silent while Robinson first yelled then either passed out or was thinking long and hard. The call ended and Sam looked at Jake expectantly.

"He's going to stop by Murphy's office. He'll leave your name out of it but mention during the investigation Kendall's name popped up and then reveal what Kendall had said. It's just going to be a short fact-finding mission, see how much Murphy wants to disclose. Until we have a positive I.D. of the victim, he can't do much more."

Sam couldn't hide her pleasure at the possible outcome.

Jake stood, grabbed her hand and pulled her from the couch. "Tone down your glee, Sam. Remember what you said about bad karma. Now I'm taking that shower and you're going to wash my back."

18

Robinson lumbered into Murphy's office and announced, "We have a tentative identity on the body found at the Embers Hotel."

Murphy leaned back in his leather chair and motioned for Robinson to close the office door. A mail clerk was parking a cart by a staff member's desk. Once the door was firmly closed, Murphy tapped his Mont Blanc pen on a yellow lined pad of paper filled with campaign strategy notes. "I thought I instructed Homicide to backburner that case," Murphy snapped.

"They did," Robinson replied as he wedged himself into a barrel chair in front of the desk. "But not before they questioned a few people. Benny's techs are working with that computer identification software to try to get a digital image from the skull. Meanwhile, someone you know personally mentioned a woman named Alicia Prince."

The chair stopped rocking and the Mont Blanc hovered in mid-tap. Murphy slowly straightened feeling a cold press down on his shoulders. He spent several minutes staring at a spot on his desk before emitting a hoarse whisper that sounded like "my God."

"I'm hoping you can clear up a few details, Dennis. With the campaign and all it won't be long before the shit hits the fan."

"Did Benny give a time of death?"

"Not yet. He's still waiting on tox reports and there are a lot of unknowns. According to John Kendall..."

"My uncle? You spoke to my uncle?"

Robinson ignored the question so he wouldn't have to admit that Sam had met with Kendall. "He says the stairway to the fourth floor was still in use when he closed the hotel but in photos when the next buyer purchased the hotel the entrance had been walled up. When was the last time you saw Alicia Prince?"

Sweat started to glisten on Murphy's forehead. "God, I only knew her for a few short weeks. We went out a couple times and then I went to the police academy. Never saw her again. That had to be in 1976."

"Do you know anything about her family, where she was from, any known relatives in the area?"

"Like I said, I barely knew her. I'm sure my uncle mentioned I worked at the hotel during summer breaks when I was in college. I dated a lot of girls during that time. Alicia was just one of many."

"And you got along? No hard feelings when it ended?"

Murphy looked up sharply and glared at Robinson. "What are you insinuating?"

"Only covering bases, Chief. We may have to bring this case off the backburner. Press is going to want to know why it was shelved, especially now with knowing you and the deceased had dated and you may have been one of the last people to see her. And you know how they love rumors."

"Damn." Murphy tossed the eight-hundred-dollar pen on the desk and leaned back in his chair. "I certainly don't need this now." He took a deep breath and appeared to shrug into a damage-control vest. "Let's hold off on any further action until Benny has a firm cause of death. What about a DMV or passport photo, something to confirm her identification other than my uncle's aged memory?"

"Department of Motor Vehicles has a number of Alicia Princes but none of the photos match our victim's age or skeletal features."

"And what would those features be if a relative hasn't positively identified the body?"

"Between twenty and thirty years of age, around five foot six, no previous broken bones or congenital defects."

"That's it? Well then, no sense chasing our tails until we have a better idea on time and cause of death. And have Benny give those results directly to me."

* * *

Ten minutes after Robinson left Murphy's eyes were still focused on the first sentence of compaign notes. But it wasn't words he was seeing. Alicia's face was materializing in all its beauty. Why now? Why after all this time? He pressed the heels of his hands to his eyes. A headache was building fast. The election was the least of his worries right now.

"Are you okay?"

Murphy looked up to see Ruth, his secretary, standing in the doorway.

"You look like you've seen a ghost." Ruth set a cup of coffee on his desk. Her nails were short but manicured. She wore no nonsense shoes more fitting of a Russian guard. Her brown hair had little style much less shine. "That reporter is on Line One." He thanked Ruth and watched her walk out of the office.

Murphy had gone the route of cover girl assistants and found them both lacking in I.Q. and, more importantly, looking better than he did on his best days. He was glad he had fired the previous assistants. They were way too tempting and now that he was running for mayor, his personal life would have been placed under a microscope. He wondered how many indiscretions Schuler had indulged in. It was all laid out in that stupid self-aggrandizing book he wrote. Pretty smart on his part. And he was sure that ass of a campaign manager, Lukavich, was poking under every rock in Murphy's past.

The incessant blinking of the Line One button reminded Murphy that Bennett was on the line.

"Rafe, what can I do for you?" The chief listened as Bennett described Schuler's town hall meeting and the subject of eminent domain.

"Do you agree that the city should kick residents out of their homes?" Rafe asked.

"I agree that we have to do all we can to revitalize the downtown area but I really dislike using eminent domain as a last resort. Alternative housing, at the city's expense, should be offered."

"As well as businesses?"

"There are a number of available commercial properties banks would be willing to get rid of. Many of them have apartments above the businesses that are larger than the houses those residents now own. The city should do everything in its power to offer acceptable alternatives. But," Murphy added with a chuckle, "I'm not the mayor yet so there isn't much I can do but offer my personal opinion."

"Thanks for your time, Chief Murphy."

Murphy was actually reciting Mayor Jenkins' opinion on the subject even though some members of the council, including Schuler, disagreed with the mayor. He looked down at the notepad, unaware he had been scribbling a name. He quickly ran his ink pen through it, obliterating the name of Alicia Prince.

* * *

The Ritz Carlton was pricey but he liked the restaurants, gym, and other amenities. And he hated to admit it, but it was what he was used to. Price was never factored in when he traveled. He had packed a few pair of pants, shirts, some turtlenecks if it turned cool, a jacket and a couple sportscoats. If he needed more he would just go shopping. His bank had finally transferred funds to the bank across the street. He had already spent a bundle tossing money around town for whatever tidbits of information people could provide. And one call was about ready to make his generosity worthwhile.

When the cell phone rang he checked the screen.

"Bennett." Rafe could barely hear the caller. "I hope you aren't in the office." He sat in front of his laptop and checked his web site for news. Whenever he was on the road, there were eyes and ears back in Tampa to keep him updated.

"Oh, no. I'm walking to Starbucks to get my boss a coffee." Cory Isaacs worked in the mailroom at Headquarters. Just by hanging around the elevator and the restaurants where the office workers frequented told Rafe a lot about which worker needed the money most. Cory lived with his girlfriend and had a baby on the way. Being a mail clerk didn't exactly pay enough to cover bills. And Rafe was very generous. A few hundred in Cory's hands with a promise of a thousand dollars if he had a worthwhile tip, might prove to be the best investment.

"Make sure no one's around," Rafe cautioned.

"I'm walking through the park to get to the Starbucks but thought what I heard while passing the chief's office might be useful. He was talking to Captain Robinson at the Sixth. The door was closed but I was dropping off mail in the office next to the chief's. They were talking about the Jane Doe case. It seems one of the previous owners of that hotel was the chief's uncle."

"Did he mention a name?"

"I guess the chief used to work at the hotel, too. Not sure what he did."

"A name. Was his uncle's last name Murphy, too?"

"No. His aunt's last name was Murphy but I can't remember the uncle's name."

"Did he happen to mention where the uncle lives?"

"He's in one of those homes, you know, for old people."

"A nursing home?" Wait. It couldn't possibly be. "Or was it an assisted living facility? Was the uncle's name Kendall?"

"That's it. The chief worked at the hotel during summer breaks. But here's the best part. According to the uncle, the chief dated a girl named Alicia Prince. The captain wants the chief to tell everyone before it gets leaked, but the chief still wants the case on hold. Since the victim hasn't been positively identified, he felt it was too premature to release her name."

"Are you sure that was the name...Alicia Prince?" Rafe typed the name in the search line. He didn't recall anyone missing by that name. "You are a wealth of information, Cory. Tell you what, I'll meet you at the Starbucks. Don't acknowledge me. Don't look in my direction. I'll slip you a copy of today's paper with an envelope inside."

Rafe folded the phone and shoved it in his pocket. Why hadn't John Kendall mentioned that Chief Murphy was his nephew? Had he not asked the right questions? Or was Kendall covering for Murphy?

19

The next morning the article Rafe had written for the on line edition appeared on the front page of the print edition. The *Post Tribune* was filled with the Jane Doe story mentioning Dennis Murphy, his uncle, and the tentative identification of Jane Doe as Alicia Prince. Rafe had even made a last minute call to John Kendall to verify what he had learned and to quote him in the paper.

"I told you that reporter was hungry." Tom leaned back, feet on the desk, front page of the morning paper spread across his lap. "We didn't have to lift a finger."

"Damn cops. All this time, clawing his way to the top. I bet Murphy has more than one dead body in his closet." You would have thought Schuler had just won the election the way he was smiling, all teeth, eyes bright. "Can't wait for Bennett to ask me for my reaction."

"Oh, no." Tom pulled his feet off the desk and folded the newspaper. "Whatever you are thinking of saying, don't. You want to remain above the fray. This is an ongoing investigation that you would not feel right offering any kind of an opinion. Bennett, editorials, public opinion, let it all unfold as these things always do. You come out indicting Murphy and you are going to look like the bad guy."

Schuler hated to admit it, but Tom was right. He kept one eye on the television set hanging on the wall. Why weren't there any camera crews parked in front of Murphy's house?

"I know what you are thinking. It's too early. Eight o'clock in the morning they are probably more apt to catch the chief of police at the office."

"It should still be on the local news." Schuler flipped through the stations shaking his head at the ineptitude of the media. "If it were me they'd be camped at my back door. What the hell is this?" He threw the remote control on the desk. "It's the mayor. Jenkins' tentacles are still working even if he's on his death bed."

Tom glared at his boss.

"What?"

"You need to speak as though there is a hidden microphone somewhere. You can't go making accusations."

"Fuck that. This is my office. I can say whatever I damn well please. If anyone is bugging this place they better start reading the files on Watergate. I'll sue the bastards for every dime they have." He rolled his sleeves up and loosened the tie. Schuler's hair had been trimmed, eliminating the patented comb over, and he had left his Rolex watch in a drawer at home, all Tom's instructions to relate better to the voters. Something on the television snapped Schuler to attention. He picked up the remote and turned up the volume. "Here we go." On screen Chief Dennis Murphy was pulling into his underground parking space at Headquarters amid a trailing swarm of press which was held back by the gate and two squad cars blocking the swarm from entering.

* * *

Murphy took the private staircase to his office. It was bad enough he only had three hours of sleep after Bennett's call and had to sink his face into ice water to get the puffiness down. That bastard reporter had called the mayor, too, for his reaction. Bennett didn't even have the decency to let a sick man rest.

Then Donna had badgered him all night for every minute detail of his life with Alicia Prince even though he hadn't met Donna until eight years after Alicia. Then Mayor Jenkins had called telling him to make this go away. Course, he never once asked if Murphy had done it. Maybe in some people's minds it was a given.

When he couldn't sleep past four in the morning, Murphy spent time drafting his press release. Jenkins demanded that he read it to him first and to make sure Murphy's attorney read it over so he didn't implicate himself or the department in any way. Then Donna demanded to read it. Thank God, Deena, their daughter, was working for Northwestern University in Qatar halfway around the globe and wouldn't hear about this on the news.

Around six this morning, while re-writing his statement for the tenth time, Murphy had an epiphany which he added to his statement without the mayor's or his attorney's knowledge. He then informed the front desk to herd the reporters to the press room where he would make a statement and answer questions at ten o'clock.

Believing in punctuality, especially when it came to cameras, Chief Murphy entered the pressroom at the exact hour. He recognized representatives from Chicago television stations and newspapers. There were only two local newspapers but reporters from surrounding towns were also present. In all, it was standing room only. Ruth dusted off the podium and set a glass and pitcher of water on the table to the right of the podium. Murphy again silently patted himself on the back for hiring an efficient rather than attractive secretary. Whatever R-rated image these reporters had in their heads about Murphy's taste in women was nipped in the bud by taking one look at his secretary.

"Thank you, Ruth." He made sure to give the impression he was a wonderful boss to work for. Ruth gave him a sympathetic smile. Murphy pulled out a copy of his statement, then handed a file folder to Ruth asking her to hand out copies to those in attendance.

"Ladies and gentlemen, thank you all for coming. Regarding the revelations which unfolded recently, I would like to offer the following information. From 1964 to 1982, John and Ann Kendall, or MK Enterprises, owned the Embers Hotel. During two of my high school years and throughout college I worked at the hotel doing odd jobs. I waited tables, carried luggage, cut the grass, whatever help my aunt and uncle needed. It helped put me through college. Since I was majoring in law enforcement and criminal studies, and while awaiting my acceptance into the police academy, I also worked as a part time security guard at a local bank. It was there that I met Alicia Prince. We dated for a few weeks. It wasn't serious and we broke it off when I was accepted to the academy.

"There has been a lot of speculation about the body found in the hotel several days ago. The body has not been, and I repeat, it has NOT been positively identified as yet and to continue to speculate until we know beyond a reasonable doubt her identity, I would hope that you treat this story as exactly what it is...speculation.

"As far as Miss Prince, I knew she was twenty-one and an art student at a local junior college. We dated for a few weeks and parted as friends when I left for the police academy. This is an ongoing investigation and until we know who owned the hotel when and who did the renovations, we can't give you any further information. I do find it quite curious though," and this was Murphy's last minute epiphany, "that in several weeks the city will be bulldozing the hotel, a project spearheaded by my opponent in the mayoral race. If it hadn't been for the animal control officers discovering the body, Councilman Schuler would have had one helluva spectacle for the six o'clock news. I believe he is one person my department will want to ask what he knew and when he knew it." There, he said it and the press was sitting up like baby birds waiting for more. Cameras were flashing, recorders were taping.

And now the questions started flying. If he had expected them to question him further on his suspicions about Councilman Schuler, he was sorely disappointed. A young woman who looked more like an editor for a college newspaper jumped to her feet.

"Chief, weren't you the one who shelved the case in the first place?"

"My medical examiner didn't discover any signs of foul play. There is a homeless shelter a couple blocks from the state line. It was at first thought the victim was a homeless person who had died of natural causes. At the present time my medical examiner hasn't been able to determine when the victim died nor cause of death. I felt this case was low priority and wanted my detectives focused on more current crimes."

Rafe Bennett stood and Murphy mistakenly believed he had already won him over. "When you worked for your aunt and uncle, Chief Murphy, you lived in that fourth floor apartment, didn't you?"

"On occasion."

"That isn't what your uncle said. You lived at the hotel full time during college breaks."

Murphy jabbed a finger at the smartass. "You bothered an elderly man in a nursing home? A man whose memory can't be trusted?"

"Is that a yes or a no?" Bennett asked.

"No." He scoured the room. "Next question."

Bennett wasn't letting up. "So she was just someone you could use and abuse."

If Murphy was hoping for a volley of questions to pick from, they weren't coming. The room was quiet, hanging on Bennett's lead. It was so quiet he could almost hear the tape recorders running.

"As I said, my uncle's memory has been failing for years. Our homicide unit will continue to investigate the case and try to locate and question anyone who might have additional information."

"And that means you, I take it?" Rafe pointed a pen at Murphy. It wasn't so much the pointing that irritated Murphy as it was the smug smile on the reporter's face.

The chief looked past Rafe as he told the room, "Thank you again for coming. Our press liaison will issue statements as we know more." With that Murphy left the room amid a swirl of murmurs. He rushed past Ruth's desk as she said, "Mayor Jenkins wants you to call him and your attorney is on line three."

"Coffee," Murphy barked as he went into his office. "And if Bennett comes anywhere near my office door, shoot him."

20

Sam wished she had taped the news conference. To watch Murphy squirm sent a thrill through her entire body. *Now let's see how he likes it*, she thought. The public scrutiny, doubts from fellow police officers, stares from the public. Sam had been subjected to the same thing after she had been accused of shooting a cop in the back. First came the suspension then the hearing before the Board of Police and Fire Commissioners. But there had been a long gap between the suspension and the hearing, leaving her to deal with the stares and whispers, the worry over whether she would be reinstated and how she could prove her innocence. There was one person who had held onto a videotape proving her innocence and that was Murphy. His disdain for his predecessor who had been Sam's godfather ran long and deep and spilled over to Sam. Even with Chief Don Connelley dead, Murphy never let up. Almost made Sam suspicious that there was something else at work here.

Her euphoria was building. She wouldn't have to raise a finger. Between the press and Councilman Schuler, Murphy didn't stand a chance. His wife would probably leave him, too, once she saw her chances of living in the mayor's mansion evaporate. How delightful. But something Murphy said at the conference started to nag at her, something about a planned demolition that Schuler had arranged. Did Schuler know more than he was letting on? Did he know the deceased?

"STOP IT!" Sam yelled at the room. She didn't want the doubts, only the possibility of his guilt. Who else deserved it more than him?

* * *

Robinson looked around the conference room for a suitable chair. Every chair had arms on it and his bulk needed more room to spread.

Ruth, Murphy's secretary, backed into the room dragging an armless chair. "Thought you could use this, Captain."

"Almost afraid to sit on such a plush thing." Robinson parked himself down anyway. He studied the room with a shake of his head. "Place sure is four star." Murphy spared no expense when it came to Headquarters. From the cherry wood table to the paintings on the wall and the thick carpeting, Robinson doubted any prisoner had tread, puked, or peed in the place. Not like the Sixth which needed a wrecking ball as badly as the Embers Hotel.

"How about coffee, soda, water, anything?"

"Bet you got some great snacks in that kitchen of yours, Ruth," Robinson said with a chuckle.

"I'm sure I have something coming out of the oven in a few minutes."

Murphy slipped in like the slippery eel he was. "He won't have time to eat. Just bring coffee, Ruth." He closed the door behind her. "Fill me in on what we know so far." He sank into the throne chair at the head of the table with a long sigh.

Robinson bit back the retort that there wasn't much to tell since Murphy killed the case, literally. He summarized what was in the file before reporting on Benny's examination of the body. "Not much else to tell since we have been working on other cases, you know, keeping a high police profile on the streets."

Murphy waited while Ruth set coffee and cups on the table. Once Ruth left and the door was closed, Murphy announced, "Mayor Jenkins wants me to have as little to do with this case as possible since I knew the deceased. He wants you to keep him updated on the investigation. The less involvement I have the less chance of any accusations of mismanagement. He said if things get a little too dicey he may be forced to bring in the State Police to take over the investigation and we certainly don't want that."

"That is usually the procedure." Although Robinson wanted to also remind him that desk duty or several days off is given to the rank and file.

Guess it didn't apply to brass. "How is Mayor Jenkins doing?"

"He leaves for the Mayo Clinic in a few days. The treatment planned looks promising. While he's gone the deputy mayor will take over. People keep saying he's on his death bed but I don't believe it. It will be a long recovery which is why he wants to stay at his Hilton Head home."

"And what about you, Dennis?"

"Jenkins wants me to take a few days off, go fishing, but that's not me. I need to keep busy. My wife is going to go visit her sister for a few days."

"A little rough at home I take it."

"She already had the drapes measured for the mayor's mansion. Didn't once ask how I was doing or give a hint of encouragement. Just wanted the sordid details of a relationship that ended eight years before I even met her. Women."

No matter what anyone thought of Murphy, Robinson felt for the guy. No one should have to have their life turned upside down when he is innocent. With that reminder, Robinson opened up his notepad.

"Chief, I need to know all those sordid little details."

* * *

"Can you believe it?" Jeff Schuler had been pacing the office for the past hour, still fuming over Murphy's insinuation at the press conference that Schuler knew something about the body found at the Embers. "The actual gall of that man. When I'm mayor I'm going to see to it that he can't even be a dog catcher in this town."

Tom grimaced at his boss's gloves-off attitude. "Don't forget, the council is heavy on the mayor's side. They may not approve anything you want to do."

"I know those guys. Once I'm in, they'll follow my lead."

Yeah, right, Tom thought. He was beginning to wonder how Schuler will deal with a loss if he isn't elected. Suspicions started to nag at him but he had to find a delicate way to word it. While Schuler continued to pace and mumble, Tom searched for the right words. He wasn't sure there were any. Instead he remained silent and let things unfold. It didn't take long.

"You get a hold of that little shit reporter and make sure he understands I never met the deceased, the wrecking ball date wasn't made by me; it was scheduled by the demolition company and was supposed to take place six months ago. For a chief of police, the protector of the people, to jump to such an outrageous conclusion proves he has no business being the mayor much less the police chief." Schuler pointed at the pad of paper in front of Tom. "That was perfect. Write it down. It will be my mantra whenever the little twerp shows up for a comment."

21

"Hey, that your little guy?" Frank motioned at the monitor where Abby's smiling face could be seen behind a bouncing Dillon who kept trying to reach out to the monitor.

"Has he grown, Mom?" Sam asked. "I could swear he looks taller."

"It's only been a week, Samantha." Abby's fingers were clamped between Dillon's grasp. His chubby cheeks smiled with sheer baby joy. He had Jake's soft brown eyes and, thankfully, his hair. She couldn't picture him with curly Raggedy Ann or Andy hair like hers.

Alex poked his head up in the background. His gray hair hung in two braids on his shoulders. He had a dark, olive tan and dark eyes that were distrustful of any non-Indians. "Have you killed the lawn?" To Alex the landscaping was his pride and joy. The gardens displayed color nine months of the year.

"Frank and I made our own nine hole golf course while you've been gone." Jake enjoyed the verbal sparring he and Alex engaged in. All Alex did was narrow his dark eyes. "How are things back home, Abby?" Jake knew Abby wielded a bit of power on the reservation and she wasn't bashful when it came to exercising her point of view.

"The Council is behaving itself. The casino revenues have been put to good use building a medical clinic and a library. The school is taking a little longer. Everyone is bickering over how many amenities to include."

Sam waved at the monitor hoping to catch Dillon's attention. "Mom, what's in his mouth?"

"Oh, I almost forgot." Abby lowered Dillon's bottom lip. "Show mommy, Dillon. Show mommy your very first tooth."

"Tooth?" Sam tried to hide her disappointment but it was difficult. Tears welled quickly and when she spoke it came out in a squeak. "He cut his first tooth and I wasn't there to see it?"

Jake stood back, a puzzled look on his face. "What's the problem, Sam? He's going to get thirty-one more." He wasn't sure if it was Abby painfully closing her eyes, Frank sucking in a lungful of air, or Alex's chuckle that gave him the first hint that he had made a major marital faux pas. He guessed it was more the shock of silent horror on Sam's face. Whatever it was, he felt his brain cells falter and steer off their logical train track.

Sam backed away, not even saying good night to Abby or Dillon. She practically ran down the hall, grabbed her keys off the rack, and charged out the back door.

Jake turned back to the monitor where Abby was shaking her head. "We may need to have a talk," Abby said.

"I don't understand."

"I know you don't. Samantha will come to her senses."

"It's that men are from Mars, women are from Venus thing," Frank said. "You are going to have to read that book."

Jake wasn't one to walk on eggshells. To him it was logical. What's one tooth when you are going to have thirty-two, not to mention that Dillon will lose the baby teeth and sprout more? Why witness something that is just a normal growing process?

Abby said their good nights and Jake turned the computer off. Frank slapped him on the back and with a hopeless shake of his head, left Jake to teeter alone on a proverbial narrow precipice.

* * *

Sam drove around for thirty minutes, not wanting to go home just yet. How insensitive could a man be? She didn't want to stop by Jackie's because that would be the first person Jake would call, if he bothered to even look for Sam. Izzy's was also out of the question. Too involved in her own emotions, she didn't notice the car trailing her from Chasen Heights. If she had been in a normal frame of mind she would have suspected not one but two cars a safe distance behind her.

The parking lot was filled since the Embassy Suites received spill over from the casinos in Northwest Indiana. There were annual high stakes Texas Hold'em tournaments going on in all of the casinos. Hopefully, most of the guests were at the casinos so she could find a dark corner of the bar in which to sulk.

She made a detour into the restroom to make sure her mascara wasn't streaming down her face. It only needed a little repair work. She pulled the banana clip from her hair, wet her hands and ran them through to untangle the curls. At Jackie's insistence Sam had started carrying a conditioner in her purse. She squeezed some into the palm of her hand and again tried to coax the curl from her long hair. It helped a little.

Checking her reflection in the long mirror by the door, she wished she had worn all black so she could fade into the shadows. Instead she was wearing tan corduroy cropped pants and brown knee high boots. Her peasant blouse kept sliding off one shoulder. If only she had grabbed her leather jacket before fleeing the house.

"Oh, well. Deal with it." She sniffed back the tears, gave herself a backbone lecture, and exited the restroom.

At least a few things were going her way tonight. The bar hosted few patrons and there was a booth in a dark corner available. Sam tossed her tote bag on the bench and slid in, making sure she had a view of the entrance.

The waitress set a napkin on the table. "What can I get you today?" She wore a tuxedo top that was cut just low enough to show the butterfly tattoo on her right breast and just high enough to leave a bare midriff above black satin shorts. Sam ordered a tall vodka and tonic.

While waiting for her drink Sam noticed a few of the people in the bar were eating. Most of the food choices looked like appetizers, some smelled like hot wings. Sam could swear her eyelashes were melting from the spicy odors. One couple at the bar was groping each other and providing entertainment for two guys dressed as if they had spent the day golfing and the afternoon drinking. The female half of the gropers Sam suspected was a hooker. When Sam had worked undercover she had seen many of the girls dressed in similar tube tops with skirts cut so short it was a wonder they could sit let alone bend over. The man with his tongue in her mouth wore a business suit and a bad hairpiece. He was about fifty pounds overweight with cheeks that quivered when he spoke.

Sam found herself checking the girl's ankles and arms for bruising from needles. She was so painfully thin Sam doubted the breasts squeezing out of the tube top were real. The mirror behind the bar reflected the woman's face. It was difficult to tell her age. Her body wasn't wrinkled but her face told a different story. Sam would place her money on crack cocaine. Now the portly gent's hand was going up the woman's tube top. The bartender motioned to a man in a dark suit who had just entered the bar. The man had vice or hotel security written all over him. Sam slid further into the booth and watched as security leaned between the two of them and then grabbed the woman firmly by the arm and led her out of the bar.

The waitress returned with her drink. Sam paid her and returned her attention to the scene at the bar. Mister Portly set his sights on two young girls sitting in adjacent bar stools. They grabbed their drinks and fled for a table in the enclosed patio. When he started to survey his next target, Sam pulled a notepad and pen from her tote bag and busied herself with notes on the Embers Hotel. She felt her Taurus 9mm at the bottom of the bag held snugly in its holster and resisted the urge to slap it on the table as a threat should the porker lumber over.

Most of the notes she wrote after visiting John Kendall were scribbled. Now that she had quiet time, she ripped out the scribbled pages and took time to write her notes legibly. John Kendall was an interesting character. He had genuinely enjoyed the era when the Strip was at its peak. He may have only been a kid when his parents first took him to the hotel, but the memories stayed with him and years later the hotel's history influenced him to purchase the Embers.

The biggest puzzle for now was the wall that had been added, obviously by someone who wanted to hide what was on the fourth floor.

It could have been innocent enough. Maybe new owners didn't see a need for people to venture up there. The hotel was empty for several years after the bank foreclosed on it. Who knew about the fourth floor and who had access to the hotel?

The arrows all pointed to Dennis Murphy. Of course, Sam had a reason she wanted the arrows to point toward him. If there really was karma, Murphy was long overdue for his share.

The waitress appeared and placed a room keycard on the table. "Are you Mrs. Jake Mitchell?"

Sam looked from the card to the waitress and felt her heart start to flutter. "Yes."

"A gentleman asked me to give this to you."

She stared at the key, not even noticing that the waitress had walked away. How did Jake find her? Then she mentally slapped her head. The GPS tracker. Of course! And here she didn't think Jake had a romantic bone in his body. By the time the elevator deposited her on the eighth floor with her drink and keycard in hand, Sam had already forgiven Jake for his insensitivity, knowing a man single for thirty-four years wasn't going to instantly grow paternal and marital antennae. He had to ease into it, trial and error. And she had to be patient. Abby would be proud of her.

Sam located Room 808 and slipped the keycard into the slot. When the light turned green, she turned the handle and walked in. The room was palatial, more a suite than a simple room. There was a gleaming chrome and glass bar to her left, a king sized bed in a room to the left, and in front of her was a couch, loveseat, entertainment center and a desk. The man at the desk turned and stood up.

"Oh crap." Sam turned and stalked toward the door. But he was quick and had his hand braced against the door before she could turn the knob and flee.

"Sam wait, please."

Please? He had never used please before. Matter of fact, he had never used Sam before. It had always been either Casey or her or you.

"Just give me ten minutes or at least until you finish your drink. I deserve at least..."

"YOU deserve?! You know, Chief, you are about two seconds away from wearing this drink."

"All right. That was a poor choice of words." He took in a deep breath and wiped an arm across his forehead. The air was downright chilly in the room yet there were beads of sweat on his face. Murphy had his tie loosened and the top button of his shirt unfastened. "I need your help," he whispered.

Sam knew it was hard for him to ask help from anyone. To Murphy it was a sign of weakness to not have all the answers, to not be in total control. Probably the most difficult thing Murphy would ever do in his life would be to ask for her help.

"Ten minutes." Sam stalked back into the living room and sank onto the love seat. "And turn the damn air conditioning off." She pulled out her notepad and pen.

Murphy pushed the controls on the thermostat hanging on the wall. "I really appreciate this, Sam. I know you don't owe me anything."

Sam checked her watch. "Nine minutes."

Murphy sighed heavily but caught himself from showing his usual impatience. He sat just as heavily on the couch cattycorner from her. "I'm sure you watched the news conference this morning. Everything I said is true. I dated Alicia briefly. Yes, I lived in the fourth floor apartment while I went to college. However, once I attended the police academy and started work at CHPD shortly after, I never stepped foot in the place again, never saw Alicia again."

Sam checked her watch and realized she hadn't been taking any notes. "I'm not hearing anything new here, Chief."

"I want to hire you to find out who is setting me up. My suspicions are Jeff Schuler but I don't know how to prove it. You can do what it is you do." He motioned with his hand as though searching for the right descriptive words.

"That isn't how it works," Sam explained. "I don't just pick things out of thin air. What I glean isn't always the full picture. Contrary to public opinion, I don't have a crystal ball." And there is the fact that she hoped he was found guilty and sent away for a long time.

"But you are a private investigator. You have unscrupulous ways of getting to the truth."

"I hope there was a compliment in there somewhere." Sam checked her watch again. "Oops, times up." She marched to the door, leaving her untouched drink on his coffee table. She hoped it would leave a very large ring.

"Sam," Murphy said as she stepped out into the hallway. "Here." He shoved a wad of money into her hand. They all looked like one hundred dollar bills. "I want to give you a retainer."

She shoved the money back. "I'll think about it and let you know my decision tomorrow morning."

Murphy pulled out a business card from his shirt pocket and handed it to her. "My cell phone number is written on the back."

22

Sam set Murphy's business card on the desk. A part of her wanted him to dangle in the wind, let him take his chances. Another part of her, though slim, was feeling guilty as hell for wanting him to dangle. She had forgotten to ask about his uncle, about any personal information he might have on Alicia or who would have wanted to harm her.

She wandered into the kitchen to make a cup of tea. Jake obviously hadn't waited up for her nor was there a note on the counter. Sleep was the last thing she wanted to do when she was this wound up. There were too many unanswered questions floating in her head. When the microwave beeped, she dropped a tea bag into the cup, then opened the silverware drawer. But she wasn't paying attention and opened the dish towel drawer instead. Poking out from under one of the towels she saw the locket. She grabbed it and her tea and took them into the study.

The locket felt hot to the touch and the same vision of a log cabin in the woods flashed before her eyes. Was Alicia showing her that she lived there or her killer had a log cabin? Why didn't she ask Murphy if he owned a cabin?

"No," she said to the empty room. Murphy is the last person in the world she wanted to help. She checked the clock on the wall. It was eleven thirty. Sam picked up the phone and dialed. It took two rings before it was answered. Abby always was a light sleeper and she wouldn't want the phone to wake up Dillon.

"Samantha. Is everything all right? Don't tell me. You and Jacob had a fight."

"No, not at all." She told Abby about her trip to the hotel. "Thought for a moment it was Jake who had passed the room key to me. I thought that was so romantic and spontaneous but it was too good to be true. I think I was more upset that Dillon didn't seem to miss me."

"Oh, sweetheart. Of course he does. He looks around for you constantly so we keep appeasing him with new toys."

The silence stretched on as Sam listened to Abby's patient breathing. "Mom, if there was someone you truly despised but you had a chance to help him or her, no matter what that person did to make your life miserable, would you help?" When the silence continued Sam rambled on. "I know that is such a stupid question. I don't think you despise anyone and not one person despises you. And you help people because it is what you do."

"There are a couple people on the Council who try my patience but I have to give them time to come around to my way of thinking." Abby laughed lightly.

Abby was so diplomatic that Sam wondered why none of it had rubbed off on her.

"I can only think of one person who annoys you that much, Samantha. What has your police chief done this time?"

Sam explained about the body found at the Embers, Murphy's relatives owning the hotel at one time, and how Murphy was now under suspicion. "He thinks someone is setting him up and he wants to hire me. Can you believe it? After he withholds information that would have cleared me in a murder investigation, he wants my help."

"Ummmm."

Sam stirred her tea and waited. Other than "ummmm" Sam wasn't sure what was going through her mother's mind.

"The fact that it's midnight and you are anguishing over this tells me, Samantha, that you have already decided to take the case."

"I have?"

"No matter how you feel about Chief Murphy, this case has piqued your interest. Whatever you find out will either clear him or prove him guilty. As I have told you in the past, don't listen to the suspects, listen to the victims."

Sam stayed up for another hour after her call to Abby. She sat on the couch staring at the whiteboard. She checked her notes three times but not one thing jumped out at her. She had meant to go up to bed but time got away from her and she woke up to the whirring and banging from the refuse truck out on the street. Her eyes snapped open. Garbage pickup was normally at eight thirty in the morning. Had she slept that late? She staggered to her feet and checked the clock behind the bar. It was eight forty-five. Jake hadn't even awakened her. Maybe he didn't know if she came home last night. Good, let him think she was out all night.

She bounced her way from door frame to door frame and into the exercise room where the wall mirror almost made her scream out in fright. Her hair was a mass of tangles and haloed around her head like Methuselah. She used the bathroom, washed her hands, brushed her teeth, splashed water on her face, and stared at the horrors of sleeping with eye makeup on.

She stumbled to the kitchen. The coffeemaker had half a pot of coffee in it and a dish from something that resembled scrambled eggs was in the sink. She zapped a cup of coffee in the microwave and looked around the counter for a note from Jake. *Sorry* scribbled on a napkin would have been nice. The microwave beeped. Sam doctored up her coffee with cream and sugar then almost dropped the cup when she saw the *Post Tribune* unfolded and spread out on the island counter like a massive billboard.

"WHAT?" On the front page was a picture of her standing outside Murphy's hotel room, a wad of bills being handed to her. The headline read, *"Our Future Mayor?*

"Oh my god." How had she missed that? Had someone used a cell phone to take their picture? Then they would have known Murphy was at the hotel. Had someone followed them? Did Murphy set her up? No. He had enough problems without infidelity charges lobbed his way. There wasn't a name on the by-line but she knew people at the *Post Tribune*. After all, her father had worked there for years.

She ran to the study and grabbed Murphy's business card. He answered on the first ring.

"Did you see the front page?" Sam yelled. No "good morning," "how are you," "yes I'll take the case."

"I had nothing to do with it. I already heard an earful from my wife."

"How did that happen?"

"Obviously someone followed me. It sounds like something Schuler would cook up. Then they leaked the picture to the newspaper."

"These are my terms and there's zero room for negotiation. We meet at noon in the conference room at the Sixth Precinct. Nothing against the baby dicks. I know this was originally their case but you need your best on this. As of right now, Jake and Frank are back in Homicide. And finally, I want the absolute truth from you. Every slimy detail no matter how embarrassing. I'll see you at noon." Sam hung up and checked the front page again. At least she wasn't wearing a tube top.

23

"Come on, Jeremy. Don't be so pokey." The boy struggled to peddle his bike. The gravel was biting at the tires of his Huffy, jerking the wheel and threatening to toss him over the handlebars. He checked behind him and saw that his brother had given up riding on the gravel and was now walking beside the bike. Dirt and stone clung to his bony knees. Jeremy had obviously fallen but he wasn't crying...yet.

"It's hard, Billy."

Billy climbed off his bike and waited for his brother to catch up. He would get into trouble if he didn't keep an eye on him. Being the oldest at ten, Billy was always picking Jeremy up, dusting dirt from his clothes, and wiping tears from his face. He didn't like it when kids called Jeremy a sissy because he was always falling. Mom said Billy was the same way when he was seven.

"Leave your bike there, Jeremy. We'll walk to the bridge, then come back and get our bikes."

Jeremy seemed thankful to release the bike that seemed to weigh more than him. They were headed to the wooden bridge which stretched over a marsh. The bridge was nothing more than pieces of wood strung together with rope. They had found it by accident a couple weeks ago while looking for rocks to put in their rock polishing machine. The marsh resembled a swamp with vines and moss drifting from the trees like some Tarzan jungle.

"Do you think there are alligators in there, Billy?" Jeremy ran to catch up with his brother.

"Alligators aren't this far north. They are down in the Carolinas and Florida." Billy prided himself in knowing interesting tidbits of information. He liked to watch the Discovery channel. He sniffed the air and wrinkled his nose. "I think this area used to be the local garbage dump. Boy does it smell." He watched Jeremy stumble and catch himself. "Tie your shoelaces."

An expletive spilled from Jeremy's lips, a word he wouldn't dare let his mom hear. He tried not to kneel on the gravel to tie his shoes but it was hard. His eyes drifted to the ditch in front of him. There was something there. He slowly stood and took a step closer. The smell was getting stronger.

"Jeremy, hurry up."

"What is that?" Jeremy took another step closer then croaked back a gasp. "A body."

"What?" Billy came up short and looked where Jeremy was pointing. His eyes grew in size, not sure if he could trust what he was seeing. It didn't look like a person. The skin was all yucky and the eyes looked filmy as if they had rolled up in her head. He could tell it was a woman by the way she was dressed. "Let's get out of here."

* * *

Sam arrived an hour earlier so she could transfer her notes to the whiteboard in the precinct's meeting room. Sergeant Scofield deposited a cup of tea on the table saying, "Nice picture this morning, Sam."

"Well, you know me and Murphy. We have to grab what private time we can."

Scofield barked out a laugh. The history between Sam and Murphy was well known in the precinct and half the city so she didn't have to explain the picture to everyone.

She stepped back and studied the board making sure she had included all of her notes. Daytime temperatures had been hovering in the sixties so she had accepted the official start of fall and dragged out her suede slacks and sweater coat. Her medicine bundle slapped against her chest as she rummaged in her tote bag for a banana clip. She gathered her hair in the clip, careful not to catch the one long earring of beads and feathers.

Captain Robinson lumbered in holding a thermos-size coffee cup.

"Nice picture in the paper, Sam. Hope he paid you enough."

"Murphy's so cheap I had to pay him." Sam turned to find Jake standing in the doorway, a look on his face that was so blank Sam wasn't sure what to make of it.

He had gone home to change from the tan uniform to dress slacks and a blue Henley shirt. He set a coffee cup on the table. "How long has it been going on, Sam?"

"Since I was seventeen. I don't know if it's the Ken doll hair or manicured nails. There is just something about him."

Frank wove his way around Robinson and Jake to take a seat at the table. "I really appreciate you going all out to get us back into Homicide, Sam. Or do I mean giving out?" His high-pitched giggle elicited a rolling thunderous chuckle from Robinson and a smile playing at the corner of Jake's mouth.

"What's so amusing?" Murphy barked from the doorway. Silence greeted him. He took a seat where he had a full view of the whiteboard. The desperate man from last night had morphed back to the demanding tyrant. Sam knew this side of him quite well. He may have given her a peek at his weak side last night but he would never part that curtain for anyone at the precinct.

"I need a cup of coffee before we start, Sam," Murphy said.

And now he was putting her in her place as a sign that the side of him she saw last night would never be revealed again. That's fine. She could play that game.

"Sure." She called Scofield and asked for a pot of coffee, cream and sugar.

"For crissake," Murphy sputtered. "We aren't going to be here all afternoon."

"I wouldn't be too sure of that."

"Should Brainard and Jackson be here?" Murphy asked.

"They pulled another case this morning. Couple kids found a body in that unincorporated area on the north side." Robinson slid papers across the table. "Take a copy of the autopsy report on Alicia Prince in case you don't already have one."

Sam's eyes slid briefly to Jake who had an undecipherable expression on his face. She wasn't sure if he was thankful he no longer had to chase dogs or curious how she ended up in a hotel room with Murphy.

"Benny didn't find any conclusive cause of death. There weren't any wounds, ligature marks, tattoos, or birthmarks. Exact time of death is also inconclusive so we can only go by the approximate date the fourth floor was walled up. Tox reports were negative. Can't get fingerprints or dental to confirm identification either and lord knows, by looking at her, even her mother wouldn't be able to give a positive identification. She is basically mummified." Robinson shoved a stack of photographs across the table.

Murphy searched through room photos until he found the ones of Alicia. For the first time in his professional career he turned his head. It was difficult to think that the woman he had once loved had been reduced to what he was seeing in front of him. This couldn't possibly be her. "Any luck finding a relative to confirm the identity?"

"Not yet." There was a knock at the door. Robinson crossed the room and opened the door. He took the tray from one of the clerical staff and set it on the table. A tangle of arms reached for cups and carafes. There was silence for two minutes while everyone doctored their coffee and mainlined much-needed caffeine.

"Any results from Benny's new facial reconstruction software?" Sam asked.

"It's a new toy so we have to give his people some time," Robinson admitted.

"Was Alicia Prince her real name?" Jake leveled an unsmiling glare at Murphy. Sam wasn't sure if that was for her benefit or if he really was pissed.

"That's the only name I knew her by."

"How could she, here in the Midwest, become mummified?" Frank asked. "Once it started to warm up wouldn't decomposition have started?" Frank reached over for the coffee carafe and refilled his cup.

"It was a very secure and weatherproofed room, from what the crime unit boys said, and it would have had to have been to preserve her that well. And with a very long and cold winter, lack of insects and animals to degrade the remains." Robinson shrugged. "It's not impossible." He turned to Murphy. "Have anything to add, Chief?"

"I want Jeff Schuler turned upside down and inside out. Find out who scheduled the wrecking ball, what firm he has been negotiating with, if he has invested even a dime in the last company to own the hotel. He is a manipulative bastard and will do anything to get elected mayor."

"Chief, maybe you should look back at some collars you've made," Robinson suggested. "See if someone made payback a priority in his life. Do you recall receiving death threats any time in your career?"

"Who hasn't?" Murphy rubbed his face with both hands. With a career spanning over thirty years, there were a lot of files to go through.

Sam wasn't ready to let Murphy off the hook. "What else do you know about Alicia? Where did she live and work?"

"She was an art major at the community college."

"Or so she said."

"She had no reason to lie," Murphy argued.

"Are you sure about that?" Robinson chimed in.

"Back to where she lived." Sam could tell Murphy was being defensive and wondered why. Other than defending his innocence, was there an underlying reason?

"She had an apartment over on Garfield. I was never in it, though. As I said, we only dated a few times."

Sam saw Jake's pen moving continuously across his notepad. Was he doodling or actually finding what Murphy was saying interesting?

"She never mentioned her parents or where she was born, what high school she went to?" Jake was treating Murphy like he would any suspect.

"Was she even from around here?" Frank asked.

Murphy checked the tabletop before leaning his expensive suit fabric on the wood. He was never sure what bacteria was floating around the

Sixth Precinct. "This is a relatively useless exercise. Without positive identification, we are wasting a lot of time."

Sam studied Murphy and wondered how he ever thought no one would find out. She reached into her tote bag as she said, "Did Alicia have a nickname for you?"

"What?" Murphy looked around the table as though not sure who had asked the question. "No, of course not."

"She didn't call you Slick?" When Murphy's face turned ashen, Sam knew she had her answer. The men looked at her quizzically, wondering where that name was coming from. Sam opened the locket and set it on the table in front of him. "According to your Uncle John, this is a picture of you and Alicia. On the right side is engraved, *Love Always, Slick.* Fourteen carat gold chain and locket the size of a half dollar. Pretty expensive present for someone who only knew the woman briefly."

"Where did you get…?" Murphy stammered, then realization struck him. "You took an item of evidence off of the deceased?" He turned his wrath on Jake. "You let a civilian into a crime scene?"

Jake said nothing but Sam could hear a soft exhale of breath and imagined her husband just washed his hands over his face.

"And you lied about how close you two were," Sam replied although she knew it was a weak excuse. "Do you want to correct your earlier statement that you barely knew the deceased?"

"We went to the show once, dinner twice. That's it."

"And how many visits to your apartment or a motel room?"

Murphy didn't have a response. He stared at the picture in the locket. "So you showed this photo to my uncle and that's how he identified Alicia."

"First he identified you, then he remembered the name of the girl he says you were head over heels in love with."

"We'll take it from here, Sam." Jake was morphing into lead detective mode.

"Chief Murphy hired me to clear his name so I need every sleazy detail. I told him last night he wasn't to hold anything back. Which reminds me, I need a three hundred dollar retainer."

"You're a consultant for the department. Just turn in your time sheet with Robinson like you always do," Murphy said.

"I don't think so. If the case is turned over to the state police, my hands would be tied. But if you hire me as a private detective, I have free rein. So pop open that checkbook."

Sam not only was being dismissed, but Murphy was also not going to pay her out of his own pocket. "If you lied about how long you dated, what else are you lying about?" Sam ripped the locket from Murphy's hands. "This is mine for the time being."

"That's evidence."

"It's not logged in so it can't be used as evidence. You should thank me."

"Shit." Murphy pulled out his checkbook, scribbled out a check and handed it to her. He stood, jamming the checkbook back into his pocket. "I have a meeting. I want to know every detail of the case as it proceeds. Is that understood?" He charged out of the room, letting the door slam behind him.

Robinson leaned forward and grabbed his head, as though expecting his brains to start leaking from his ears. "What do you think?" he said. "Is he telling the truth?"

Frank and Jake said nothing. Sam grabbed her tote bag and stood. "He's still holding back on something. Not sure what, but I will find out."

<h1>24</h1>

"Tell me again how you lured him to your love nest at the Embassy Suites last night?" Jackie was a little too enthused about the front page story, but then, that was Jackie.

Sam glared at her friend from across the table. They were seated at an outdoor café not far from Jackie's store. "I would rather talk about your new found friend, the black Adonis."

Jackie ignored her comment with a wave of her hand. "What did Jake say about you and Murphy?"

"Nothing yet. I haven't had two minutes alone with him. Other than finding the morning paper spread out on the kitchen counter, I didn't have a hint he knew anything about it. If it had been Jake who rented a hotel room I wouldn't be in this mess."

"That's not Jake and you know it. So what's your next move?"

Sam pushed her empty glass of iced tea aside. "I'm going to pay Schuler a visit, maybe talk to the uncle again. Here I was getting Jake and Frank back into Homicide but do you think they appreciate it? No. Jake dismisses me like I'm some nuisance."

"Well, he did call you first when they found the body. I bet he was none too happy that you took that locket from the crime scene."

"It was the only thing in the room I got vibes from. Once it was logged in as evidence I would have never seen it again."

"Still."

Sam was tired of talking about Murphy and the case. "What about your stalker? Seen him or her lately?"

Jackie shuddered at the reminder. "It's more a feeling. I started looking at every shadow like you told me to but I was making myself nuts. Can't live that way."

"Did you tell the captain?"

Jackie shook her head. "Not yet, and don't you either."

* * *

Sam walked into Schuler's campaign office. It was a cramped space filled more with boxes and supplies than bodies. Three campaign workers looked up when she came in. They couldn't have been any older than college age. Working on a campaign probably gave them credit in their political science class. Two guys were folding flyers while a girl with pierced eyebrows was making phone calls. Schuler wasn't there and she didn't see the guy who was his campaign manager, Tom something.

"I'm from Kelly Girl. Someone asked for a typist?" With the number of people a candidate hires for a campaign office, Sam doubted anyone would question temps.

"Finally," the boy wearing the U2 tee shirt said. "Help yourself," he added with a wave toward the computer. The three appeared to have an earlier agreement: When someone showed up to hold the fort, they would take a break. They announced they were going to lunch and left her to her devious tasks.

Sam clicked on explore and checked the different files that had been created. There appeared to be ad copies and campaign letters. She clicked on correspondence. The drop down menu revealed a ton of letters. "Wonderful, I'll be here all day." She spent the next twenty minutes skimming through the letters but not one looked suspicious. She found one document listing contact phone numbers but that was also lengthy and the heading identified the people as contributors. If Schuler hired anyone to set up Murphy it would be very easy to bury that contact in a list of contributors. But it would also be dumb. She went back to the main screen and typed Embers in the search screen. After several seconds that reaped her zilch. If Schuler was involved in anyway, he wasn't keeping the evidence on this computer.

The door opened and Sam looked up to find a startled Rafe Bennett.

"Hey." He motioned to her with his notepad. "Aren't you the lady in the photo?"

"Gee, and aren't you the guy with a camera stalking people? You know there are laws against harassment."

Rafe took a seat and folded the notepad to a clean sheet. "I've been checking up on you."

"There are laws against that, too." Sam closed out the open files. The last thing she needed was for Bennett to see what she was looking at. "You seem to have an unusual dislike for Chief Murphy."

"Just doing my job. So...." He let that word hang in the air while he motioned around the room in a gesture she was supposed to understand. When Sam didn't bite, Rafe asked, "What are you doing here?"

"I figured I got some money out of one candidate yesterday, I thought I'd get some out of Schuler today."

Rafe laughed. "You're kidding, right?"

"Hey, you tell me. Your front page photo and story certainly gave your readers that impression. Why look surprised?"

"OK. Let's start over." Rafe jumped to his feet, walked out the door and back in. "Well, if it isn't Sam Casey, former detective sergeant who was cleared of murder and now works as a private investigator, who has an unusual method of obtaining information and solving crimes, and who has one helluva set of legs and isn't half bad to look at."

"Don't forget the part about a husband who's former FBI, six foot two and two hundred plus pounds of solid muscle."

"Yes, there is that. Certainly don't want to piss him off."

"Too late."

Rafe's face drained of all color. "Really?"

"I trust you are here to question Schuler regarding the Embers Hotel."

"That was one of my questions, that and if he knew the deceased."

"You do know the body hasn't been positively identified. Just because the photo in the locket..."

Rafe's head snapped up. "What locket?"

"Oops." Sam playfully touched her lips. "Did I say locket?"

"Why you clever little…" Then it dawned on Rafe what she was up to. "Okay, what do you want?"

"You are obviously here to question Schuler. I'd just like to know if you find out anything." Sam saw Schuler's car pull up to the curb. "There is an outdoor cafe several doors down from Jackie's Boutique. Meet me there for an iced tea when you are through here." She grabbed her tote bag and stood. "Just don't pass me any money in public. You never know who might be snapping pictures." She hustled past an awestruck Schuler and Tom Lukovich, leaving Rafe to try to explain her presence.

* * *

"Off the record," Sam repeated as she handed the opened locket to Rafe.

He was quiet as he studied the picture. There was a certain sadness in his eyes but he must have realized Sam was watching him because he quickly snapped the locket closed. "About all I can tell is it's old. Who did you say she was?"

"Alicia Prince, although it hasn't been confirmed yet."

"So it's possible it could be someone else."

A hand reached down and snatched the locket right out of Rafe's hand. "HEY!" But his mouth snapped shut when he saw who was looming over him.

Sam followed Jake's movements as he pulled out a chair and sat down. "How did you know where to find me?" she asked.

"I used my spidey senses." Jake turned his mirrored sunglasses on Rafe. "How much did you tell Clark Kent?"

"We're in the sharing stage of our relationship. He was just telling me how angry Schuler was when he found me in his campaign office."

"Behind the desk, using his computer," Rafe added in an attempt to divert Jake's attention from him. Jake's sunglasses zeroed in on Sam. But the two must have bonded because Rafe jumped to Sam's rescue. "I told

Schuler that when we arrived his workers were taking up all of the chairs and the one behind the computer was the only one available. Sam was done with whatever she was stealing by the time Schuler showed up." Rafe flashed a dimpled smile.

"I'll ask for the last time...how much did you tell Clark Kent?"

"I told him about the locket, OFF the record," Sam stressed. "In turn he told me Schuler's response to Rafe's questioning."

"Which was?" Jake queried.

"*I know nothing*, just about sums up what Schuler said, deleting the expletives he spouted toward his accuser," Rafe replied. "I bet you could go Jack Bauer on him and get some information. How about it? Are you hauling him in?"

"No comment," Jake said.

"Hey, come on. I've been fair with your wife."

"Which part? The one where you followed her to a hotel and plastered her picture on the front page?"

"I wasn't following her. I was following the chief who was following her. I just happened to be in the right place at the right time."

Jake dangled the locket in front of Sam, then snapped it back into the palm of his hand. "I need to get this to Benny so he can compare it with his composite." Jake turned his mirrored sunglasses again on Rafe and added, "BEFORE we can make a positive identification."

"Isn't there some conflict of interest if the same department as the accused does the investigating?" Rafe asked.

"He isn't accused of anything yet."

"Too bad." Rafe sounded genuinely disappointed.

"Will I get it back?" Sam called out as Jake departed.

Jake said nothing.

* * *

"No negligible fingerprints, no blood, no weapons found. She died of natural causes. What other explanation is there?" Frank tossed the box down and rummaged through the stack of newspapers that were taken from the apartment. He had taken over one of the night detectives' desks in the outer office. Adhering to Murphy's recent edict, the desks in the outer office were cleaned off of everything but a calendar and an in and out box.

Andy and Maury were gathered around Andy's desk, their suit jackets flung onto the backs of their chairs, short-sleeved shirts crisp and colorful. "Are those newspapers from the hotel?" Andy asked.

"Yeah. Did you know the murder rate in Chasen Heights was zero back in seventy-six? Were you two even born then?"

Maury appeared to mentally calculate the years. "Actually, no."

"Maybe they just hid the bodies better," Andy offered.

The *Post Tribune* wasn't very thick back then but a by-line caught Frank's eye—Samuel Casey. "What was daddy dear up to back then?" He scanned the article which mentioned a Brinks truck robbery. Sam's father had investigated the theft of close to a quarter of a million dollars from the truck but authorities suspected the real target was the bank which held millions of dollars from the Sin Strip business owners after a successful holiday weekend filled with guests from a large convention in Chicago. "Bet those thieves are soaking on the bottom of Lake Michigan wearing concrete shoes."

Captain Robinson walked over and took a seat in an armless chair next to the desk. "Burning the midnight oil, boys? I'm impressed." He glanced down at the empty yogurt containers in Andy's trash can. "You eat that shit? It tastes like wallpaper paste."

"It's healthy," Andy said. "You just have to eat the flavored ones."

"I'll take a pass." Robinson wrapped his fingers around the opened box and tugged it down to see the contents. "These the papers from the Embers?"

Frank flashed the newspaper at him and plopped his legs on the desk. "Some thieves ran off with a quarter and change from a Brinks truck, shot and wounded a cop. Sam's father was investigating the theft." Frank told Robinson about the holiday weekend. "There was at least twenty million dollars in the bank. But they must not have expected a security guard to be on duty."

"Did they catch the guys?"

Frank tossed several subsequent issues at him. "Haven't found out but help yourself." Frank folded up the newspaper and grabbed another off the stack. "Did you know that a gallon of gas was forty-five cents in seventy-six and you could buy a Plymouth for just three thousand bucks?"

"Yeah, and I'm sure the medium salary was only sixteen thousand." Robinson opened the paper and scanned through the front page. "Here we go. J.J. Perez and Mickey Donovan. Perez was found dead of a gun shot wound. Mickey Donovan was tracked down the next day. Neither one had the money on him. Donovan claimed he wasn't near the bank but eye witnesses said otherwise."

"I trust Donovan didn't get off on a technicality."

"Mickey Donovan?" Andy asked. He typed the name into the database and the information popped up. "Took five years to bring him to trial. He was given fifty to life with parole after twenty years. Would have been the death penalty had the cop died."

Robinson continued skimming the article written by Sam's father. "Donovan claimed he didn't know who killed his partner. Casey suspected there was a third player, the brains behind the job but the hired help screwed it up."

"Twenty million." Frank shook his head. "Somebody definitely screwed up. Donovan's lucky the cops found him first."

Robinson turned to the baby dicks. "What about your catch this morning?"

"Elderly female, contusions on the face." Andy handed a report to Robinson who wheeled the chair over and grabbed it. "Benny isn't sure if the injury was caused from a fall or if she was stuck by something. There is a photo in there of the mark left on her face. A lot of gravel and rocks in that area."

Robinson studied the photo, turning it around to look at it from different angles. "Benny have any idea what might have been used?"

"Not yet." Maury walked behind Robinson and pointed at the victim's face. "Benny thinks she might have been struck first, then suffocated. She was dumped like a bag of garbage. Nothing in that area so she had to have been driven. Was well-dressed. Got the pearls going and the lacey dress."

"Pearls?" Frank set the newspaper down. "Let me see that photo." He grabbed it from Robinson and studied the face. "Too decomposed to verify the face but those pearls look like the ones worn by a lady missing from the Shoreline Shelter. Her name is Eleanor something. Talk to Marie Bakowski, she's the director. And there's a Lucille who is a friend of Eleanor's."

The two were in their suit coats and headed for the elevator before Frank finished his last sentence. "Glad to be of help," Frank called out as the elevator doors closed.

Robinson wheeled back across the aisle. "Love it when my crew works together."

"Whoa." Frank pulled his feet off the desk and sat up. "Captain, they interviewed the bank's part-time security guard. Guess who it was?"

25

Jackie set the alarm then locked the front door to her boutique. Although she lived above the business, she had a taste for a double latte from the coffee shop down the street. Car horns beeped as she sashayed down the block.

Ignoring the horns, she took her time as she walked past the strip malls. The clothing and jewelry stores were closed as were the lock and key shop and hobby store. Across the street teens were mingling in the parking lot of a Burger King. Lamon had called earlier to say he would call when he dug himself out of the pile of evidence from the Embers case.

A soft purr from a car engine cut through the traffic noise and fading laughter from the teens. At first Jackie dismissed it as a vehicle slowing down for the stop light up ahead but from her peripheral vision she saw a car idling in the parking lot of the cleaners at the end of the strip mall. The cleaners closed at six o'clock so it couldn't be the owner. She knew every business owner in her strip mall and what time the businesses closed. It helped to have extra sets of eyes watching out for suspicious people.

Jackie pulled her cell phone from her purse, remembering what Sam had told her. First, she pretended to be on her phone, then she pressed a button on the side of the phone which started the camera. As she slowly pulled the phone from her ear, she made sure the front of the car showing the license plate was on the screen, then pressed the OK button to snap a picture. She wished she knew her cars better. About all she could tell was that it was black in color and it had a moon roof. Whether it was a Ford or Chevy, she didn't know.

Jackie crossed the street at the light receiving more honks. She probably shouldn't have trotted the last twenty feet. She felt her girls leaping toward her neck, the bra unable to contain the weight. Maybe her skirt was conservative but the cut of her jacket and the camisole underneath weren't.

She found a table near the window to drink her latte while people watching. Her gaze drifted to the parking lot across the street but the black car was no longer there. "Just my imagination." Probably someone who pulled over to make a cell phone call, she thought. She pulled out her phone, brought up the photo, and forwarded the picture to Sam's Email address. Hopefully, they could get a clear plate number. The car was too far away but she was sure the photo could be cropped and the image zoomed or whatever it was computer people do. Jackie included a text message to Sam to let her know she had Emailed a photo to her.

The walk back was thankfully boring. She didn't see the black car anywhere. Back on her side of the street she made a mental note to talk to the management company about leaving on more outside lights after closing. She was all for conserving energy but saving a life seemed a little more important at the moment, not to mention being able to find keys in her purse.

Jackie's Boutique occupied the end unit of the strip mall. It provided parking not only in the front but also the side of the building. She dug through her purse and pulled out her keys. One light at the back of the building illuminated the back door. Just as she jammed the key into the dead bolt lock, she heard the soft purr of a car engine. She turned just in time to see the black car, lights off, drifting by, then speeding off down the alley behind the next building.

* * *

His feet shuffled as he made his way along the uneven sidewalk. The jacket had tattered patches on the elbow and itched like hell. But he had to keep up his appearance as a homeless man, unshaven, a soiled fishing hat on his head, and jeans threadbare at the knees and cuffs worn ragged. Bums leaned in doorways as he walked past, their odors turning his stomach. What worthless pieces of humanity. That was one reason he didn't dress nicer. The bums would be hitting him up for money to feed their habits. He should put a gun to their heads and put them out of their misery.

There hadn't been much action around the hotel. The story had been pretty much buried and would have stayed that way had it not been for the explosive revelation that Murphy had known the deceased. How utterly satisfying to see his picture paying that hooker money. Strange thing was she didn't look like a hooker. She looked like the same woman who had been snooping around the hotel after the body was found. He hated not knowing what was going on.

He turned a corner and waited. Couldn't trust that he wasn't being followed. How he missed that old biddy tailing him he'll never know. Two stupid kids had to go and find the body. With any luck the cops won't be able to identify her but there was that L word again. There were other shelters in town but none as close to the hotel as this one. No, he would just have to keep his eyes and ears open, maybe spend more time in the garage. After all, it wouldn't be the first time he slept in his truck.

He entered a side door to a garage he rented. There weren't any ground level windows so curious eyes wouldn't be able to detect the vehicle this seemingly homeless man owned. It was a used truck he had purchased for five hundred dollars from a farmer in another state. Although he wasn't fond of the make or model, the windows were tinted the darkest under legal limits. No sense letting his fellow homeless buddies see him with a vehicle.

The fake beard had to go. He took it off and shoved it in the glove compartment. Next, he exchanged the fishing hat for a Cubs baseball cap. The wig would stay. The gray ponytail served a purpose. Now for the jacket. He laid the itchy sport coat on the passenger seat, then slipped into a blue jean jacket with an American flag on one shoulder and MIA-POW on the other. No one would mess with a vet.

There was one place he was sure to get the latest scoop on the Embers case. It was going to be a risk but such a tantalizing risk. He had been hesitant to ever step inside for fear of drawing attention. As he sped down the alley he didn't notice the floral hat he had discarded drifting in the backdraft.

* * *

Rafe walked down the hall past three hotel rooms and knocked on the door. It was opened quickly and he stepped inside.

"There was a locket found with the body. It's her."

Two hands flew up to stifle a scream.

* * *

Heads whipped toward the door when he walked into Izzy's, but he kept his head down and shuffled in, thankful there was an open seat at the bar. A mirror behind the bar would help him keep tabs on the patrons. He slid onto a bar stool surprised to find the two dog catchers sitting right next to him, at least they looked like the dog catchers who had discovered the body. But they weren't in uniform.

"Hey there, soldier. What can I get you?" The bartender was as wide as a refrigerator and as mean looking as a bull dog.

"Hey, Izzy," one of the dog catchers yelled, lifting an empty beer glass. "When you have a chance. No hurry. Get our military brother first."

Soldier, that's what he had hoped for. A little respect, and from a black dude too. How times have changed. What a far cry from when our men in uniform came home from the Vietnam War. He cupped his ear as though he hadn't heard Izzy.

"Little shell shocked, huh?" Izzy said a little louder.

"Miller Lite." He would rather people thought he was a bit deaf. That way people would leave him alone so he won't have to answer questions. To add a little extra mystery to his persona, he squinted as though the lights were too bright, then slipped on a pair of sunglasses. Made it easier to scope out the faces without people wondering why he was curious.

Izzy placed the beer in front of him. "There you go, buddy."

He toasted the dog catcher's reflection in the mirror, then took a long swallow of the foamy beverage. In the mirror he was able to study the reflections of the patrons. There were couples huddled around pizzas and guys playing darts. Most of the men had their eyes glued to the television set which was televising a baseball game. He could tell which of the guys were cops by the bulge under their shirts which hung outside their pants. He dragged a bowl of popcorn closer and started munching.

He could hear laughter from another room which he assumed was the restaurant. A figure emerged from the doorway to the restaurant. It was the reporter, Rafe something. He remembered seeing him on television. He walked up to the two dog catchers as though they were his best friends, draping an arm across each of their shoulders. "Jake, Frank. How are Chasen Heights best detective sergeants doing?"

Detectives? Not dog catchers? He kept his sunglasses anchored at the mirror, watching the three men carefully.

"What's up?" Rafe raised his glass and ordered a beer, jamming a thumb toward the detective named Frank. "Put it on his tab."

"Thanks, Rafe. I love moochers," Frank said.

The other detective looked all business. He was studying reflections in the mirror, too, and looked suspicious of everyone. The eyes were like cyborg's shifting from one end of the long mirror to the other.

"Anything new to report?" Rafe asked after Izzy set his beer on the bar.

"You know we can't talk shop, Rafe," Frank said. "Besides, everything comes out of the chief's press liaison."

"Yeah, but the chief isn't exactly in charge any more, right?"

Neither detective replied.

"Okay, what about your wife, Jake? Does her crystal ball tell her anything?"

Huh? The vet sipped his beer while his eyes, hidden behind the sunglasses, watched closely.

"Speaking of the devil." Frank swiveled in his chair while the vet eyed the woman who had just entered. It was the same woman who had gone into the hotel before the crime scene techs arrived. Why would a cop call his wife out to a homicide? He saw several hands wave at the woman and even more appreciative stares dart her way.

"I had a feeling you two would be here." She scooted the reporter aside and draped an arm over Jake's shoulder.

Izzy sidled up before she opened her mouth. "Sam, you are looking great. The usual?"

"Yes, please."

Rafe said, "We were just talking about you."

"I bet."

Frank's cell phone rang. He pressed a finger to one ear so he could hear. "Yeah, babe." He was doing more listening than talking. "Just finishing my beer. I'll leave in a minute." He hung up and slipped his phone in his pocket.

"What is that now, two calls or three?" Jake said referring to the number of times Claudia had called.

"You are so lucky to have a wife who used to be a cop," Frank said. "Sam doesn't bug you about where you are and when you are coming home." Frank could only vent with other cops. Claudia didn't want to hear about the daily grind Frank went through. She didn't want to know the details and wanted Frank to leave everything at the office so to speak. Sam was eager to hear all the dirt, every bullet, every punch, every bone and blood splatter.

"Cut her some slack, Frank," Sam said. "For one thing she tries to make the home a place where you are insulated from all the grief you encounter at work. She also knows you take twenty minutes to drink one beer so she assumes one hour and three beers is enough time to vent. I also think she can tell by your voice if you need more time to vent or if you are just kicking back and getting plastered."

Frank slid off of the bar stool. "As long as you put it that way, I guess I'll stop off and pick up a bunch of flowers for my better half." He gave a wave to Izzy and left. Sam slipped onto the empty bar stool and slid the vodka and tonic in front of her.

Rafe ordered another round and settled between the two bar stools. He set a twenty on the bar saying, "So, Sam, do the dead really talk to you?"

The vet looked up sharply, watching the images in the mirror behind the bulk of the bartender. He wished fatso would move.

Sam smiled and sipped her drink.

"Come on, Sam. I've leveled with you. The paper said twenty-three bodies were buried in Pine Grove. Couldn't miss that headline."

Huh? Now the vet's beer glass hovered over the bar, the condensation almost causing the glass to slip through his fingers.

"It didn't come from us or our department," Jake explained. "But we couldn't stop the rumors from the police departments on the scene."

"Do you know how valuable your talent would be in finding missing people?" Rafe appeared genuinely impressed. "You should be working for the FBI."

"No thanks. One agent in the family is enough."

"Former agent," Jake reminded her.

FBI? Fuck me. The vet finished his beer, left a dollar on the bar, and headed for the door.

Rafe's phone rang. He pulled it out and checked the screen. "I have to take this. Nice talking to you."

"I think he might be a little upset that we wouldn't share any information," Sam said as Rafe left and walked through to the restaurant.

"I'm sure he'll get over it."

Izzy reached over to remove the empty popcorn bowl. Sam grabbed the vet's empty beer glass to push it closer to Izzy. It was then that she saw bars. Had the veteran been in prison? The patch on his jacket did say *POW-MIA*. She turned toward the door, hand still clasped around the glass. Through the wall of windows she saw the vet standing outside staring at her. Then he disappeared from view.

* * *

He started up the truck and peeled rubber from the curb. His eyes snapped to the rearview mirror, expecting the cop's wife to come running down the alley in hot pursuit. What the hell was that all about? The dead speak to her? Is that why her husband called her out before calling the crime techs? And why did she look shocked when she touched his beer glass? Did she see or sense something? And that nosy reporter better watch his step. If he screws up the plans he has, if he gets in the way... but he didn't want to lose focus, not now.

<h1 style="text-align:center">26</h1>

Robinson closed the door to the conference room where the usual faces assembled. He tossed a new file folder onto the table. It was bright lime green. Murphy turned his head quickly, as though the colors were burning his retinas.

"I had a sit down with Jeff Schuler. He didn't arrive in our fair town until twenty years ago, never met Alicia or anyone in her family. He was very cooperative so I have no reason not to believe him."

Murphy was surprisingly quiet. It wouldn't have surprised anyone in the room to learn that Murphy had already checked Schuler's background. Schuler's published memoir described every detail of the councilman's life. "I went through the files of my prior collars. What few jump out at me I gave to Andy Brainard to check out. I have to say, though, not one looks promising. Either they were in prison when Alicia died or not living in the area." Murphy pointed at the green folder. "What have you got here?"

Robinson opened the folder and handed Murphy a glossy eight-by-ten photo of Alicia Prince. "Benny's computer expert finished playing with their facial recognition software. The composite made from the skull confirms that the photo in the locket matches the victim found in the hotel. However, we couldn't match Alicia's description with anyone by that name in Social Security nor any pictures in the DMV database. So either Miss Prince didn't have a Social Security number or she wasn't whom she claimed to be."

All heads swiveled to Murphy. "Hey, as I said before, when you are in your twenties you are lucky to ask for someone's first name, let alone her last. And I had no reason to run a background check on her."

He tossed the photo on the table where Sam quickly grabbed it. "Did you ever take Alicia anywhere other than your apartment?" Murphy glowered at her. "Hey, I'm being paid to ask questions. I'm not asking what burger joint you took her to. I'm curious if you took any out of town trips, maybe a resort, little island weekend."

"Right. I had money to go off to Hawaii every weekend." Murphy studied a piece of lint which dared to land on his suit sleeve. He flicked it off and watched it drift to the floor. "My aunt and uncle owned a summer cottage up in Wisconsin. Alicia and I went there a few times."

"A log cabin?" Sam asked.

"Yes." Then Murphy's cop curiosity kicked in. "Why did you say log cabin?"

Sam shrugged, not ready to play her hand yet. "Aren't all cabins in the woods made of logs? Where at in Wisconsin?"

"Just past Milwaukee in an unincorporated area. It's not on Lake Michigan. It's more inland. There's a good fishing stream nearby but mainly it's a great place to relax. My aunt was into bird watching and my uncle liked to sit on the deck and watch the flowers grow. I never went back to the cabin after Alicia and I broke up. My uncle sold the place a couple years after that."

"I'd like the address," Jake said, tapping his pen on the table.

"Why? Like I said, my family sold it years ago."

"Come on, Chief," Robinson piped in. "Think like a cop. There might have been neighbors who had seen Alicia. Maybe she went to a store nearby, got friendly with someone, confided a little about her background."

"That was years ago. The nearest neighbor was at least a mile away, as was the nearest grocery store."

"You don't think she hopped in the car and took a ride while you napped or went on a nature walk without you?" Frank suggested.

Murphy glared at them across the table. "What is this? A witch hunt? My own officers have me guilty before trying to prove my innocence."

"Chief, when you asked for my help I had just one condition—don't lie to me. You said you barely knew Alicia, only dated a couple times. Yet your uncle claimed you two were hot and heavy for weeks and you bought her that expensive necklace. Now, is there anything else you might be holding back?" She could see his hands ball into fists. But then he took a deep breath and his hands relaxed.

"I'm sure I don't need to tell you, Sam, that guys tend to inflate their egos a bit. At any age they don't want to admit some woman dumped them. Alicia disappeared out of my life. No phone call, no note, nothing. It was easier for me to shrug and say, 'we barely dated, she meant nothing to me, on to the next conquest.' In reality, I was devastated. Yes, I fell fast and hard and it hurt like hell when she left."

"You didn't put out a missing person report?" Robinson asked.

Murphy's phone rang. He checked the screen then said, "I have to go. I'm late for a budget meeting."

"I think you better cancel it," Sam said. She was overstepping her bounds and bringing up something personal that was better left said in private but she couldn't stop now. "My father skewered you in those articles regarding the Brinks truck robbery. He kept focusing on how the part-time security guard took an extended break right before the robbery went down."

"I remember that case and I know what you are thinking." Murphy ran a hand over his silk tie. How like him to be more concerned with his appearance than the case building against him. "I was in the washroom and showed up just as the robbery was taking place. Matter of fact, I thwarted the robbery."

"According to the workers my father interviewed, a beautiful blonde showed up and you left with her through a side exit and didn't return for half an hour. Seems to me she timed it just right."

Frank added, "The paper did say it was odd the robbers hit the Brinks truck when there were millions in the bank."

Murphy didn't hide his anger. "As I said, my return obviously thwarted the robbery."

"Which could have been prevented had you not been conveniently lured away by an offer of afternoon delight by a woman whom you knew absolutely nothing about. Sounds like you were set up, Chief." Sam glared back, still stinging from her realization that the chief's animosity toward her father had carried through all these years.

Robinson laid two pictures on the table. "Do you recognize either of these two men?"

Murphy studied the photos and slowly nodded. "There's something familiar about them. They robbed the Brinks truck?"

"J.J. Perez and Mickey Donovan. Perez was killed after the robbery. Donovan was captured and prosecuted." Robinson placed another photo on the table. "This is Donovan the day he was released about six years ago." Prison time and aging had transformed Donovan from a long-haired hippie to a balding man with sunken eyes and a sallow complexion. The left eye drooped, as though being dragged down by the scar just above the cheekbone.

Murphy ignored her and looked at his detectives. "Do we have an APB out on Donovan?"

"Yes," Robinson replied.

"Then I think we are through here." Murphy pushed away from the table and stood. "I have to get to that budget meeting."

"Chief," Robinson started, "my men are only doing their job."

Murphy paused for a few seconds, then nodded. That was as much of an apology as they would ever receive.

"The address," Jake reminded him.

Murphy rattled off the address and brief directions on how to get there. After he left the room, Jake turned to Sam. "He's still holding back."

"Probably."

Robinson said, "Doesn't surprise me. It's probably killing him to be interrogated by his own people. I feel like we have to drag every piece of information out of him. So I say, yeah, he's still holding something close to the vest. Where next, Jake?"

"I want Benny to send Alicia's picture through the pipeline, see if she pops up in any police departments in the country," Jake said. "We aren't sure exactly when she died, don't know of any surviving relatives. My gut tells me she was part of the theft ring. Could have been her job to keep the guard busy while her partners did their thing."

Robinson shoved the photo into a separate folder and handed it to Jake. "Before you make a trip to Wisconsin, go show the eight-by-ten photo to Murphy's uncle," Robinson suggested.

27

"I don't feel comfortable riding with a bottle of liquor in the trunk," Jake said.

"My dear husband. The man who genuflects at the tablet of laws." Sam studied her hunk of a brute as they drove toward South Bend, Indiana to visit John Kendall. She was text messaging Jackie with the bad news that the photo she took of the car wasn't clear enough to get a license plate number.

"I'm happy," Frank said from the back seat. "I've got the chocolate malt balls."

They spent the one hour drive reviewing the various owners of the hotel and what Sam had learned during her first visit with John. Murphy's uncle was more than happy to have guests again for lunch. John was sitting at his usual table with another man.

"Hey, Sam. Hope you don't mind. After you were here the first time, I looked up a friend who was a cop back in the Seventies. He's retired Sergeant Jerry Zuniga. He's up here from Florida visiting relatives. Thought he might be able to help you out."

Gravity had been pulling down hard on Jerry's cheeks during the years making him look like a basset hound. His skin was tan and leathery and there was power in his handshake.

"I trust, Sam, your friends can imbibe in my special lunch beverage," John said as he accepted the paper bag from Frank.

"Sorry, but we're on duty," Jake admitted. "Sam isn't driving so I'm sure she'll join you."

"Don't get heavy-handed on me, John." She watched John pour and raised a hand to signal him to stop. "Thank you." She stirred her drink while the waitress set their plates of cheeseburgers in front of them.

"Hope you don't mind. I took the liberty of ordering lunch for everyone. Their burgers are rather good," John said. "Hope no one is a tree hugging veggie."

"Been there as ordered by the missus, done that. Not my thing," Frank said. "This looks great." As an afterthought, he handed John another bag. "Sorry, I got a little hungry on the ride down so you'll find some of those malt balls missing."

"I hear you guys have a possible murder case on your hands," Jerry said.

Sam could see a spark in his gray eyes, a spark that never seemed to die out even after retirement. "We believe so."

"I can tell you from experience, John's nephew may have been an arrogant know-it-all in his youth, but he would be the last person I would accuse of murder." Jerry fished the lime out of his glass and set it aside.

"No one is accusing him," Jake said. He wanted to add 'yet' to his comment but decided against it. "Tell us about Sin Strip, Jerry. I've read some of the newspaper stories when the Strip was being closed down. Most everyone sounded as though they were in mourning."

Jerry nodded with a sigh. "It was an exciting time, I can tell you that much. There were some problems but the businesses basically policed themselves. We just tried to keep the peace, make sure everyone was safe."

"Have you always lived in this area?" Sam asked.

"Sure. My ancestors came over from Germany in the late 1800s. My grandfather road his bike to Standard Oil. Made less than five bucks a day, which was the highest rate for a skilled laborer. A lot of farms in this area, then the railroads came and with it more industry. You hear people belly-aching today, they should have lived back then. My grandfather worked as much overtime as he could. Bought one of the first mass-produced cars in the country, an Olds Curved Dash for just six hundred and fifty bucks. Can you beat that?"

"Life expectancy was forty-six," John countered.

"What do you expect? People died from diarrhea back then."

"Yeah, diarrhea of the mouth."

John and Jerry roared with laughter.

Frank asked, "When did you move down to Florida, Jerry?"

"One week after I retired at fifty-five. I owned a couple acres down in Florida for years. Use to set up my trailer on vacations. Great fishing down there. Then the place started building up, people got uppity about what type of housing was allowed. Thought I better get something built before the prices started skyrocketing. Got one of them pre-fabs that was just coming out. Suited me fine. Wife wanted something fancier. But she really hated the heat."

"She didn't like you too much either," John said with another bark of a laugh.

"Well, there's some truth to that saying. Cops and cops' wives stray more often than an alley cat."

Sam detected a bit of remorse in Jerry's voice. "I don't think that's always true. There's probably a percentage in every line of business. Look at doctors and their wives, lawyers, actors, athletes, even office workers."

Frank pushed his plate away with a gratifying sigh. "Cops, though, have more to lose. Both the cop and the spouse are armed."

Sam shifted a side glance toward Jake. "And I am getting better at the shooting range."

One corner of Jake's mouth twitched again. "Who opened the first strip joint?" Jake asked in an attempt to get the discussion back to Sin Strip.

"Manny Corsini." Jerry pawed through the debris on the table looking for an ashtray.

The waitress pushed a cart close to the table then cleared away the plates. Everyone ordered another drink. Sam opted for an iced tea. Jerry raised a cigarette toward the waitress who handed him a tin ashtray. When the waitress left, Jerry passed his glass of tonic water to John. Once it was significantly spiked, Jerry took the glass back.

"Anyway," Jerry continued as he lit a cigarette, "Manny started the ball rolling. It was like the morning after a frost. There was only one mushroom one day and the next day the whole damn forest is filled with them. The Strip seemed to sprout up overnight. We had more liquor licenses per capita than any other town in the country. Just three blocks but with all the lights and people you'd a thought you was walking in downtown Vegas. I didn't become a cop until the fifties, but those old timers on the beat had the stories to tell."

"Remember Louie the Hawk?" John asked. The two men started roaring with laughter. John turned to his guests. "Louie had eyes like a hawk and a beak to match. He ran the mobile poker game. Different location every night. Word of mouth was the only way you heard about it. Cops had a devil of a time keeping up with the locations and Louie knew every move the cops were going to make."

"Sounds like he had a friend on the inside." Jake lit up his own cigarette and shared Jerry's ashtray.

"If there was, it wasn't me," Jerry said. "Oh, there were all kinds of rumors."

"One or more of your mayors went to jail, right?" Jake said.

"For only being in town seven or eight years, you certainly know the history," Sam commented.

"Where were you before?" Jerry asked.

"With the Bureau."

"THE Bureau?" John leaned forward as if he somehow missed some sign on Jake's forehead.

"Can't you tell?" Frank said with a laugh. "He hasn't cracked a smile since I met him."

"Well, I hate to tell you this, G-man." Jerry blew out a puff of smoke. "They had some feds on the payroll, too."

Jake finally did crack a smile. "I hate to tell you this, Jerry, but those guys were on the inside. Who do you think brought down your mayor?"

There was a second of stunned silence, then the two old guys burst out a volley of laughs.

"Did any of those poker games make it to the Embers when you owned it?" Sam asked.

"Sure. Matter of fact, we had tournaments in one of the ballrooms. Authentic poker tables, bars set up, waitresses walking around taking drink and food orders."

"Police didn't hear about them?" Frank reached over and grabbed several malt balls from the bag in front of John.

"Oh, yeah. But we had a lookout. The previous owners built that fourth floor not just to hold their high stakes games but that wall gave cover for someone to be a lookout. Cops never checked the fourth floor for gambling. The ballroom was another story. The lookout would phone down and in the blink of an eye table tops were placed on each table, concealing the poker chips and cards. Drinks and plates were placed on the tables as if all that was going on was a banquet. Those who felt comfortable with the raid, stuck around. Others who were more prominent members of the town and didn't dare chance the cops would discover the ruse, snuck down into the basement and out the hidden exit which leads to the gardens. There they would just stroll or sit and watch the gardens as though completely oblivious of anything illegal taking place in the hotel."

"Can the door be seen from the outside?" Sam asked.

"Only if you know what to look for. It's an old delivery door which hadn't been used since they put in that bay of delivery doors in the back. The double doors are made of steel. No door handle so you needed a special key inserted into a concealed keyhole to get in from the outside."

John waited for the waitress to leave, then added a couple shots of vodka into his glass.

It was obvious to Sam the waitress knew what John was doing because she always left room for him to add the liquor. "How do you get to it from inside?"

"Downstairs passed the laundry there's a storage room. Dennis used to use that entrance, then take the service staircase to the second floor. That way he avoided his aunt seeing him at the front desk."

"Who else knew about that exit?" Jake asked.

"Jeez, everyone who used it. But there were only two keys. You had to slide a piece of metal to the right to access the key hole. It used an old style skeleton key."

"So your nephew had the other key?" Jake asked.

John set his glass down and studied Jake. "I told Sam, Dennis may be a lot of things but a killer he isn't. I helped raise that boy after his parents died. When he was in his early teens, I had to talk him into being our lookout on the fourth floor. He didn't feel good about doing that. And when he was in college and decided to go into law enforcement, I couldn't even get him to call the players to let them know a game was scheduled."

"I take it that is a yes." Jake stabbed the cigarette butt into the ashtray.

"Love can make people do stupid things," Frank said. "Could have been an accident. Maybe she fell and hit her head."

Jerry was shaking his head back and forth, jowls quivering with every movement. "I have to agree with John. Dennis was a straight arrow. A clean cut kid who could have easily been swayed by the questionable characters roaming the streets. But when he was focused on something, when he had his mind made up, nothing would get in his way. And murder would have never been his choice."

"You didn't see how he was with Alicia?" Sam asked. "That 'I'll die if we ever part' feeling?"

"Well, I never met this girl personally but the few times I saw Dennis he always had his nose in a book, always studying," Jerry added.

"Show him the picture," John suggested.

Sam pulled a folder from her tote bag. "You couldn't be positively sure it was Alicia's photo in the locket so we had a digital reconstruction done. This picture is larger and clearer." Sam handed the photo across the table.

John slipped his glasses on. "Yep, that's Alicia."

Jerry patted his pockets and pulled his glasses from the left shirt pocket. He slipped them on his nose and took the picture from John.

"What did you say her name was?"

"Alicia Prince," Sam replied.

Jerry shook his head, the jowls shuddering and wobbling. "No, no. I've seen her before. Alicia wasn't her name. It's..." He tapped the picture several times. Sam leaned closer as though hoping to pull the name from his lips. "Jeannie. No." He grimaced and squinted as though squeezing life into his brain cells. "She was Gus Barlucci's daughter." His eyes brightened as the brain cells clicked. "Gina! Gina Barlucci."

28

"Barlucci of the East Coast Sicilian mob?" John asked, his mouth gaping.

"Who was Gus Barlucci?" Sam asked.

"So Alicia wasn't Alicia," Frank said under his breath.

"One guy you didn't want to mess with if you lived in New York City. He was never in our neck of the woods," Jerry clarified. "I had heard he had a son who was a total screw up. Wanted his own territory but his father wouldn't even let him pick up his dry cleaning. Young Tony wanted to prove himself, bring his style of business to the Midwest, right to our front door."

"What business was that?" Jake asked.

"Drugs and prostitution. Tony believed drugs was the big moneymaker, which it was. But back then the club owners in Chasen Heights had enough to handle with gambling and strip joints. I believe our chief of police gave Gus a call when he spotted Tony scoping the city out. Gus swooped in and dragged the kid out of here. He brought his daughter and wife along with, like it was a family vacation. They were headed to Chicago. The wife wanted to do some shopping so he had his driver take the women to Chicago and Gus sat down with some of the business owners to assure them he wasn't moving his operation out of the East Coast."

"You're sure this is the girl you saw?" Frank said.

"She was still in high school at the time but already a real looker. She and Tony were close. She and her mom felt sorry for the screw up. Guess he had that wounded puppy look. Tony was a few years older than Gina." He handed the picture back to Sam. "If she came back into town in the mid Seventies, I didn't hear about it. But wherever Gina was, Tony was always close by. If you ask me, they did not act like brother and sister."

"He was doing his own sister?" Frank's look of revulsion brought laughs.

"Didn't matter. She was adopted. They weren't related," Jerry explained.

"But still." Frank reached over and grabbed more malt balls.

Jake asked Jerry, "Is there anyone whom you know who might have been close to the Barluccis?"

"Sure. There was a cousin of the Barlucci family who lived in Jersey. Tom DeLeo, I think."

Jake reached across the table and handed Jerry his business card. "Give me a call if you learn anything or if Tom feels comfortable talking to me. We are trying to get a relative to fly in to claim the body."

"Not quite sure how to find him but I can make a few calls." Jerry tucked the business card in his shirt pocket.

Sam asked, "Do you think Dennis knew of the close relationship between Gina and Tony?"

"I was pretty busy with the hotel," John replied. "I'm pretty sure I never saw a third party lurking around when Gina was in the hotel, but that's something you'd have to ask my nephew."

"Do you still have that skeleton key?" Sam asked, "or did you give it to the next owner?"

"Nah," John said waving a dismissive hand through the air. "Once we filed for bankruptcy I didn't give a second thought to that exit. Have no idea where that key is now."

* * *

"What do you think?" Frank asked from the passenger side of Sam's Jeep. Jake was driving and Sam was busy organizing her notes in the back seat. "Jealousy can make a man act rashly."

"Anything is possible," Jake said. He was itching to have a cigarette but didn't want to smoke in Sam's Jeep. "He hasn't been completely honest with us so far."

"Would have been a perfect setup. Gina distracts Dennis with her body while her brother and his friends rob the bank."

"They planned to rob the bank," Sam piped up from the back seat. "Maybe Gina had a change of heart which is why Dennis came back early. The thieves were only able to rob the Brink's truck. That might have made them upset if Gina didn't hold up her end of the plan. They lost out on millions of dollars."

"Still, that was 1976. The fourth floor wasn't walled up according to John." Jake patted his pocket as though assuring himself he didn't leave his last cigarette back at the assisted living home.

Sam leaned forward, placing an arm across the back of each of their seats. "Time to check out that log cabin."

29

Robinson gave his blessing for the trip to Wisconsin so the next morning Jake, Frank, and Sam headed out early, making just two stops on their way to Petawka, Wisconsin.

They slammed out of the Ford Taurus and walked slowly toward the log cabin. The deck was the same one Sam remembered seeing when she first touched the locket.

"Someone is keeping the area neat and trim," Frank said. They could smell the scent of fresh mowed grass. The log cabin sat on one acre surrounded by blooming perennials which hugged the wrap-around porch.

"The family owned about five acres." Jake studied the wooded area around the cabin trying to get his bearings. The scent of moisture and wet leaves drifted through the air. There was water somewhere close by.

"Who owns it now?" Sam asked.

"According to John Kendall, he sold the cabin to Genesis Enterprises." Jake climbed the deck and peered into one of the windows. "Wausaw Realty rents some of the properties around here year round. But, they have never rented this property. The office manager will be back around lunchtime and will see if she can find out more information on the property."

"How do we get inside?" Frank pressed his face against another window. "Looks neat and tidy in there but the furniture looks a bit outdated. No glasses or papers lying around.

Jake grabbed the door knob and turned. "Who leaves their door unlocked?"

"You're kidding." Frank joined Jake at the door and entered behind him.

Sam studied the deck, the planter of dried flowers hanging above the railing. A chair made of twigs sat in a corner of the deck, dried flowers clinging to the arms. She didn't like the chill spreading over her body as she crossed the threshhold into the living room. A large stone fireplace was in the corner of the room.

"Nice ceiling." Frank craned his neck to the big paddle fan hanging from the ceiling. "Looks like a loft up there."

But Sam's eyes were on the leather couch where an afghan with a rustic scene lay across the back, the same afghan she had seen before. Sam needed to feel the warmth of the sun. She left the house and walked out into the yard, her arms wrapped tightly around her midsection. Flowers cascading from planters looked neglected as weeds crowded out the blooms. She looked back at the house with the tall windows overlooking the yard. Weathered lattice surrounded the bottom of the deck probably to keep out the animals.

She walked the perimeter, amazed at the care someone had taken to trim around flower beds and decking. The realtor had said a service had been hired to fertilize and cut the grass and also plow the long drive in the winter. Sam reached the start of the thick underbrush and wooded area surrounding the property but something was pulling her back. A slight breeze rippled through the thick underbrush. It barreled past her ruffling her feathered earring and tousling her hair. It settled near the ground where errant blades of grass and leaves circled in a crazy waltz, then picked up the beat. Whispers followed. Sam could barely make out distinguishable words but could swear they were in Lakota. It was obvious the spirits wanted to get her attention.

The leaves and blades of grass danced across the lawn but appeared to have a target in mind. Sam hesitated, then slowly approached a rock garden where tall grass stood like sentries. The grass began to sway yet Sam no longer felt a breeze. Stones were stacked on top of each other like a...the word tombstone flashed in her head. The grass and leaves sprayed across the foot of the rocks, scattering in a six foot area.

Sam didn't hear the two men approaching until Frank said, "House doesn't look like anyone has lived there in a while."

Sam ran her gaze around the backyard. "Have you seen any shovels around?"

"Shovels?" Jake pulled his sunglasses off and stared at the rock garden.

"Oh shit," Frank said. "Don't go pulling this crap on me, Sam. I can't take another twenty-three bodies."

"Not twenty-three. Only one, I think." She expected her logical husband to protest. Instead, he marched off to a shed in the corner of the property and returned several minutes later with two shovels.

"Oh shit oh shit oh shit. Damn that black cat." Frank rolled up his shirt sleeves and yanked one of the shovels from Jake's grasp. "You better be wrong."

Jake studied her for several seconds before putting his sunglasses back on, then started digging.

It took them thirty minutes before a fabric that looked like blue jean material was exposed. Another sixty minutes of painstakingly removing the dirt with spoons until they exposed the front side of a corpse.

"Male, about six feet," Frank said. "Who wants to check the pockets?"

Sam retrieved latex gloves from the trunk of the Taurus, then tossed them at Frank.

"Dammit, Sam. You found the body, you check the pockets."

"You're already down in the grave."

Frank tugged on the gloves, muttering, "Damn black cat. It's still haunting my life." He squatted down and carefully shoved his hands in the pants. "Nothing in this pocket." He winced as he lifted one side of the body to check the back pocket. "Nothing here either. Wait." He hefted the body up a little farther. "Got a wallet." He carefully opened it and chuckled. "Well, well. Meet Tony Barlucci."

30

Rafe Bennett was waiting for Robinson when he returned from lunch. He crooked his finger and had Rafe follow him to his office. He pointed at a chair in front of his desk. "Let me guess. You heard we have a possible identification for Jane Doe, aka Alicia Prince."

"I can't seem to find the police chief anywhere to ask for his reaction."

"This is all off the record, Rafe. I don't want to read any quotes from me in tomorrow's paper. Agreed?" Robinson thought the reporter looked tired. He was probably burning the midnight oil on this case and hadn't taken time to shave, unless he was going for the popular rugged look.

"Agreed."

"A cop who had met the Barluccis years ago identified the composite photo as Gina Barlucci. We have confirmed the photo with DMV and passport photos." Robinson figured Rafe was actually going to be true to his word because he wasn't taking any notes.

"And Murphy had no idea that the woman he dated was Gina Barlucci."

"None whatsoever."

"Do you believe him?"

"Have no reason not to. Even his uncle only knew her as Alicia." Robinson was curious about Rafe. Reporters were inquisitive but there was something different about this one. For one thing, the night patrol officer who had taken Rafe on a ride-along stated that the reporter was very knowledgeable about police terminology and procedures. Here Robinson had predicted this town would eat Rafe alive, but the reporter was proving him wrong.

"There are a few things you need to know about Dennis Murphy," Robinson explained. "He went through six partners when he was a patrolman, three when he was in robbery. He had a high closure rate while in Homicide. Murphy has a line that cannot be crossed. One partner wanted to use him as an alibi while he cheated on his wife. Murphy wouldn't go along with it and told the partner's wife. One partner slipped a few pieces of jewelry from a house. Another planted a gun on a suspect. Murphy made a lot of enemies during his career but he would never cross that line."

"I hear he plays politics as slimy as Jeff Schuler. Doesn't he have a moral line for that?"

"That's different. Political games are just that. He plays hardball with the best. If he has one fault it's that he is very vindictive when crossed. You know the adage, 'Don't get mad, get even?' Well, that's Murphy." Robinson was thinking specifically of Sam's father and godfather. Murphy was passed over for chief originally and blamed Sam's father for the scathing articles written years earlier. When Connelly and Samuel Casey were out of the picture, Murphy turned his wrath on Sam. But that wasn't public knowledge.

"Seems to me a vindictive person is someone who would kill Tony and Gina Barlucci."

"Murphy is not a killer. I would stake my career on it."

"You may have to, Captain."

* * *

They sat huddled on the top stair of the cabin's porch waiting for Petawka's Deputy Chief Chet Toomey to finish checking their I.D.s. He was a suspicious cop, which wasn't unusual. After all, Jake and Frank were way off their beaten path, hadn't given the deputy a head's up when they came to his town, plus they had dragged along a civilian, as Toomey had called Sam. He had chuckled when she showed him her investigative consultant business card.

"So," Frank started, "when the questions start flying out of the deputy's chubby little mouth, what do we tell him?"

"The truth," Jake said, as though he had never considered anything else. "No sense getting off on the wrong foot."

"Too late for that," Sam said.

"He's only doing his job."

Frank said, "Yeah, but even we would have asked questions first rather than growling, 'shut up and give me your identification.'"

Jake's phone rang. He checked the screen and said, "It's the realtor. This is Detective Mitchell." He listened but his face revealed nothing. Sam could only tell by the slow grimacing blink that Jake didn't like what he was hearing. "You are sure about that? John Kendall and his wife are the ones who sold the cabin, right?" Jake ran a hand through his hair. Sam looked at Frank and the unspoken assessment was this didn't look good at all. "And you have faith in your records...I know you have only been there for a year...yes." Jake let out an exasperated breath which was certain to be heard on the other end. "Tell me this much. Was the sale made in person or through the mail?" He pulled a pen from his shirt pocket. Frank handed him his notepad. "And what was that date?" Jake scribbled on the notepad then thanked the young woman. He folded his phone and clipped it back on his belt.

"That didn't sound good," Frank said.

"It wasn't. According to her records there has been only one owner after John Kendall and that was his nephew."

"Wait," Frank popped off the stoop as though stung. "Chief Murphy owns this property? But he said..."

Sam didn't like the direction this case was headed in. Frank dropped back onto the porch as the chief returned.

Deputy Toomey leaned one foot on the porch stairs, forearm on the top of his knee as he handed their I.D.s back. "Tell me again what prompted you to look for a body on property that doesn't belong to you."

Jake started to tell him the details of the case they were working on but Toomey stopped him.

"First things first, son. What I need to know," Toomey looked toward the yard where the remains of Tony Barlucci were being hefted out of the grave, "is how you looked at all this property and went right to that area. Could have been a family dog buried there seeings how them stones are piled up like a marker. Someone tell you where to look for a body?"

This was not a conversation Jake cared to have but there wasn't a delicate way to put it. Sam jumped in as he hoped she would.

"My relatives told me," Sam replied.

Jake grimaced. That wasn't exactly how he would have hoped Sam would put it.

Toomey clicked his pen and put it to paper. "And what are their names?"

"They're dead." Sam enjoyed the reactions from people and tried to hide her smile.

The pen was clicked repeatedly as Toomey waited. One bushy eyebrow jutted up as he tried to encourage her to fill in the blanks.

Frank cleared his throat. "Did you read about that case in Pine Grove, Indiana, a few weeks back where they dug up twenty-three bodies?"

"Yeah. They found the victims of the I-80 killer." Toomey watched as Frank jerked his head in Sam's direction. Toomey's eyes widened and he pulled his foot off the stair as though trying to put distance between himself and Sam. "You're her?" His head swiveled from the coroner's wagon to the backyard.

A woman in a dark pantsuit, jacket sleeves rolled up, was pulling off latex gloves as she approached. "Hey, Toom. Nice little job you gave me." She handed him a zip lock bag containing a bullet.

"Well, you know me, Nettie. Hate to see a woman with time on her hands." Toomey motioned to the group on the stairs. "These here people brought trouble from Chasen Heights, Illinois. Mighty nice of them to give us a little puzzle to solve." He introduced them to Annette Simmons, the county medical examiner. "Got anything interesting to tell us?" he asked Nettie.

"Victim was shot with a twenty-two. Been dead anywhere from five to ten years. Can't give you anything firm till I get him back to the shop."

They remained silent as the gurney rolled by. "Could have been shot right by the gravesite and pushed in. Hard to tell. Find anything in the house?"

"I got two people looking through it now. Water isn't on. No clothes in the closets. Doesn't look like it's been lived in," said Toomey. "No signs of a struggle, no blood. Victim wasn't killed inside."

As the men rolled the gurnee into the wagon, Nettie said, "I have to escort Mister Barlucci to the morgue. Are you going to join me for the autopsy?"

"Yeah, yeah. I'll be there. Just get the coffee on." He waved her off but there was a smile on his face as they bantered back and forth.

"I'll scrape it into a cup for you." Nettie chuckled as she walked off.

"I don't suppose we can join you during the autopsy," Jake said.

"Wishful thinking, son. We have a lot to discuss before we get to that phase. We tend to move a little slower up here. Nettie probably won't start the autopsy until tomorrow. Maybe if I sweet talk her she might start today."

A uniformed officer exited the house and handed several magazines in a zip lock bag to Toomey. "Thought this might be important, sir. Found them in a desk drawer."

"Thanks, Bill." Toomey turned the bag over and checked the mailing label. "Law Enforcement magazines. Know this guy?" He held up the bag where the three could see the address label.

"He's our police chief," Jake said.

"I think maybe we better take a ride to my office and sit down for a little chat."

31

"Well, looks like I got a simple case compared to you." Toomey paced a circle around the room. The Petawka Police Department didn't have a conference room. The building was a converted gas station and could have come right out of a Mayberry television studio. Two desks butted against each other while Toomey's desk was in a small room to the right of the entrance. A uniformed cop was at another desk answering phones. A door in the back led to what they assumed were the jail cells. They couldn't tell since Toomey hadn't given them a tour of the facilities.

Toomey pulled three chairs near the center of the room while he hefted one cheek onto the corner of a desk. There wouldn't have been room for all of them in Toomey's office which looked no larger than a walk-in closet. "Hope you don't mind," he said as he pressed the button on a tape recorder which was the size of a toaster.

Jake spent thirty minutes explaining the case thus far. The chief had interrupted a number of times to ask questions which stretched the agony of the wooden chairs to one hour. Frank had called Captain Robinson from the car on the ride over to update him on what had been found on the property. Robinson was going to make a visit to Murphy's office for a little one-on-one.

"Looks like your chief is in a bit of a pickle."

Sam remained silent. She was still trying to wrap her head around all the lies Murphy had been spewing. Did he ask for her help only to discredit her when all the truths started piling up? That sounded like Murphy. She wanted to be seething with rage but something wasn't adding up, she just wasn't sure what.

"Miss Casey?"

"What?" Sam had been unaware Toomey had spoken to her.

"Listening to your relatives again?"

Now would have been a good time to carry her gun. "Yes, and you wouldn't believe what they think of you."

This brought a chuckle from the deputy chief. "I asked if you had a more logical way for me to explain how you happened upon the deceased."

"No," Sam smiled sweetly. "There isn't a logical way to sugar coat it. The press doesn't need to know the details. Once it is mentioned that he was from the Barlucci family they will have enough meat to chew on for a while."

"If you say so." Toomey pressed the off button on the recorder. "I would appreciate it if you could stick around until my clerk types up your testimonies, then you can sign them and be on your way."

* * *

It was dark by the time they headed home. Sam tried sleeping most of the way but phone calls between Frank and the captain kept interrupting her attempts. The lull of the car's movement wasn't enough to help her drift to sleep. It always did its magic on Dillon. But Barlucci, the magazines found in the cabin, and Murphy's name as the current owner conflicted with her belief that someone had orchestrated an elaborate setup.

They were just minutes from home after dropping Frank off at his house when Jake saw the headlights growing in the rear view mirror. "There's a squad car behind us."

"I'm sure it wasn't your lead foot. Far be it for you to go over the speed limit." Sam turned around to see the squad car race up the lit brick drive. The wrought iron gate closed behind them.

Jake pressed another remote and the garage doors opened. They pulled into one of the empty spaces as the squad car made the turnaround and stopped at the front door. Motion detector lights blazed across the property and as they exited the garage a figure stepped out of the passenger side of the squad car. To their surprise the squad car took off. The wrought iron gate worked on a sensor for those exiting the property.

At the front door stood Chief Dennis Murphy with a briefcase in hand. But as they approached Sam saw it was a bit larger than a briefcase.

"Oh, sweetheart," Sam said with a sigh. "I told you never to stop by when my husband was home."

Murphy grumbled something unintelligible. Jake said nothing. "I had no place else to go. The press is parked at my home, the mayor suggested strongly that I take a leave, Schuler wants me fired, and the press would find me at any hotel I tried to stay at. Since we have a lot to talk about," he turned slightly and looked up at the house, "damn you have a big place...and you definitely have room, I thought..."

"Have you tried the homeless shelter on State Line?" Sam asked. Murphy wasn't amused.

Jake turned the key in the door, then pushed his way through. "We definitely have a lot to talk about but right now is not a good time. We have been on the road since seven o'clock this morning."

"That's fine with me." Murphy trailed behind them through the sitting room, the dining room, and into the kitchen. "I have spent all afternoon on a conference call with the Board of Police and Fire Commissioners and the mayor. They want me to pull out of the mayoral race. My poll numbers are plummeting. My wife won't answer my calls." Murphy stopped as they reached the kitchen. "Hell, this house is big. I had heard it was huge, but damn."

"Don't make yourself too comfortable." Sam stood in front of the patio doors and pointed toward the yard. "Alex's carriage house is out back. You can stay there. Don't make a mess and clean up after yourself or he'll have my head."

Murphy squinted at the yard lit up with landscaping lights. "I can barely see it. Is it in the same county?" He looked toward the garage. "What's there? Is that an apartment over the garage? I can stay there, right?"

"There isn't a bathroom or shower," Jake said. "Just a couch. It's my planetarium."

"You have a telescope up there? Suuweet."

"Or hell," Sam mumbled. "They are bonding over constellations. Have fun boys. I'm going to bed."

32

Sam hadn't expected to wake to the smell of bacon. For a drowsy second she thought Abby was home but then she heard male voices, more than two, and wondered who else had shown up. She quickly showered, tamed her wet hair with conditioner, jumped into comfy jeans and a pullover and headed downstairs.

"Morning, Sam."

"How's it going, Sam."

Her head swiveled at the amount of testosterone seated around the dining room table. Jake, Murphy, Captain Robinson, Sergeant Dorsey, and Frank were passing plates of food back and forth.

"Who cooked?" Sam pulled out a chair next to Robinson and across from Murphy. Someone had made scrambled eggs, hash browns, bacon, and French toast.

"I took cooking classes years ago with my late wife," Robinson said. "Between the chief and me, we pulled it all together."

Everything looked good and while Jake explained that he had brought everyone up to speed on what transpired yesterday in Wisconsin, Sam loaded her plate, then poured a glass of orange juice. Sergeant Dorsey was presenting the Baby Dicks' report on several issues. They had verified that Dennis Murphy's name was the only one on the mortgage for the cabin. Their research had shown that Genesis Enterprises, whom John Kendall thought he had sold the cabin to, never owned nor bid on the property.

"Who paid the real estate taxes on the place?" Sam attacked a breakfast that looked almost as good as Abby's.

"Good question." Robinson looked at his detectives.

Frank thumbed through his notepad but shrugged. "All the realtor knew was who currently owned the property and whether all taxes were current and they are."

"Do you remember paying annual real estate taxes?" Robinson asked Murphy.

"No, but I don't handle the bill paying in the house. Donna does. I'm not sure I can even get her to take my calls."

"Well, try a text message, or check your bank statement from last month. See if something jumps out at you," Robinson suggested.

"One interesting tidbit they found out," Dorsey continued, "was that Mickey Donovan, one of the men who had robbed the Brinks truck, was released from prison about six years ago."

"Can we back up a minute?" Sam said. She looked across the table at Murphy. "You had denied that Gina tried to distract you so the bank could be robbed. But suppose that was the original plan. You returned early and screwed up their target of millions of dollars in the bank. They had to settle for the Brinks truck. If Donovan and Perez knew the plan was screwed up by you and Gina, isn't it possible Donovan might be behind this?"

"Yeah," Robinson piped up. "Donovan could have been after his share of the money but Tony and Gina spent it so he kills them. And now he's on a mission to pay back everyone who ruined his promising life so he looks you up. What better payback then to let you spend some time in jail, blame the two murders on you?"

"Except," Jake reminded them, "Mickey would have been in prison so he couldn't have killed Gina."

Frank intercepted the platter of French toast as it made its way around the table. "So maybe Tony killed Gina and then after he was released from prison, Mickey killed Tony. He had a lot of time in prison to think of how to frame Murphy."

"But he didn't know Murphy," Sam said. "Do we know if Tony visited Mickey in Prison?"

"If he didn't, I'm sure he found a way to get messages to him." Jake searched for the plate of bacon, finding it hidden under the plate of hash browns. "I do wonder how Mickey would have gained access to the hotel."

Sam studied Murphy as she poured another glass of orange juice. He was being very quiet. "Did you give Gina a key?"

"No," Murphy snapped.

"What about your magazines that were found at the cabin? They were only a couple years old."

"I've had that magazine stolen from my mailbox on more than one occasion, Sam. All I would do is call and complain. So they started sending them to me at my office," Murphy explained. "And it isn't hard to type an address label and slap it on a magazine."

That was logical, Sam thought, or a good cover.

"You still don't trust me, do you?" Murphy's question silenced the room.

"Do you blame me? We don't exactly have a great history. I always thought it was your animosity toward my godfather that spilled over to me but then I found my father's articles where he felt you knew more than you let on and dogged you about it, dropped hints in those articles that you might have taken a part in it. A man who would hold that kind of a grudge against an enemy's daughter..."

"Yes, I'm an ass. The politics of this job has morphed me into someone I'm not too proud of at times. But your father never once corrected his assumptions or apologized for almost ruining my life. I almost didn't make it into the academy. I hired you because I knew if there was any truth to what you do or..." he waved his hand around as a way of describing the indescribable, "...anyway, it would be the time for you to prove your, uh, talents," he added, for want of a better word.

Dorsey motioned for the carafe of coffee. "Guess now would be a good time to ask Sam her, uh, take on all this." He passed the carafe to Robinson.

"I wish it were that easy. I saw lilacs spread around the apartment and pictured Gina at a log cabin. That and the locket with hers and the chief's picture are about all I can contribute right now. What is puzzling, though, is the date of the newspapers left in the apartment. Gina couldn't have died in 1976 because John still owned the hotel and the fourth floor was accessible. The killer wanted us to know about the Brinks truck robbery."

"All to start suspicion pointed in the chief's direction." Robinson pushed his plate away. "What a mess."

Murphy shifted uncomfortably and cleared his throat. "I may have left out a small detail."

Five heads swung up to meet his gaze. Jake reached over and clamped a hand on Sam's forearm, as if expecting her to lunge across the table at Murphy. "Now would be a good time to lay everything out on the table," he told Murphy.

Murphy poured himself another cup of coffee. It seemed as though he were conjuring up the courage to admit a mistake. "When we parted that day Gina asked me to call her later. I was so busy with the reports and answering police questions that I almost forgot. It was getting dark out when I finally headed home to shower and change. I saw Gina climbing into her car in the parking lot of a liquor store. Traffic was too heavy for me to cross lanes and intercept her before she drove off. But I followed her, thinking I'd be able to catch up. When I finally did, she was pulling into a motel parking lot. She used a key and entered one of the rooms which I found strange because she had an apartment, or so I thought.

"I drove around for about a half hour, debating whether I should walk up to the door and knock. Instead, I stopped at a pay phone, looked up the name of the motel, then asked for her room. They didn't have anyone registered there by that name. By this time I was livid with rage. I know that's hard to believe."

Sam was sure her eyeballs were rolling back in her head but she bit her tongue and let him finish.

"My rage got the best of me. I sped over to the motel, kicked in the door. I didn't even bother knocking. Gina was sitting on the bed in her underwear with another man. They were surrounded by money, like they had had a damn pillow fight with bags of money. Well, I knew immediately I had been used and that the money was from the robbery. Gina looked shocked and called out my name. I didn't care to hear anything she had to say. Thoughts of what this would do to my chances of getting into the police academy even took a backseat to my feelings."

"You didn't call the cops?" Jake asked.

"No. I couldn't do that to her. I just stumbled out of the motel and found the closest bar. I never saw or heard from Gina again. I figured they caught two of the guys, at least one of them alive, and that should take any suspicion off of Gina."

"Any normal man would have been angry enough to kill them both." Robinson eyed him across the table. It was a theory Sam was sure everyone was thinking.

"If I were to look at it as a cop, sure. I would have the suspect in the box for hours. But I didn't kill them. I would swear on my parents' graves."

Sergeant Dorsey handed Murphy an eight-by-ten photo. "Is this the man Gina was with?"

There was a hint of residual anger on Murphy's face as he looked at the photo of Tony Barlucci from 1976. "It looks like him but I can't be one hundred percent sure. I only saw him briefly."

"We need to talk to this Tom DeLeo when he gets into town," Jake suggested. "Maybe he can help us piece together Tony and Gina's whereabouts in 1976. I'm sure they didn't stick around town."

"Who's Tom DeLeo?" Murphy asked.

"Once we knew Gina's real name, we were able to locate a relative," Robinson explained. "Her parents are deceased, but Tom DeLeo is an uncle and he will be arriving in town to take the body back to New Jersey."

"If Tony hired Donovan and Perez, why didn't they turn him in when they were caught?" Frank asked.

"Maybe Tony promised Donovan a bigger share if he kept his mouth shut," Sam said.

"Or he put the fear of God in Mickey. There might have been a number of Barlucci family members or henchmen in prison who could get to Mickey should he open his mouth. Maybe when he was released, Tony wouldn't give his share or didn't have it to give."

"Or maybe," Jake added, "Mickey knew where all the money was so if Tony wanted to see his share he had to make sure Mickey remained safe."

33

Rafe raised his microphone to catch Schuler's comments. It was an impromptu press conference being held at Schuler's campaign office. Members of the press who had not arrived early enough were standing outside on the sidewalk.

"I am calling for an emergency Council meeting today to demand the resignation of Chief Dennis Murphy. There is enough evidence now that to have him continue in his current position opens up the entire department to allegations of favorable treatment."

"Do you think he should step down from the mayoral race?"

"Have you spoken to him about this?"

"What does the mayor think? Has any member of the Council discussed it with him?"

The questions were coming fast and furious. Rafe just hoped his tape recorder didn't fizzle because he couldn't write notes fast enough.

"The decision to step down is Chief Murphy's to make but sometimes what a candidate wants and what is right for the city are two different things. We can't have this city's reputation tarnished by scandal. We have had enough of that over the years. The people of this fine town need to let their elected officials know how they feel."

Rafe suspected there was a separate dictionary for politicians. The words they used, the cadence of their speeches, the condescending tone that could make someone puke. Didn't they know it all sounded pre-packaged and as trustworthy as a gang banger in a gun shop?

Rafe shouted out, "Aren't people innocent until proven guilty?"

Schuler glared at him from the podium. Microphones were thrust closer to the candidate. "This is not a question of guilt or innocence. That's up to a court of law. This is about honesty. Chief Murphy swore to uphold the law yet when it came to being honest about his knowledge regarding a robbery, he chose to remain silent. Now a body is found buried on property he owns. If we can't expect honesty from our top law enforcement officer, where is this city headed, ladies and gentlemen? And now we want to elect him to head this city?"

"Perhaps efforts should be made to find the one man who might know more about what happened in 1976." Rafe checked his notes. "This Mickey Donovan. What are the police doing to find out his whereabouts?"

"That's a question you'll have to ask the deputy chief who is in charge in the chief's absence."

Rafe chuckled. "You are a member of the Council and you don't even know there isn't a deputy chief? That spot was never filled because the Council eliminated that position in the last budget cuts."

This got everyone laughing. Rafe may not have been in the city long but he had definitely done his homework.

Schuler's lips strained to smile but his eyes were seething. "That's something I'm sure a hot shot reporter like you with lots of time on his hands would be able to find out...the whereabouts of Mickey Donovan."

Touché.

* * *

The man chewed the bacon slowly while watching the press conference on the television set. He had slipped out the back door of the shelter when he saw the two cops who were investigating the old biddy's death. Marie had asked anyone who had anything to tell the police to stick around. That was his cue to leave and drive over to a diner for breakfast. He had mumbled the expected condolences so he didn't draw attention to himself.

To his recollection, he hadn't said more than two words to the old biddy while they were at the shelter. It was when she had followed him to the garage that he almost lunged at her on the street. It had been hard to hold back, to not drive off and find another place to live. Not that he needed to stay at the shelter. There was enough money to get by but owning a home or renting required identification and that was something he didn't want to submit.

Living in the homeless shelter let him come and go as he pleased, no one bothered him, no one cared to look him in the eye. Even on the streets, passersby pretended he wasn't there. He was treated the same way he treated the drunks and drug addicts wandering the alleys and streets. The only difference was he didn't belong here, which pissed him off even more. He shouldn't have to stand in a damn soup line with the rest of the dredges of society. He had learned a lot in prison. The main thing was that payback was a bitch.

* * *

"Hey, Cleo. You don't have any more presents to bring mommy, I take it?" Jackie bent over the cat which sported a new diamond studded collar. "You are such a good little girl and look at me, talking baby talk to a cat."

"I think she got them all," Armando said. "The mice are gone, the storage room is completed. All that's left is for me to buy you dinner as a thanks for giving me a job."

Jackie straightened and graced Armando with one of her patented smiles. "Dinner? Hmmmm. How tempting. Tell you what, though. I have pretty expensive taste in restaurants so I would never dream of depleting your well-earned finances. How about I make you dinner? I have the wine and the fixings. All I need is for you to bring that Adonis body of yours."

"Hey." Armando flashed one of his own wide grins. "You're the boss lady."

* * *

Sam was too antsy to sit and wait for the autopsy report on Tony

Barlucci. Even Jake and their company had returned to the office, except for Murphy who was still using her property as a hideout. She would have to remember to check to see if the chief planted any listening devices in her house. It wouldn't surprise her.

Sam parked her Jeep behind the Embers and entered the hotel with the use of her lock pick. The door closed behind leaving her in complete darkness. She made her way down the narrow hallway to the lobby where windows provided sufficient light. Now she just had to find the door to the basement. John Kendall had given a vague idea where the storage room was which lead to the escape exit to the gardens. Finding it in the dark was going to be a challenge.

Sam was tempted to make her way back to the fourth floor but wanted to check out the basement first. She clicked on her flashlight and headed down the stairs in search of the fuse box.

The hotel had a creepy silence to it, not like the last time she was here when voices from Jake and Frank filled the air. Now every creak and structural groan was magnified. There was a musty smell which wasn't unusual in places that had been closed up this long. The halogen beam sprayed light on the marble stairs and walls as she made her way down to the basement. It smelled even more damp and musty on this floor. Shadows curled around doorways and corners as she moved the beam from side to side. She finally located the fuse box. Lights flickered weakly, not sure if they had the energy to stay lit.

The concrete floors were worn down by years of wear. Sections had been painted gray at some point, flakes accumulating in corners. Footsteps sounded overhead, or was it her imagination? Sam stopped to listen for several seconds. She thought she heard the creaking of a door but after several minutes of silence she chalked it up to her imagination.

At the end of a corridor Sam saw the sign for the laundry room in front of a double swinging door. John Kendall had told her to walk through the laundry to the store room. The room beyond the door's windows was dark. Great. Now she had to find another set of light switches. Sam clicked on her flashlight then slowly pushed the doors open. The large room was vacant except for concrete platforms which might have housed the washers and dryers. She turned toward the wall to find a light switch but instead found a face. Sam screamed and pulled the Taurus from its holster, her thumb flicking off the safety. But as she gathered her composure she could see it was a mannequin, probably used when alterations were performed on uniforms.

She holstered her gun and sank against a wall, waiting for her heartbeat to return to normal. On her left was a row of switches. She hit them all and watched as fluorescent tube lighting flickered and danced along the ceiling. She brushed imaginary flecks from her pullover as though her fear could be that easily removed. Moving through the room she saw long tables against one wall, imagining they were used for folding. Steel poles ran from one end of the room to the opposite side, used to possibly hang uniforms after steaming them.

She reached a corridor at the end of the room. To her left was a stairway which, according to John, led to the second floor. To her right was a large storage room, it's shelves and racks standing empty. Beyond the room and down a short corridor was a set of double doors. They were heavy and made of steel. Sam turned the door knob and had to pull hard to get the door open. Its hinges were old and rusted, scattering flakes on the concrete floor. Just as John had mentioned, there weren't handles or doorknobs on the outside. A bell on the side was near a faded sign. Sam could only make out several letters and was sure it said *Deliveries*.

She propped the door open with a brick and walked outside and down a cracked concrete drive. The gardens were a jungle of overgrown weeds and grass. Yellow stalks had given up their attempt to hold dead blossoms erect and lay passively on the ground. Stone walkways meandered around stagnant ponds and silent water fountains. Hostas that should have been separated annually blocked walkways with their large leaves. It was a huge garden and she could imagine a carpet of lush grass without a hint of a dandelion back in the hotel's early years. She turned and studied the opening. Vines crawled along the walls, its roots ripped from their anchor when she opened the door. Sam walked back the way she came, through the laundry room and back to the lobby. Her eyes automatically lifted to the mezzanine area and without a second thought, found herself climbing the stairs.

The broken drywall had been removed as evidence, the stairs vacuumed by the crime scene investigators. But it wasn't specks of dust or overlooked evidence Sam was seeking. It was Gina. Her body was still in the morgue awaiting the arrival of any relatives to claim her and return her to New Jersey.

The wooden stairs did little to muffle her footsteps but it was the eerie silence of the hotel that let her hear all the minute creaks and groans, and especially the rattling of drawers and shoes on hardwood floors coming from the fourth floor.

Sam kept her back to the wall and stepped only on the sides of the stairs as she made her way up to the apartment. Who could be in the hotel? The killer? Slowly she pulled the Taurus from its holster. How would someone gain entry? Did the back door not close behind her? She hadn't stopped to check, just assumed it locked automatically. Or did someone have a key?

The door to the apartment was ajar. Sam reached the top stair, kept her gun hand low against her thigh, then stole a glance into the room. She didn't see anyone. If her heartbeat would quit pounding in her ears she would be able to listen for movement. But there wasn't any. Had the intruder moved to the back bedroom? Cautiously, Sam pushed the door open and as she stepped into the room she saw movement from behind the door, someone with a gun pointed at her.

She swung the gun in his direction when the man yelled, "Sam, it's me. Don't shoot."

"Jesus, Rafe. You scared the hell out of me. What are you doing here and what are you doing with a gun?"

Rafe dropped his hands on his knees and gulped volumes of air. "Let me catch my breath. Holy crap."

Sam holstered her gun and did a quick check of the room. Rafe was alone. The place wasn't trashed so she wasn't sure what he was looking for. "Well?" she prompted.

"I have a license." His gun disappeared under his jacket. "I was across the street interviewing some of the residents. I wanted to see if they remember anyone coming and going from the hotel on a regular basis. Then I saw you drive by. Where have you been? What else is there to see in this mausoleum?"

"The basement. My curiosity got the best of me so I went exploring." Sam didn't care to tell him about the back door. Instead she led him out of the apartment and back to the lobby. They stood in front of the large window by the entrance. Across the street and past the front lot they could see the Shoreline Shelter two blocks away. "Make any headway at the shelter?"

"Too many people transitioning in and out. Many of the people don't use their real names or can't remember them. Even the director has only been in charge for a year. "

Rafe stepped closer. There was something about the crisp cut of his jaw line that reminded her of someone, maybe Jake. His eyes were penetrating, perhaps a talent only reporters and cops have.

He stared at her for several seconds. "You saw something up there, didn't you?"

"I saw a lot of things since the body was found. Gina tossed a path of lilacs in the hallway which told me either she was killed in the spring or there's another reason she wants me to focus on the spring. Lilacs bloom in May. I saw a log cabin which led us to Murphy's cabin in Wisconsin. I saw Gina with piles of money around her."

For a brief moment, anger flashed in Rafe's eyes, then just as quickly disappeared. "She didn't look like someone who would be involved in a robbery. The woman in the photo looked so innocent." He shook it off with a laugh. "What about me? Did you get any vibes from me?"

Sam would have thought Rafe was only curious but there was a line of worry etching across his forehead. "Doesn't work that way. Mom says someone has to be dead or just evil for me to detect anything. Mom, on the other hand, she's..." It had always been a problem describing Abby.

Few people knew of Abby's powers and she preferred it that way. "Let's just say it doesn't matter if you are warm or cold to the touch."

"Guess I'm glad she's out of town."

Across the street the vet was leaning against a light post, smoking a cigarette, his eyes directed at the hotel. "Did you meet him?"

Rafe studied the vet in Sam's crosshairs. "No. Do you know him?"

"Not sure. I could swear he was the same guy sitting next to me at Izzy's."

"Well, let's go check him out."

They hustled to the back door, making sure the door locked behind them. But by the time they reached the front of the hotel, the vet had disappeared.

"Probably wasn't the same guy. When I saw him he had on a jean jacket with MIA-POW patches on it."

They made their way to their vehicles. "What about Lucas Rucker? Have you been able to give him some media coverage?"

"My editor liked the interview I did. I have pictures of the proposed youth center and how it impacts the businesses and families affected by eminent domain. I also have a challenge to the city fathers to create a campus that would be a boilerplate for other cities to follow."

"How so?"

"Take the youth center. It's supposed to have a gym, sports field, large screen TVs to watch movie events, serve meals, have things for the kids to do rather than hang out on the streets. But why not add vocational courses? Make it the Youth and Vocational Campus with a building for the arts, one for recreation, and one for vocational courses. Those businesses that don't want to leave because, let's face it, the cost to rent commercial property in another part of the city is horrendous, far outside their finances. Let's house those businesses in the vocational building and teach the kids about motorcycle maintenance, car maintenance, and cabinet making. Woodworking can be part of the curriculum. And what boy doesn't want to learn about refurbishing a classic car?"

"That's ingenious. But what do you do about their houses? They currently live above their businesses."

"There's an empty warehouse just a block from here. It isn't that old and the owner donated it to the city. Why not turn it into loft apartments or condos? If they leave it reserved for staff, such as teachers, the city can use federal funds to do the refurbishing and modifications. There are three floors so they can fit probably twelve units in the building. The city can charge dirt cheap rent because part of it will be subsidized by the government. Lucas and the other business owners can teach one or two classes a week and work their businesses out of the vocational building."

"You should present that to the mayor so he can introduce the changes before he leaves office."

"Right. And be the heartless guy who bothers a sick man."

"He's still a politician. Even on his death bed Mayor Jenkins wouldn't turn down a suggestion for the Jenkins Youth and Vocational Campus."

Rafe slowly smiled. "You are almost as devilish as me. Does your husband know we are so well suited for each other?"

Sam stopped abruptly, turned and looked back at the nearby buildings.

"What is it?"

Her eyes swept the windows looking for figures staring from behind partially closed curtains, faces obscured by baseball caps. "I don't know. It feels like someone is watching us."

34

"Have a seat." Captain Robinson motioned to the conference table as he escorted the woman into the room. Sonya Lucci could have been a face off of a box of pasta. She was portly, wrapped in what looked like a house dress, and wore her steel wool hair pulled back in a bun. Either she had very good genes or she used her money for face lifts and possibly a villa in Sicily rather than Fifth Avenue clothing and jewelry shops. There was an aloofness about her that made it hard for Jake to get a read on her. "You know Tom DeLeo, I take it." Seated at the table was a wisp of a man in a clerical collar. His eyes appeared too close together and he blinked nervously behind wire-rimmed glasses.

"Tom!"

"Aunt Sonya. Haven't seen you in a long time. How did you hear about Gina?"

"In the news." Sonya took a seat next to Tom.

"Miss Lucci, Mister DeLeo, you have my department's sincere sympathies on the loss of your loved one." Captain Robinson introduced his detectives to Gina's relatives. "For the record, could you please state your relationship to the deceased."

"Gina was my niece," Sonya replied. "Her father, Gus, was my brother."

"Is Lucci your married name?" Frank asked.

"No, I shortened it so no one would know I was related to the Barlucci family."

That tossed a red flag in Jake's mind. "And why was that?"

"Prostitution, gambling, drugs, you name it. I didn't approve of what my brother did. I never talked to the authorities, though. Wouldn't squeal on him, if you know what I mean. After all, we were still blood."

Robinson leveled a gaze at Tom. "Mister Deleo?"

"It's Reverend Deleo, but you can call me Reverend Tom."

"Reverend?" Sonya snorted. "Vera told me you got your license on the Internet. May as well have gotten it in a Cracker Jack box."

"I'm ordained by the Lord's Secular Center."

"More like the Center for the Gullible," Sonya said under her breath.

Robinson steered the conversation back to Tom. "How close were you to the deceased?"

"I am Gus Barlucci's nephew. His wife, Vera, is my mom's sister. We are, or used to be, a very big family. Tony was a few years ahead of me in school. Gina was a sweet girl. I have known her since high school."

"He also was in love with her." Sonya clasped her hands on the table. Jake noticed the large emerald rings on her fingers. "They played doctor when they were eleven."

Tom sighed. "We were typical inquisitive kids." He turned his attention to the detectives. "Gina and I hung out in high school. She was very shy. Her parents died in a car accident when she was eight. Aunt Vera always wanted a daughter but after Tony was born she couldn't have any more children. She read about Gina in the papers and wanted to adopt her."

"That kid started out as trouble."

"He wasn't a very good influence on Gina," Tom conceded.

"They didn't get along?" Although Jake knew the answer, he wanted to see what their guests had to say.

"I wouldn't say that," Tom replied.

"Got along too well, if you ask me." Sonya tapped her nails on the table. They were long and thick, like the sculptured nails the clerical staff sported. All Jake knew was that they cost a lot and looked as thick as sheet metal. Sonya's were painted a bright red. She may dress like a housewife but the jewelry, hair, and nails told him different.

Frank looked up from his pad of paper. "How long were Gina and Tony closer than brother and sister?"

"They weren't related," Tom argued.

Sonya stared at him with a look of annoyance. She turned back to the detectives as though they had more common sense. "He was sniffing around her the minute she turned fifteen. I told Gus and Vera it didn't look right. But they said I was reading into it, I had a dirty mind, that they were close the way a brother and sister should be."

"What about you, Reverend?" Robinson asked.

Tom shrugged. "I asked Gina how she felt about Tony. She said she loved him like a brother. She relied on him for everything. Help with homework, take care of guys who bothered her at school and in the neighborhood."

"Which he gladly did because he was jealous as hell if anyone looked sideways at Gina," Sonya argued.

Jake definitely wanted to get these two in separate rooms. "How did you get along with each of them, Sonya?"

She sucked in a quiet breath and dammit if it didn't look as though Sonya was about to start sobbing. "She felt sorry for me. I was the old maid of the family, the childless aunt and I thought of her as the daughter I never had. I couldn't stand to see the way Tony treated her." Sonya fumbled in her purse and pulled out a hankie. "Tony saw me as a wedge between him and Gina and I admit it. I was."

"And how did Tony treat her?" Jake asked.

"Like dirt," she spit out. "Gina would never admit it but I just know he beat her. She'd hide bruises by wearing long sleeves or high collars."

"Didn't her father see those injuries?" Robinson asked.

"He was too busy with the business. And Vera thought the sun rose and set on her son's ass. She said I was just jealous because I didn't have kids of my own."

"Was that true?" Jake wondered why Jerry mentioned that the reverend would be the one with all the family secrets when it was Sonya who couldn't stop trashing the family name.

"I loved that girl. She wasn't blood but I swear she looked just like me when I was her age. We could have been mother and daughter and I hated the fact that anyone would harm one hair on that girl's head."

"Why didn't she tell her parents if Tony was roughing her up?" Frank asked.

"Gina protected Tony."

"She loved him," Tom offered.

"She feared him," Sonya countered. "It made me crazy that my brother didn't believe it."

"Maybe it's because your marriage ended after two years because your husband beat you. Admit it, you hate men," Tom challenged. Sonya ignored him.

"I take it things were strained between you and your brother," Robinson said.

"Quite. I needed to put distance between me and Gus. So I changed my name and left town. Never told anyone where I was going."

"Where did you go?" Robinson asked.

"Phoenix."

"Did Aunt Vera know where you went?" Tom asked. "No one ever talked about you."

"We didn't part on good terms, as I'm sure your mother told you."

Frank asked, "When was this?"

For being so talkative, the detectives were surprised Sonya had suddenly grew silent. She reached across the table and grabbed the pitcher of water, taking her time to fill her glass. Jake started to wonder if she either had to jog her memory or make up a good lie.

"It was after Gina's son died."

35

The men were stunned. Reverend Tom studied his hands splayed on the table. Surprise was not evident on his face. Robinson cleared his throat and said, "Son?"

"Let me back up a bit." Sonya took a long swallow of water before continuing. "Gina and Tony came back to New Jersey in 1976." The mention of that date had the detectives exchanging glances. "I remember because it was the year the anniversary celebration took place. They had been gone for three years with no explanation where they had been, not even a postcard, just a phone call from Gina to Gus and Vera when the mood hit her. But Tony was bragging about how he had come into a bunch of money." This again had the detectives exchanging glances. "She wasn't home no longer than a month when she announces she's pregnant and Tony was the father."

"You didn't help things any with your 'I told you so's,'" Reverend Tom interjected. "The only reason you kept your mouth shut after they returned is because Gus threatened to cut all ties with you."

"That's true," Sonya conceded. "Gus wouldn't let me near Gina or the baby if I kept bad-mouthing his precious son. So yes, I kept my mouth shut even after the shotgun wedding and Gina's numerous black eyes which she claimed she walked into a door, the baby accidentally punched her, or her numerous excuses for the bruising. But it was when I started seeing bruises on that beautiful little boy that I started screaming again." Sonya buried her mouth in the hankie.

Robinson stood and stretched. "I think we all need a ten minute break about now." He looked over at Jake whose eyes had hardened at the mention of abusing a child. "Jake, get a cup of coffee or a cold drink."

"I think I need something stiffer," Jake replied. He made a trip to the bathroom, then slipped into his office to make a call. "Hi, hon. Do me a

favor? Call your buddy out in Phoenix and have him check out a name...
Sonya Lucci. I want to know everything, when she moved there, where
she lived, what she did for a living, anything he can dig up." He didn't
explain anything further to Sam but promised to fill her in when he was
through with the interview.

He walked over to the break room to grab a Pepsi. Sergeant Dorsey
waved him over as he passed his desk and handed him a sheet of paper.

"Thought you'd like the rap sheet on the good reverend."

"Thanks." He glanced over the list of misdemeanors, teenage pranks,
and drug possession charges which were dropped, probably after an
influential uncle donated money to some judge's campaign coffers.

They reconvened around the conference table. Jake set the report on
the table and sat down. "Where were you during all this time, Reverend
Tom? You didn't see what Sonya saw? You didn't try to intervene?"

"I was busy. Besides, Tony and I weren't that close any more, not
after Gina left."

"He wasn't a good influence on your teen years either, was he?" Jake
handed the rap sheet to Robinson but not before Tom and Sonya caught
the name at the top of the sheet.

Robinson picked it up and studied it. "Well, that must have pissed
you off."

Sonya showed a touch of sympathy as she patted Tom's hand. "Tony
was a bad influence on a lot of the neighborhood boys. Tom was a good,
clean, decent kid. Tony could turn even the strongest of them. Look what
he did to Gina."

"I don't think he had to do much to Gina," Tom said. "She liked bad
boys, much like you, Aunt Sonya. You met your husband at a motorcycle
rally in South Dakota from what I heard."

Sonya nodded with a smile. "That's true. That's why I saw a lot of
myself in Gina and I knew exactly where it was heading."

"What was the son's name?" Frank asked.

"Anthony. Tony wanted everyone to call him Tony Junior but I
refused to. I always called him Anthony. Sweetest boy, nothing like his

father, thank God."

"How old was Anthony when he died?" Frank asked.

Sonya looked up, a puzzled look on her face. "Oh. Well, he got sick when he was seven, some type of cancer. The doctors tried everything for almost two years. The only thing left was a bone marrow transplant."

"That was when all hell broke loose." Tom leaned back and folded his arms. A body language expert would say he was protecting himself for what might come next.

"What do you mean?" Robinson asked.

"Neither Gina nor Tony were a match," Sonya said quietly. "That is when Gina announced that Tony wasn't the father."

36

"There's no way of knowing if Murphy was the father, right?" Sam asked. Robinson and Jake exchanged a silent communication. "Hey, don't hold out on me now. For all his faults, Murphy is still my client." They sat in the dining room watching as Murphy hoofed his way down the asphalt path from the carriage house. After the first night in the observatory without a refrigerator to raid and unable to convince Sam to let him sleep in "the mansion," he had decided to try the carriage house.

Jake set three beers on the table. Robinson grabbed one and twisted the cap off. Jake did the same.

Murphy entered the dining room and grabbed a beer. "I see I'm just in time." They settled around the table, Sam with her glass of tea and a puzzled look. Murphy took a long swallow while his eyes searched the faces of his captain and lead detective, then swung to Sam. "What?"

Sam shrugged and gave a nod across the table to her husband. "Well?"

Robinson gave Murphy a brief rundown on their conversation with Gina's cousin and aunt. Murphy listened with vague interest as though they were giving a weather forecast, whether because it was over thirty years ago or he was tiring of the entire predicament. Then Robinson mentioned that Gina and Gus had a baby.

"So? I told you they looked pretty intimate in that motel room."

"You said you never saw her again after seeing her in the motel room in 1976," Robinson said.

"That's right."

"According to her aunt, Gina's son had cancer and needed a bone marrow transplant. Neither Gina nor Gus were a match."

Murphy crossed his arms and waited. Patience was never his strong suit. The subject was beginning to bore him, until Robinson came to the punch line.

"According to the aunt, Gina came back to Chasen Heights to see if the father of her baby would agree to be tested." Robinson waited.

It was so quiet Sam thought she could hear the plants in the Florida room growing. Murphy's skin had turned a tinge of gray. She remembered her godfather, the former chief, telling her how much Murphy wanted to have a son. It didn't make him love his daughter any less but a "dad always wants a son," Chief Connelly had said.

"She didn't call to tell you she was coming?" Robinson prodded. "This would have been 1985, '86."

"A son?" Murphy whispered. His hand shook as he placed the beer bottle on the table.

"Chief," Robinson tried again to get an answer. "Did she call you to tell you she was coming back?"

"No. As I said before, 1976 was the last time I saw Alicia, I mean Gina." He raised pleading eyes toward Sam. "Can I get something a little stronger?"

Jake rose from the table, grabbing the empty bottles. "I think we can all use something a little stronger."

Ten minutes later with various mixed drinks in hand, they sat in silence waiting for Murphy to speak. Color had returned to Murphy's face and his voice and demeanor were all business. He was analyzing the situation with a cop's eye. "So Tony might have convinced Gina that he should accompany her, maybe offering to call me and have us meet at the hotel. My guess is the hotel was between owners and he found a way into the hotel. I don't know. Maybe Gina got my keys from me when we dated and made a copy of the key to the back door. If Tony was as jealous as the aunt says he was, he was probably irate when he found out the baby wasn't his. But I've seen guys like that. We all have. Friends claim the boyfriend/husband/significant other is such a nice guy and they don't believe he could be an animal. It takes everyone by surprise."

"We still have the problem of Tony's murder," Sam reminded him. "Deputy Chief Loomis hasn't been in touch with you, Chief?"

But Murphy wasn't listening. He was still trying to digest the news.

* * *

Rafe slammed out of his car and looked around the dimly lit street. He had received a phone call earlier from someone claiming to have information on the Brinks truck robbery which took place in 1976. Rafe had asked if he was Mickey. He had rambled a string of questions but the caller ignored them. All he said was to meet him. Rafe had suggested the mall parking lot where there were lots of cameras. But the caller shot that down. No surprise. Instead, he wanted to meet in a forest preserve parking lot. Not a good idea.

He exited the hotel parking lot having finished a late dinner. How stupid of him to agree to meet him at night, and without a witness. At least he had a gun should he need it. His car was parked at the fringe of the lot. As he crossed the lot he saw a shadow move from behind a tree, or were his eyes playing tricks? Maybe he shouldn't show up. Let the guy call him back, then he would demand that he meet in daylight, in a public place, like the park.

The shadow moved again, or at least he thought it did. He checked the surrounding lot. Other than a couple on the far side, he didn't see anyone else, but negative vibes were nagging at him. Rafe opened the car door and took a second to check the parking lot one more time. That was when he heard a blast and felt a pain slice through his head. He fell against the opened car door and slid to the ground.

37

Murphy entered his house through the back door. The rooms were familiar to him so there wasn't a need to turn on the lights. The house smelled of lilacs from the candles Donna would use. Funny, he had been the one to suggest what scent she should buy. It had never dawned on him before why that particular scent appealed to him the most.

He crossed the kitchen and entered the living room with its high ceiling and stone fireplace. The house was almost three thousand square feet. All the interior decorating had been left up to Donna and they had hired a landscaper to design the outside. Neat and orderly...too bad he couldn't say the same about his life.

Murphy tossed his jacket on the couch then slid down and sat on the floor. He was dressed in a jogging suit and gym shoes and doubted anyone in the precinct had ever seen him dressed so casual. He brought his knees up and rested his chin on his knees. He needed to think and he did his best thinking in the dark. Gina had been pregnant. The news just about rocked him on his ass. It wiped out all of the pain he felt after seeing her in that motel room with Tony. But why did she stay with Tony? Why hadn't she returned to Chasen Heights? Now he was thinking like a jilted lover. She couldn't return here because she would have been arrested. It was best that she stay away.

And what about Donna? When he put it under a microscope, he had to admit what attracted him to Donna was that she reminded him of Gina. She also had blonde hair and blue eyes and was the first woman he met since Gina who brought any feelings of love out of him. He couldn't even be honest with Donna now.

It also fueled an anger in him that was hard to tamp down, and he had no place to direct that anger. Tony was dead. Gina was dead. Their son was dead. His neat and orderly life was falling apart.

* * *

Sam didn't know why she felt compelled to stop by the hospital. Rafe was just another nosy reporter. She should unplug the police scanner from her Jeep and avoid hearing up-to-the-minute reports. The emergency room was relatively quiet but it wasn't a comfortable place for her anyway. She had been a guest of this wing of the hospital on several occasions and it brought back unpleasant memories. Later, probably closer to midnight, there would be more action when accident and domestic violence victims were hauled in by EMTs.

The fish in the tank across from her appeared to hover and stare from behind the glass. It was a salt water tank with some of the most beautiful fish she had ever seen. It served its purpose as a distraction from what was happening down the hall. At the moment it did little to distract Sam from the question of who would want to harm Rafe? Maybe the better question was how many people had Rafe pissed off? Jeff Schuler or his campaign manager who found Rafe to be a royal pain in the ass? Or what about Lucas Rucker? He appeared to have a short fuse and maybe Rafe wasn't working hard enough to stop the demolition of Rucker's house. And then there was Chief Murphy. Sam doubted it was a matter of Rafe being in the wrong place at the wrong time.

The double doors down the hall opened and two EMTs walked out. Sam recognized them but didn't remember their names. She hurried toward them and was surprised they knew her.

"Hey, detective. What brings you here?"

The names on their badges were T. McNeal and R. McNeal. Now she recalled they were brothers. "Did you bring in Rafe Bennett?" Sam asked. Tom and Rick, she suddenly remembered. They were identical twins who were quite easy on the eyes. Matter of fact, each year they graced the firemen's calendar which was sold as a fundraiser for the local food pantry. Definitely not hard on the eyes at all.

"The shooting at the hotel? Yeah," Tom replied.

"Shot in the head," Rick added. "Two of the nightshift detectives grabbed the case. I heard them say it wasn't a robbery because he still had his wallet, money, credit cards. Even his rental car wasn't taken."

"The doctor say anything?"

"Nothing other than she's surprised the guy's still breathing," Rick said.

Sam thanked them and waited for the doctor, although she knew she would only disclose information to a relative. But there might be someone who would know. She pulled out her cell phone and called the editor at the *Post Tribune*. Tristan Price was a relic who had been at the newspaper since the Stone Age. She gave the receptionist her name and asked to speak to T.P. She could almost feel the wires melting from his shrieks.

"Who the hell you calling TP, you little squirt?"

Tristan's colorful vocabulary had always made her father grimace since it was often used within earshot of his young daughter. Sam had heard someone in the office call Tristan T.P. behind his back and she had picked up on it, not realizing it was short for toilet paper.

"Hey, if the T.P. fits as they say." Sam smiled at the curmudgeon, picturing him in his starched white shirt and bright red suspenders, feet up on the desk and, since it was after eight o'clock at night, a glass of scotch on the desk.

"Seems as you've grown taller your mouth has grown bigger."

"Well, I am my father's daughter."

"So you are. And what are you crawling on your hands and knees begging for this time?"

"I never beg. Maybe bribe, but never beg."

"Bribe my ass. More like blackmail."

Sam couldn't help but laugh. He knew her too well. "One of your reporters was shot tonight. Thought you might have the name of a next of kin."

"He's dead?"

"No, but since I'm not a relative I doubt I'll be able to get info out of the doctor."

"What's the name?"

"Rafe Bennett."

"Who?"

"Rafe Bennett. He created some political blog site and has been freelancing for the *Post Tribune* covering the upcoming election and now the latest scandal with our police chief." She heard him talking to someone in the background, asking for Rafe's file.

"Okay, let's see."

"You're really on top of things, T.P. Don't even know who's working for you."

"Keep giving me lip and I'll hang up on you."

Sam heard the rattling of ice in a glass, then papers rustling.

"Pretty impressive background. He worked for the *Tampa Daily Times*. The AP picked up quite a few of his stories. I never know what Human Resources is doing. As long as they aren't hiring full-time people they can do what they want."

"Any relatives listed on his resume?"

"He wrote *deceased* by the parents' names."

"Did he reference anyone at the *Tampa Daily Times*? They might have the name of a relative other than parents. If you could call and get a name I'd be forever in your debt."

"No references. HR isn't picky when it comes to freelancers we pay by the word. And you think I have time to make calls for you? You're crazy. Here." Sam heard him thumbing through something that squeaked, possibly a rolodex. "Here's the number for Lars Senik, you lazy bum."

"Such sweet talk." Sam wrote down the number for the editor at the Tampa paper. "I just might get you something special for Christmas."

"Two of what you got me last year would be nice. Now get off my phone." With that T.P. hung up.

Sam smiled as she dialed the Tampa phone number. Last Christmas she had bought T.P. a bottle of scotch. This year he'll receive two bottles. His wife will kill her.

The editor at the *Tampa Daily Times* wasn't as pleasant as T.P. It was after nine o'clock in Florida and he took little time complaining about missing a deadline. "Rafe Bennett? He's no reporter, lady. Look, I have a deadline. You want to know about Rafe Bennett, I suggest you search our archives."

Sam found a computer on a desk in the corner of the waiting room. She typed in the URL for the paper. Why would Rafe lie about working for the *Tampa Daily Times*? Sam typed in Rafe's name in the search line. There were a laundry list of articles. Rafe wasn't a reporter at all. He was a former Tampa police detective who created a web site called www.findme.org. Rafe Bennett was pretty successful at finding missing people. One was a young woman who had been missing for twenty years, kidnapped at the age of five from a shopping mall in Orlando. A computer-generated picture had advanced the girl's features but it had garnered little response until Rafe changed the photo to give the girl several possible identifying features. He had a photo of a shy girl in mousy brown hair, one with blonde hair and excessive makeup. But it was the photo of the goth girl with black hair, a nose ring and several eyebrow rings that struck pay dirt. Rafe had a hunch the girl might have run away from her captor and, having little recollection of her real life, changed her entire identity to hide in the background of society.

There were other successful cases: a missing wife who left her children and her purse at home; the teenage girl who made a quick trip to the store for pop and never made it home; the single woman who was last seen leaving the health club. Few were found alive, but at least the families had long sought after answers. Sam surfed Rafe's web site which included photos of thousands of missing persons and a chat room where law enforcement and citizens all over the country could post information they felt might be of help in finding out what happened to the missing.

Sam called the *Tampa Daily Times* editor again. "Mister Senik, I know you have a deadline but I have Rafe Bennett in critical condition. I need to know why he quit the police department three years ago."

Senik sighed heavily. Sam heard a door slam in the background. "It was difficult to give both jobs his full attention and he felt he could do more good with his second job."

"How does he support himself?" Unless Rafe inherited a bundle of dough, Sam couldn't see Rafe lasting too long without a job.

"Both of his parents died when he was young so I have a feeling some well invested life insurance money might be keeping him afloat. Is Rafe causing some trouble by you?"

"He's been causing some people a huge headache which got him shot. We're just trying to find out if he has any relatives who should be notified."

"Sorry to hear that. Hope he makes a full recovery. A lot of people depend on him."

"Your paper covered a lot of his success stories. Did he tell you about his trip to Chasen Heights?"

"He told me about ten days ago that he was working a lead on a big case but he didn't give me any details."

Ten days? Something didn't sound right. "Are you sure of the date, Mr. Sinek? We didn't I.D. the deceased until a couple days ago."

"Rafe receives the police reports from all over the U.S. Wherever a body is found in an area where his stats list missing persons, he's on a plane before you can say *Beam Me Up, Scotty.*"

38

Jake handed Sam a cup of hot tea from the cafeteria. "Robinson is talking with the doctor now."

"Who's handling the investigation?"

"Detectives Chang and Rutherford. They found a Browning .22 calibre in a trash can near the hotel. Robinson sent them to Ballistics with the gun while he handled the hospital. You say he doesn't have any relatives?"

"No, but I found out something interesting." She sipped her tea as she watched Robinson lumber down the hallway, trailed by an Asian woman in scrubs. He introduced them to Doctor Lee.

"Your friend was very lucky," Doctor Lee reported. "He must have leaned out of the way at the right time. The bullet didn't penetrate the skull. It entered at the temporal bone by the right eye and traveled under the scalp exiting on the left. Your bullet is still out there somewhere but it's not in the victim."

Sam asked, "Can he talk?"

"He's still unconscious. I'll keep him in ICU overnight, monitor his vitals, then possibly move him to a room in the morning." She held up a clear plastic bag with a gun and holster. "We found this on the patient."

Robinson took the bag, thanked her, then motioned for Jake and Sam to follow him to the other side of the room away from the front desk and the television set. He pulled the gun out, discharged the magazine and checked the chamber. "One bullet in the chamber but the gun hasn't been fired. What is Rafe doing carrying a gun?"

"He's a former Tampa detective," Sam announced. She filled them in on her conversation with the editor of the *Tampa Daily Times* and the discovery of the www.findme.org web site. "Rafe arrived in town the moment the discovery of the body was announced. He has been doing a lot of digging under the guise of a reporter."

"He may have pissed off Schuler, Schuler's campaign manager and Murphy," Robinson said, "but he's also been looking under a lot of rocks for Mickey Donovan."

"Which means," Jake added, "that we need to find Donovan."

* * *

Benny studied the pictures of the body found in the uncorporated area days ago. There was bruising consistent with a struggle or her body hitting the ground or rocks. It was difficult to tell. But something was niggling at the back of his brain. He made himself a cup of herbal tea, sat down, closed his eyes, took a couple deep cleansing breaths, then looked at the pictures again. It wasn't the bruises on the wrists, nor the legs. Something else. He grabbed his magnifying glass and studied the photos closer. Then he saw it. On the back of the neck was the identical mark, and he had seen it before. But where?

39

Sam had a dream of being chased by a hoard of insects, the buzzing so loud even clasping her hands over her ears couldn't diminish it. She tried to shake herself awake but all she could muster was to roll over and find a muscular warm body to wrap herself around.

"Honey, someone's at the gate," Jake mumbled.

"Huh?" Sam struggled to lift her head to see the alarm clock on the headboard. "It's five-thirty in the morning. Who could possibly be at the gate?"

"Maybe Murphy was out barhopping all night."

"Then you better answer it because I'll shoot him." She snuggled deeper under the covers.

The buzzing came again, but this time they realized it wasn't the gate. It was Jake's phone.

"Get up. I'll be there in thirty minutes," Robinson grumbled.

In exactly thirty minutes, Robinson was hefting his bulk onto a kitchen chair. "Coffee first," he bellowed.

Sam scrambled eggs in a bowl while Jake defrosted hash browns in the microwave. She planned to throw an egg, bacon, and hash brown casserole in the oven while Robinson drank his pot of coffee.

"Throw a little cheese in that casserole, and nutmeg," Robinson said.

"Any time you want to cook for me, feel free."

"I hear Abby does just fine."

"When she's around which won't be for another week, or is it two?" Sam had to think about that. Matter of fact, it had been days since she had communicated with her mother.

"Where was your client last night while all the fun was going on?"

"Murphy? Not sure. He's using Alex's house."

"Why don't you wake him up and have him join us for breakfast."

Sam looked at Jake and shrugged. "You be the one to wake him before the crack of nine," she told Jake. She finished putting the casserole together and shoved it in the oven while half listening to Jake's call.

"He said to give him twenty minutes but he wasn't happy about it." Jake carried the carafe to the table and refilled Robinson's cup and his own. He turned to Sam. "Coffee or tea?"

"Coffee. I need to wake up." She set the timer and then joined them at the table. "Okay, Captain. You have our undivided attention. What's up?"

"Chang and Rutherford found a casing in the parking lot and the bullet in a telephone post about fifty yards from where Rafe was shot. The bullet came from the Browning .22 calibre they found near the hotel. The gun is registered to John Kendall."

* * *

Sam banged cabinets and drawers while grabbing plates and silverware. "I should never have trusted him. He knows more than he's saying. First he didn't know the girl, then he didn't know her that well, then she was pregnant and had tried to contact him. He thinks he's so smart." Before she could slam the plates on the table, Jake caught her arms and took the plates from her. She took a deep breath to cool down. She wanted to make it about her, how it would be just like Murphy to find a way to discredit her. But by making himself guilty?

"Yes, he is smart." Sam grabbed silverware from the drawer, then stopped in front of the table. "So why would he be so stupid to leave his gun at the scene of the crime?"

"Same thing I was thinking," Robinson said. "But there's more and you aren't going to like it. I'll wait 'til Murphy gets here."

Jake pulled the silverware from her hands and finished setting the table, which, for a man, meant dumping them in the middle of the table and letting everyone grab his own.

Murphy maneuvered Alex's truck up the driveway and parked in front of the garage. He scrambled out and crossed the patio. When he stepped into the kitchen, three sets of eyes stared at him. Murphy was still in the jogging suit he wore last night and a five o'clock shadow was dusting his face. He looked like one of the homeless from State Street.

He ignored their stares and snarled, "This better be damn well important."

Sam couldn't stop staring at him. Even his picture-perfect hair looked disheveled. "Chief, are you all right?"

"Just wonderful. I'm accused of murder, my wife left me, I was a father for a brief nine years, and I may have to file for unemployment. Things couldn't be better." He pulled out a chair and poured a cup of black coffee. "So what are you going to tell me that might make my life more of a shit hole than it is?"

Robinson pointed to an empty chair. "Have a seat, Dennis. Breakfast is on."

"Where's Frank? Thought you two were joined at the hip." Murphy grabbed a plate and was the first in line at the counter, although Sam wondered if he would have any appetite left when Robinson was done with him.

"Not this early," Jake said. "Benny asked one of us to stop by this morning so he was elected."

They settled around the kitchen table. Sam planned to keep her mouth shut and just let Robinson handle everything. To accomplish that, she kept shoving food in her mouth.

"So," Robinson started, "what did you do last night, Dennis?"

"I, uh." He took a sip of coffee, avoiding, unsuccessfully, Sam's eyes. "I borrowed the truck and went to my house to get some things. Ended up falling asleep on the couch."

"How did you get the keys to the truck?"

"You don't lock the patio door, Sam. Not a smart thing to do, even if you do have a monitored gate."

"Anyone see you?" Robinson continued.

"No, why?" Murphy studied the faces around the table. "What's up?"

Robinson told him about Rafe and the gun found at the scene. "Your uncle says he gave you the gun."

Murphy's fork dropped into his plate. "Wait. Are you accusing me of something?"

"Did your uncle give you a Browning .22?" Robinson tried again, speaking slowly as he would to a suspect.

"Yes, he gave me the Browning when I graduated from college, and no I don't know where it's at now. Why?"

"Well, you better jog that memory of yours because it matches the weapon used to kill Tony Barlucci up at your cottage." There was total silence in the room as Robinson poured another cup of coffee and let that tidbit settle in.

Murphy almost burst out laughing. "Unbelievable. And there are witnesses to my telling my secretary to shoot Rafe Bennett if he comes anywhere near my office. This couldn't have been better planned if I had done it myself."

Sam's breakfast was sitting like a lump in her stomach. Maybe Murphy was trying to alleviate the tension but it was beginning to look like the pressure was getting to the chief. He was as giddy as a school girl.

"Well, I have news of my own," Murphy started as he struggled to rein in the giddiness. "I have made up my mind to drop out of the race. Schuler will be so busy doing his victory dance he won't pay much attention to this investigation."

"Deputy Chief Chet Toomey is driving in from Wisconsin," Robinson said. "He has his forensics reports on Tony Barlucci completed and wants to do a formal interview with you. I trust you have your attorney on stand-by."

"Sure. He's on speed dial." Murphy flung his napkin on the table. No one would ever accuse Murphy of not being able to control his emotions. The humor was gone and the steely administrator had returned.

"Chief, my current and only client. Can you shed any light on when you saw the gun last?"

"I didn't have it when I got married. I don't think, no, I KNOW I didn't have it at the police academy. I kept it in my apartment at the hotel, in a secretary. My aunt had one of those roll top desks and I kept it in there."

"Anyone else see where you kept it?" Jake asked.

"No, no one. Wait." He closed his eyes briefly and grimaced. "I did show it to Gina. She knew where I kept it."

Robinson huffed out a squall-size breath. "And after the two of you broke up, did you notice it was gone?"

"I didn't really look to tell you the truth. I was too devastated to think straight. All I know for certain is I didn't take it to the academy." He turned to Jake who was sitting at the end of the table taking notes. "How is the search going for Mickey Donovan?" When Jake said nothing, he turned his antennae toward Robinson.

"We have zip," Robinson admitted. "Trail is cold. Nothing on the radar, never checked in with his parole officer, no record anywhere of being employed or renting a house, boat, car, nada."

"No record of his death?" When that was met with silence, Murphy added, "So he could be out there somewhere."

"Doesn't make sense," Sam said, more to herself.

"Excuse me?" Murphy's head swiveled up.

"Think about it. You never met Mickey Donovan. What axe does he have to grind with you? It just doesn't make sense unless he thinks or was lead to believe you somehow walked away with all the Brinks money. But why wait until now?"

"He was in jail," Robinson offered.

"Sam's right," Jake said. "Mickey knew Tony and Gina but he didn't know Murphy. So what's his angle? Why wait until now? How has he been surviving? What does he do for money? For transportation?"

Everyone mulled over questions that were so obvious now but elicited few answers. "Well," Murphy finally replied, "that's why I put together such a great homicide unit: Two ace detectives who haven't a clue and a mystic investigator whose mojo isn't working."

40

Frank walked into Benny's office to find Andy Brainard and Maury Jackson seated at the conference table. "Hey, guys. What have you got, Benny?"

"You were right about Eleanor Majewski," Andy told Frank. "We compared her fingerprints to those in her room at the shelter as well as the hair from her hairbrush."

"Anything found near the scene?" Frank asked. "Tire marks? Footprints?"

"It has rained since she was reported missing," Maury replied. "No usable prints and the gravel road couldn't produce any tire tracks. Her friend did find her hat, though, a couple blocks from the shelter."

"But that's not why I called you gentlemen here." Benny passed eight-by-ten photos to each of the detectives. "There is a mark on Eleanor's cheek where she was struck with something. The same mark is on the back of her neck."

Frank grabbed the magnifying glass and studied the images. "Is that a shape of some sort? Have you found anything that might make that mark?"

"Not yet." Andy studied one of the photos. "What was cause of death?"

"Asphyxiation, but it's puzzling. I can't figure out what made those marks."

"Maybe a belt," Maury offered.

"I thought the same thing, but there aren't any ligature marks anywhere on the neck." Benny rose and motioned toward the door. "Let's go take a closer look at the bodies."

Frank looked puzzled. The pictures were all interesting, but... "Wait. You said bodies. You have another victim with the same marking?"

Benny smiled the devilish one he saved for exceptionally puzzling cases. "Your Jane Doe from the Embers Hotel."

* * *

The diner was a short three block walk over the Indiana state line. He had to get away from the shelter which had been buzzing with plans for the old biddy's funeral. As long as he kept up his facade of having post traumatic stress disorder, people left him alone. He hadn't shown any violence, he had to chuckle at that, so there wasn't a reason for anyone to be concerned. It helped that he had shared a cell with a Vietnam vet so he knew how to play the part.

What concerned him now was the welfare of the other nosy person on his list. He pushed his empty plate away and signaled the waitress for another cup of coffee. The newspaper only reported that Rafe Bennett was still unconscious. If he did recover, how much would he be able to tell the police? It was too dark for the reporter to have seen him but he may have seen enough to be sure it wasn't Murphy who shot him. Couldn't let that happen. He had to focus or things were going to go downhill fast. His mom always said his bad luck was his own damn fault. But he knew better. He knew someone else was to blame.

41

While Murphy changed into what he considered a more appropriate suit for his interview, Sam left to check on Rafe at the hospital. Murphy planned to call a squad car to pick him up and take him to the Sixth which was just as well. She didn't care to be the chief's personal driver.

Rafe had been moved from ICU to a room in the new wing of the hospital. The entrance resembled a hotel lobby rather than a hospital. There was an escalator at the entrance which brought visitors directly to a large waiting room with flat screen television sets. Visitors lounged in comfort while children sat on the floor with a building block set. Sam grabbed a cup of tea from the waiting room before making her way past large urns of plants to the nurses' station.

The station was a lazy blur of flowery tunics and blue scrubs. She waited near the doorway until one of the tunics acknowledged her. "Has there been any change in Rafe Bennett's condition?"

The young woman grabbed a clip board off of the desk and ran her fingernail down a list. "He's Ellie's patient. I'll get her for you."

Sam turned back toward the rooms. A security guard sat in a chair just outside the door. As promised, Robinson had requested security for Rafe.

"You wanted to know about Mister Bennett?"

Sam stepped back from the doorway. Ellie didn't look any older than Sam. Her hair was swept back in a neat twist, not one strand out of place. The clipboard was clasped to her chest as if to keep any minute detail from Sam's gaze.

"Is he awake?"

"Not yet. It may take awhile for the body to bounce back. He rested comfortably all night, his vitals are good. He is one lucky guy."

"Can I see him?"

"He does have one other visitor, but sure. Even though he isn't awake, it might help to hear familiar voices."

The door was open and the curtain partially drawn. There was a long counter with a sink and refrigerator against a wall by the foot of the bed. Sam had heard that this new wing had private rooms. And just like the entrance, this room could have been in a hotel suite. As she approached the curtain she heard muffled cries, a woman's voice. She peered around the curtain to find a familiar face. Although Sam hadn't met Gina's aunt before, she had seen her around the precinct and Sergeant Scofield had pointed out Sonya and her nephew, Tom DeLeo. "Miss Lucci?"

Startled, Sonya released Rafe's hand and sat back, fumbling with her hankie as she dabbed her eyes. "I'm sorry. Do I know you?"

"Sam Casey. I'm an outside consultant for CHPD. Rafe and I had been working together on your niece's case." Sam pulled a chair over and sat across from her. She wondered if Sonya knew about her involvement with Murphy but decided to let that lie for now.

"Well, I guess you're wondering what I'm doing here."

"I know that Rafe worked on missing person cases so I can only assume he was working on your niece's case."

Sonya nodded behind the hankie. "I was the one who told him where Gina was headed the last time any of us saw her." She turned back to the motionless body on the bed. Rafe's head was wrapped in white bandages. He had an I.V. in his right arm and another in his left. "He looks so helpless. It breaks my heart."

"You two must have worked closely over the years."

Sonya pressed her lips together and sat straighter in her chair. If Sam wasn't mistaken, she could swear some invisible walls had just slammed in place around her. Sonya appeared to regain her composure and asked, "Exactly what is it you do for the department?"

"Currently I have been hired by Chief Murphy to investigate the false claims against him."

"Really." Sonya's glare was piercing. Sam didn't blame her. Murphy was currently the number one suspect in Gina's death. "What do you think of Chief Murphy?" Sonya asked.

That wasn't the question Sam was expecting. "He's an excellent cop, top rate administrator, handles the politics of the job with finesse. He's a hard nose, very demanding, and I haven't always been his biggest fan. But I used to be a homicide cop with CHPD and I know when someone is being set up. No matter what I may think about him, I know he isn't a killer."

"I don't really know you well enough to tell if you are good at your job or just plain gullible."

Sam left that comment alone. "What did Rafe think of Murphy? He must have reported back to you on his reaction."

She looked back at the still form lying in the bed. The heart monitor beeped in the background. It was a steady, strong beat. "He had doubts. We both would have pointed eagerly to Tony Barlucci if only he hadn't been found dead on Murphy's property."

"Murphy's uncle sold that property and it wasn't to Dennis. Someone has worked tirelessly to make sure every detail fit snugly. To me it fits way too perfect. What can you tell me about Tony Barlucci?"

"Other than he was a worthless piece of humanity and he's dead? What else do you want to know?"

"Did he ever mention Mickey Donovan? Tony cheated him out of a lot of money."

"We never knew where Tony got his money. After the baby was born, Tony and Gina lived near his parents but when Gus and Tony had a falling out, Tony moved Gina and the baby to Italy for a few years until relatives had it with him."

"Why is that?"

"Gus tried to let him work within the organization, but like everything else in his life, Tony screwed it up. Gus is the one who found him some work with another relative in Italy. I didn't hear why but within a few years Tony and Gina were back, Gina with more bruises, Tony with a ridiculous tattoo on his arm of a heart with Gina's name in it. How adolescent." Sonya shook her head in disgust.

"I'm surprised Gina stayed with him so long."

"She had no choice."

"Everyone has a choice."

"Easier said than done. Little Anthony was diagnosed with leukemia at seven. Poor thing suffered for a year before the doctors decided to try a bone marrow transplant but..."

"I know. They couldn't find a match." Sam sipped her tea while she studied Rafe's motionless body. In a way he didn't look like the same man she had met almost two weeks ago.

"Why didn't Gina return to New Jersey for her son's funeral?"

"Tony said the father refused to donate and it devastated Gina."

"That's not true," Sam said. "Murphy never received a call, never knew Gina was in town. Did she ever tell anyone the father's name?"

"No. And when Tony said Gina wanted to be alone and wasn't planning to come home yet, Gus and Vera knew Gina was dead. There wasn't any way that girl would not have wanted to be with her son while he was so ill. Tony's explanation that Gina needed her space and had to get away only convinced my brother and his wife that he was lying."

* * *

"How long have they been at it?" Sam leaned against the door jamb to Jake's office. She had passed the conference room where Deputy Chief Toomey, Murphy, and Attorney Aiden Sloan were meeting. Although Toomey preferred Sam not sit in on the interview, he did ask that she and Jake be available should he need anything clarified.

"Murphy's been in there for three hours."

"What are you guys doing for dinner? I invited Sonya to Izzy's for chicken but she declined. Said she was meeting Tom DeLeo for dinner."

Frank chuckled. "Sounds like you had an ulterior motive buried in there somewhere."

Sam shrugged. "Just thought we could pick Sonya's brain a little more. Maybe the captain wants to join us."

"The captain said he has plans with Jackie," Jake replied.

Sam knew exactly what Jackie had planned and smiled at her friend's mastermind. "For some reason I think her dinner is going to be a lot of fun."

Frank tapped on the door frame. "Have you told her yet?"

"Told me what?"

Frank chuckled. "Oh, it gets better and better. I think it's good news for Murphy."

"WHAT?" Sam dragged Frank into the office and closed the door.

Frank told her about the markings on Eleanor Majewski's face and neck and how they were identical to the one Benny found on the back of Gina's neck.

"Same killer?" Sam couldn't be more shocked than if they told her Gina was still alive. "That means he's definitely here in Chasen Heights."

"Right." Jake leaned back in his chair and plopped his feet on the desk. "Which critics could still point to Murphy."

"But Murphy doesn't know this Eleanor person, does he?"

"Claims he doesn't but until we figure out what the hell that mark is and what made it, we're just spinning our wheels," Frank commented.

"What does it look like?" Sam grabbed a paper Jake thrust her way. There were three images and it was obvious they were identical. "Looks like a pitchfork," Sam said. "Or maybe a menorah minus a lot of candles. Any idea what made them?"

"None." Jake shoved the papers back into a file folder. He pointed at a chair in front of his desk. "Where did you run into Sonya?"

Sam told them about her visit to the hospital and how Rafe's condition hadn't changed. "Would be great if he woke up and told us who shot him."

Frank said, "Depends on how far away the shooter stood. It was pretty dark out."

"I haven't seen this Reverend Tom around much," Sam said. "Seems to me when Tony was in and out of prison and shunned by his parents, couldn't he have sought refuge with the good Reverend?"

"Good point." Frank scribbled a note in his notepad.

"DeLeo said he was going to be busy making arrangements for Gina's body once it's released," Jake said. "You missed a very interesting interview with them. He and his aunt went at it for sometime."

"Uh, oh." Frank nodded toward the window where Murphy and Deputy Chief Toomey were approaching. Frank opened the door as Murphy walked on toward Robinson's office. Toomey stopped in the doorway.

"Got a minute?" Toomey stepped in and took a seat next to Sam. Frank hefted one cheek on the side of the desk as Toomey pulled folders from a briefcase that looked as though it had been through an airport baggage claim area one too many times. "Got some autopsy results on Mister Barlucci and some additional info on the case I thought might be of interest to you boys." He hesitated and looked at Sam, then added, "and ladies."

"Was Chief Murphy able to clear up any questions?" Sam asked.

Toomey snapped a sideways glance her way. "Clever way for you to be nosy, little lady."

"Inquisitive. I like that word better."

Toomey grumbled, "Just like my wife. Most cops' wives don't want to know the gory details of your job but my wife is like the supreme interrogator." Toomey folded open a notepad and leaned back. "Did come up with something you might find very interesting. Kootie Blackjack..."

"Kootie?" Frank said with a laugh.

"Yep. His real name." Toomey continued. "Kootie Blackjack was the former owner of Petawkaw Real Estate. Although the ownership records show Dennis Murphy as the current owner, I thought I'd see if Kootie remembered John Kendall, your chief's uncle."

"Did he?" Sam asked.

"Hold on, little lady. I'm telling the story. Anyway, Kootie keeps records better than the IRS. Kept everything in writing in a penmanship that would make a nun proud. His records show John Kendall sold the cabin to Genesis, as he had thought. However, they owned it for five years then sold it to Biggert Corporation, a real estate company that now rents the cabin. How records got all turned around in the existing computers to show Dennis Murphy still owning the property is a big mystery. There's been a bit of deception going on but I'm going to keep digging."

Jake said, "Someone might have hacked into the system."

"Doesn't take much. Kootie said several years back they had to fire one worker because she was taking money to falsify records."

Sam pulled the autopsy photo off the desk and studied the body of Tony Barlucci. Very little was left of the skin and muscle except where his clothes had covered the body. It was pretty much decomposed. But her eyes were drawn to the arms. She studied the dark blue skin closer, searching both forearms.

"This isn't Tony Barlucci," Sam said.

"What?" The men said in unison.

"Sonya told me Tony had a tattoo."

"Who's Sonya?" Toomey asked.

"Sonya Lucci is Tony's aunt," Frank explained. "She was close to Gina even though Gina wasn't a blood relation. She always felt that if Gina had been murdered, it was Tony who did it."

"Sonya said when Tony and Gina returned from Italy, Tony had a tattoo of a heart with Gina's name in the middle. It was on his forearm." Sam passed the photo to Jake.

"I didn't read anything in the autopsy report about a tattoo." Toomey shuffled through the papers until he found the autopsy report. "The victim did have a fractured sphenoid bone."

Sam nodded at the folder in front of Jake. "Look at Mickey's more recent photo. Damage to his left eye might have been caused by an injury to the sphenoid bone."

"Shit," Frank huffed. "Mickey's the one in the grave, not Tony."

42

"Wow!" Armando stood in Jackie's doorway, mouth gaping.

"I guess that's a compliment." Jackie grabbed the bottle of wine and nodded her approval at the selection. "I told you not to waste your hard-earned money, sugar." She turned from the door, her floral caftan flowing around black leggings. The square-cut neckline dipped off one shoulder where it was held up by a spaghetti strap. Her hair was piled on top of her head and surrounded by white gardenias. A vase of the same flowers was on the dining room table.

"You have magnificent taste." Armando closed the door and took in the fine lines of black enamel, chrome and glass. The carpeting was so white he was afraid to step on it. But then his senses picked up a variety of aromas. "Is that chateaubriand? Glad I bought a merlot."

Jackie nodded toward the bar. "Help yourself to a before-dinner drink. I'm just going to put this wine on ice."

"Do you need help in the kitchen?"

"Oh no." Jackie shooed him away. "My chef doesn't like any intrusions." She smiled as she disappeared through the kitchen door.

"Chef?" Armando moved toward the bar but stepped back to the door and slipped out of his shoes. "Damn. The lady has a chef." He opened the refrigerator behind the bar. It was stocked with beer and wine bottles. So much for being original. Wine glasses hung from a rack over his head. He pulled one down, grabbed the opened bottle of wine and filled a glass. He felt underdressed and wished he had worn a suit. His phone vibrated in his pocket. He looked at the screen, then flipped the phone open.

"What's happening?" a frantic voice said.

"I just got here. Can you not bother me demanding minute-by-minute updates?" He folded the phone just as Jackie returned.

"Hope you don't have to leave, sugar." Jackie placed a covered basket smelling of warm biscuits on the table.

"No, just checking the stock market."

"Why don't you go ahead and sit down right there." Jackie motioned to a seat next to the head table. Armando looked puzzled. There were four place settings. He opened his mouth to say something, but Jackie quickly said, "There's a lighter on the bar. Would you light the candles, sugar?" While Armando lit the two candles in the middle of the table, Jackie moved the gardenia centerpiece to the coffee table.

With the candles lit, Jackie let Armando pull out her chair before he took his own seat. The swing door to the kitchen opened and the chef backed out of the kitchen pulling a serving cart. Armando's brows furrowed and as the chef turned, the young man gasped, "Dad!"

"Good evening, Ty. Hope you haven't turned vegetarian because I only know how to cook meat." Robinson set a huge serving tray of chateaubriand in the center of the table.

"I, uh." Ty looked at Jackie whose smiling face was propped on her folded hands.

"You didn't really think I couldn't see the similarity in the voice and those massive shoulders, did you?"

"But you never, I mean." His skin started to take on a sheen.

Robinson continued to set out the potatoes and vegetables. As he pushed the serving cart to the side he said, "We have a lot of food to eat so why don't you go ahead and call Marisa. I'm sure your sister must be starving by now." He smiled at the stunned look on his face. "Go on. I'm sure she's close by. Tell her to come to the back door."

Ty fumbled for his phone, flipped it open and dialed. "Yeah, it's me. Come on up. Use the back door. Dad's here."

They could hear Marisa scream 'WHAT' from Ty's phone. He winced, closed it and shoved it back in his pocket. "Well, I guess I have egg all over my face."

Lamon walked to the monitor next to the door. Several minute's later Marisa's face appeared in the screen. He pushed a button to buzz her in, then opened the door and waited for her at the top of the stairs. "Dinner's getting cold, little girl."

Marisa stomped into the apartment and glared at her brother. "You told?"

"Didn't have to." Lamon closed the door and ushered her to the dining room table. "You didn't really think Jackie couldn't put it all together, did you? Now sit down and let's talk over dinner. Little girl, why aren't you in Indianapolis teaching school? And, Ty, I thought you got that job in Philadelphia at that corporation in their legal department? Now you two show up in Chasen Heights without even calling me. Tell me what this charade is all about, although we have a pretty good idea already."

"We took a couple weeks off for a good cause." Marisa lifted her chin, avoiding Jackie's eyes as she took a seat across from her brother. Her eyes lit daggers across the table. She grabbed the bottle of wine and filled her glass as her eyes danced around the expensive decor of the apartment. "Hooking must pay pretty good money," she said as casually as 'I like the curtains.'

Lamon jabbed a finger at his daughter. "You show her some respect. Now apologize."

Marisa's chin lifted higher in defiance. "Why? Would mother?"

"Lamon," Jackie cautioned. "Let's eat while your fabulous meal is hot. If your daughter wants to vent, fine. You wanted to know what this charade was all about so sit back and enjoy the show." And what a show it was.

Marisa sliced off a piece of steak and grabbed mushrooms, potatoes, and garlic biscuits. She looked like a longshoreman beefing up for a long trip. "All you had to do was..."

"Just stop it, Marisa." Ty turned to Jackie. "I'm sorry. I didn't just walk into your shop by accident looking for a gift for my aunt. We wanted to see who our father was so enthralled with."

"Seems to me you got just as enthralled," Marisa snapped. "If I didn't know better, I'd say she's got you under her spell."

Ty grinned. "Who wouldn't be." He flashed a shy smile at Jackie.

"Once I got to know you I understood exactly why my dad feels the way he does."

"Oh, spare me." Marisa grabbed another slice of steak and refilled her glass of wine. "You had a simple job of getting her to bed to remind dad what kind of woman she is."

Jackie and Lamon exchanged smiles across the table. He knew she wouldn't be offended by anything his daughter dished out. Jackie passed the basket of biscuits to her left. Marisa's eyes never left her brother's face as she grabbed a biscuit and passed the basket to her father.

"What she is is a great business woman." Ty grabbed the basket and took two biscuits. "Damn these are good." He pointed at his sister with the biscuit. "And who are you to pimp me out? If you had spent as much time with her as I did, you would have seen her for the beautiful, gracious, caring person she is. You should see how she treats her customers. Hell, you were one of her customers."

"Outrageous prices." She mopped up the gravy with a biscuit. "And you still owe be eighty bucks for that outfit I had to buy."

"Had to buy? You tell me you wear it every night. That it's one of the most beautiful things you've ever owned. You could have returned it."

"The bottom line is, she isn't mama." Marisa's voice broke.

"Marisa, no one can replace your mama," Jackie said.

"Don't placate me," she snapped.

Lamon placed a hand on his daughter's arm. "Your mama died ten years ago. I never loved a woman more. She gave me two beautiful children. But, little girl, she isn't coming back. I will always love her but life goes on. You can't judge women I date by your mother. I have dated scores of women since your mother died. Why now? Why did you find it necessary to come to Chasen Heights to check out Jackie?"

Ty jumped in before his sister could continue to monopolize the conversation. "Because of how you talk about her. You've never gone on and on before about a woman you were dating. We had to find out who she was and how she treated you."

"And if she was going to break your heart. I can't bare to see you torn apart again. We just wanted to prove to you that women like her don't change. If she could jump into bed with Ty without blinking an eye then she wasn't the woman for you."

"Do I need to remind you, little girl, that I am a grown man? I have my eyes wide open. And I don't need the permission of my two grown children to date anyone I want."

"I think it's my turn, Lamon," Jackie said. She looked at each of Lamon's children. "The one picture Lamon carries in his wallet is a picture of Celia with both of you at Seaworld. I think you were twelve and Marisa was ten. Those are the only pictures I have seen of you two but I knew who you were the minute I laid eyes on you. Now, I don't need to explain my life to you. You don't need to know how many cities I've lived in, how many daddies I've had, what struggles I've had. I grew up fast and learned that men most times do not think with their brains. Matter of fact, certain departments of the government found my talents to be quite useful in loosening the lips of potential threats to the country."

"Oh, right. Like you were an undercover CIA agent," Marisa said with a sneer. But neither Lamon nor Jackie responded. "You're kidding, right?"

Jackie rose from the table. "Let's get this mess moved to the kitchen, then in a bit we can have dessert and coffee by the fireplace and talk about how Ty doesn't like being a lawyer."

"What?" Lamon gaped.

Ty dipped his head as though expecting a plate to come flying across the table.

"Let's go," Jackie prompted. As she stood she caught Marisa staring at her floral shoes.

"Are those Jimmy Choos?" the young woman gasped.

"Yes. You like them?"

"Oh, my god. What size do you wear?"

"Seven and a half."

"Really?"

"She has a closet just for her shoes," Lamon said.

Marisa's eyes widened.

"Want to see them?" Jackie didn't wait for an answer, just turned and headed to her bedroom.

* * *

With the table cleared and the dishwasher humming, Lamon led Ty over to the couch by the fireplace and motioned to a chair across from him. "Okay, want to tell what this whole thing is about your job?"

"What is there to say? I'm one of fifty lawyers in a company that does title searches. It's boring, no place for advancement. And being a lawyer was your dream for me. It wasn't my dream. I feel like my talents are being wasted."

Lamon popped open a beer can and poured the contents into a glass. He would almost accept it if his son wanted to backpack across the country. "Okay. Let's have it. Exactly what is it you want to do?"

Ty took a deep breath, then looked Lamon squarely in the eye and said, "I applied to the Bureau."

"Bureau of Vital Statistics? Bureau of Motor Vehicles?"

"Pops, you know I mean the FBI."

Lamon felt his neck muscles tighten. "You know..."

"Yes, I know you want me to go into something other than law enforcement. But, Pops, it's in my blood. I have a knack for remembering details, I'm thorough, love a good puzzle. I even own a gun and I'm a damn good shot."

Lamon studied the foam capping his beer. Would it do him any good to try to change his mind? Being in law enforcement wasn't easy and it wasn't anything he wanted for his own son or daughter. He just needed to knock Ty down a peg or two. He reached into his pocket and tossed a folded paper at him. "Okay, hot shot. Tell me where those markings came from."

Ty unfolded the paper and studied a forensic photo of two victims, the odd images on the backs of their necks and another on one of the victim's cheeks. Lamon explained about the two cases, twenty-five years apart.

"Maybe a belt buckle? Were there ligature marks?"

"Already thought of that, and no. Our medical examiner didn't find any type of ligature mark."

"But they were asphyxiated."

"Until we figure out the murder weapon we can't tell for sure."

Ty studied the image, turning the page around. He splayed his hands and smiled. "Be right back."

He returned several seconds later carrying a garbage bag. He walked behind Lamon and said, "Take a deep breath, Pops."

"Huh?" Lamon set his beer down, turn a deep breath, then saw the plastic bag pulled over his head, felt it twisted in back and pulled tighter, grinding something painful into his neck. He waved his hands to stop. Ty released his grip and pulled the bag from Lamon's head. "What the hell?" Lamon gulped in air. "I don't think a knot of plastic made those marks."

"No, it wouldn't." Ty walked back to his chair, pulled off his ring and handed it to Lamon. "But this would. It's my class ring from Indiana University."

43

The next morning Sam stood in front of the white board in the study. She had changed Tony's name as the deceased in Wisconsin to Mickey's. Jake had the baby dicks working on Tony's background. Robinson was making sure not one of the latest developments would be revealed to the press or anyone outside their investigative team. If Tony was in town, he didn't want to spook him. Here they had spent all of their time and resources looking for Mickey. It all made more sense now. Tony had a bigger grudge against Murphy. Gina obviously had fallen for Murphy. She had given birth to Murphy's son. Perhaps Gina's role in Tony's life of crime was to distract security at banks and never sleep with them but somehow she and Murphy connected. This must have driven Tony insanely jealous. But patiently jealous? To wait this long to exact retribution?

And what connection did Eleanor Majewski have to Tony? The shelter wasn't too far from the hotel. Maybe Eleanor saw Tony twenty-five years ago and then he showed up in town again. She could place Tony with the body. But could an elderly woman really remember someone from twenty-five years ago? No one looks the same after twenty-five years.

Sam checked the whiteboard again. The Embers Hotel was supposed to be torn down six months ago. It kept getting delayed. If Tony came to town to have a front row seat at the unveiling of the body exposed during the demolition, he may have needed a low-profile place to stay. What if he stayed at the shelter?

Sam grabbed her purse and headed out the door just as her phone rang. Jake's name popped up on the screen. "Hi, sweetie."

"The captain discovered what caused the marks on the back of Gina's and Eleanor's necks." Jake told her about Robinson's son.

"So Robinson's son went to Indiana University and recognized the symbol."

"Right. And guess who else went to Indiana University."

Great. Of course…Murphy. "Let me guess. Murphy hasn't seen his ring in years."

"He gave it to Gina."

* * *

"Miss Bakowski?"

"Yes?"

"I'm Sam Casey. I'm an investigative consultant with CHPD. Can I ask you a few questions about Eleanor?"

"Please call me Marie." She led Sam to a table by a window. The shelter had been donated to the city years ago. It was one of the oldest buildings in town. In its early days it had served as an overflow hotel. Although it was only two-stories high, the building was longer than it was wide and could house up to eighty people comfortably.

The lobby was a mismatch of furniture and tables and served as a large dining room. Several television sets had been donated and set to various channels as residents drifted in and out of the room. "I trust you don't handle this all on your own."

"Oh, no. I have several volunteers plus many of the residents pitch in. Now, if you want to know more about Eleanor, I should probably have you talk to Lucille." She disappeared down the hall and returned trailed by an elderly woman in a crisp house dress and sensible heels.

"Miss Casey, this is Lucille Montgomery. She has been a resident for three years and was Eleanor's closest friend." Marie left the two women promising to bring them hot tea.

Sam stripped out of her sweater coat and tossed it on the back of a chair. She exchanged smiles with Lucille until Marie brought out the teapot and mismatched china cups and saucers. "I have cookies coming out of the oven shortly," Marie said. She disappeared down the hall.

"I already spoke with those nice young gentlemen. They had all of us here in the room to ask us about Eleanor."

"Detectives Brainard and Jackson."

"Such nice, well-dressed young men. Don't see that much these days."

Sam wondered what had happened in Lucille's life that brought her to this place. Weren't there any relatives to help her out, give her a room to live in? Or maybe she preferred the company of others. Some people couldn't stand silence or solitude. "I wanted to ask you a few more questions about Eleanor."

"Oh, that poor thing." A hankie materialized in Lucille's hand and she dabbed at her red ringed eyes. "She was from my generation so we had a lot in common."

"Did she get along with everyone?" Sam knew the residents had already been questioned but one never knew what fleeting memory might pop up if jogged enough.

"Only the kids bothered her. I swear parents just don't discipline their children these days. All the running, the screaming. This used to be an adults only shelter then they had to change it because of some discrimination laws."

"Do you think she might have gotten lost and walked a half mile?"

"Never. We were lucky to walk four blocks without having to hail down a cab." She leaned close so Sam could hear her whisper. Sam could smell mints and baby powder. "And sometimes you didn't dare hail a cab in this neighborhood."

"Did she ever walk by herself?"

Marie entered carrying a plate of cookies. "Can I get you anything else?" They both declined so Marie returned to the kitchen.

"Why is it so empty in here?"

"Today is free lunch day at Saint Michael's," Lucille replied. "Not that we don't have meals here. Marie doesn't provide lunch on days when there are free meals at other places. This way she can stretch the supplies."

Sam asked again if Eleanor ever took a walk alone.

"We weren't together all the time. She was pretty independent, much like me."

Sam took a bite of a chocolate chip cookie. *Damn.* She wondered how many her tote bag could hold. "I understand she was rarely seen without her hat. Do you remember where you found it?"

"Oh, yes. Two blocks down in an alley." Lucille walked Sam over to the door and pointed down State Street. "Right behind those brown buildings," she added. "The police spent a lot of time there looking for witnesses. Most of the buildings there are empty. Some appear to be garages but the police wouldn't tell me if they found any clues."

Sam had seen the police report. Andy had also asked Lucille if Eleanor had ever met Chief Murphy. Not one person at the precinct believed Murphy had anything to do with Eleanor's death but Andy had to cover all bases. It was possible Eleanor was abducted in the alley but with a lack of eye witnesses, they had little to go on.

"You said only the kids got on her nerves. But living with so many people, she must have complained about someone, especially since she has lived here for a few years. It could be someone who doesn't live here anymore."

Lucille thought about that for several seconds while she munched on a cookie. Sam grabbed the teapot and filled both of their cups. The elderly woman was prim and proper. She wore short white gloves and what looked like a vintage dress one would have worn during the turn of the century. Her white hair was pinned up with decorative hair pins.

"You know, I do recall Eleanor complaining about someone walking too heavy late at night. It would keep her up, the constant tap tapping. Sounded like someone with high heels tramping on the wooden floors."

"Did she ever see the culprit during the daytime?"

"No." She nodded toward the floor. "Everyone's shoes make noise on these floors. The kids, some of the mothers who wear those cloggy type shoes. Even Marie wears heels but she wears house slippers at night. Matter of fact, come to think of it, Eleanor asked Marie to put up a sign asking everyone to wear house slippers after nine o'clock at night."

"Anyone complain?"

"Men, mainly, and kids. They don't like rules."

"Do you recall if Eleanor had any other concerns leading up to the day she disappeared?"

Lucille finished her tea and set the cup in the saucer. "Shopping always excited her. But not the mall. Too many people. She did like flea markets, though, and garage sales. Living where we did, though, there was never a way to get around this city."

Sam didn't accomplish much by stopping by the shelter. Lucille couldn't shed any light on Eleanor's comings and goings. The detectives had already questioned everyone and inspected the alley. One bright note was that Benny now knew what left those marks on Eleanor and Gina.

* * *

He opened the refrigerator and pulled out a beer. Almost six bucks. What a rip. The room was elegant compared to the sparse furnishings at the shelter. Queen-size bed, wide screen TV, a bathroom that wasn't down the hall. And he was stuck in squalid conditions. Why was he always getting screwed? Aunt Sonya was the one who had convinced his parents that he was the evil incarnate. So many things were coming to a head. Plan ahead was one thing his old man had taught him. He just hoped he had enough bullets to take care of everyone on his list.

There was a sound at the hotel room door. He hadn't lost his touch. One of the cleaning women had believed him when he said he locked himself out of his room. How easy to fool the gullible.

A key card was being inserted. A figure in the shadows closed the door and took two steps into the room before stopping.

"Hello, Tommy. How'ya been?"

44

Jake and Frank entered the hospital room to find Rafe sitting up in bed drinking a glass of water. "Can't wait to see your new do," Frank said which elicited a weak smile from Rafe.

"Guess I'll look like you, just a shade lighter."

"Sonya, Frank is going to ask Rafe a few questions. Can we go out to the waiting area?" Jake escorted Sonya to the lounge. "Can I get you some coffee?"

"Yes, thank you."

As he filled two coffee cups, Jake noticed chairs near the top of the escalator away from the noisy television set and families waiting in the lounge. He motioned Sonya over with a nod of his head. "Why don't we sit where it's more private. I hope you take cream in your coffee."

"That's fine." Sonya dumped two packages of sugar into the coffee and then followed Jake to an alcove by the escalator. "He doesn't remember anything," she said as she took a seat. They used an end table to set their cups on.

"That's to be expected but I'm sure memories will start flooding back. I need to know more about Tony."

"Tony? Why?"

"It wasn't Tony's body in the grave up in Wisconsin." Jake watched her reaction. Denial he would expect, anger maybe. But he wasn't prepared for the shock and terror on Sonya's face.

"Oh my god. He's here, isn't he? Oh my god." Sonya's hands started to shake.

Jake moved closer and clasped her hands in his. "I need to know anything you might remember about Tony, anything he might have said, anything his mother might have told you. Did he go home after getting out of prison? Help me with a timeline, Sonya. Tony came to Chasen

Heights with Gina in 1985. That's the last time Gina was seen or heard from."

Sonya's eyes flitted around as though expecting Tony to walk down the hall any minute.

"Sonya?" Jake placed her coffee cup between her hands and waited for her to take several sips. She cradled it in her lap as she spoke.

"With Anthony in the hospital, Tony accompanied Gina to Chasen Heights to find the father. I knew something was up and told Vera Tony shouldn't be alone with Gina. When that little boy died while they were out of town, Tony claimed Gina left him, said she needed space. But we never heard from her again. Gina would have wanted to attend her own son's funeral. She practically slept in the same bed with him while he was sick. Gus and Vera finally believed everything I had suspected of Tony. Tony returned home a few times, all beaten up and broke. We suspected he was gambling, got into trouble with some loan sharks. Still claimed he hadn't heard from Gina. Gus was furious, refused to bail him out of his problems any more. Tony got in trouble for theft or embezzling, I'm not sure. But Gus wouldn't spend money for an attorney."

"That must have made Tony angry."

"Oh, you don't know the half of it. Vera said Tony would call from prison screaming at them, threatening them. Gus died while Tony was in prison. Tony was all about payback, retribution. He expected loyalty from those closest to him, like he was some godfather-type."

"Did he try to find you?"

"I never wrote a return address on my letters to Vera. I had a friend who traveled a lot on business. She'd take my letters and mail them from whatever state she was in."

"You never slipped and gave clues where you were living?"

Sonya's eyes snapped to the escalator, focusing on visitors carrying flowers and towing children. "No, not at all. And Vera always destroyed my letters after reading them."

"When did Vera die?"

"About a year ago."

Jake checked his notes. Where has Tony been all this time? Letting vengeance and anger build? His father and mother both turned on him, the woman he loved had loved someone else, and with Gus and Vera dead, Murphy seemed to be his next target. But why now? He had years and many opportunities to pay Murphy a visit.

"I think I've seen him." Sonya's voice was so quiet, Jake wasn't sure he heard correctly.

"What did you say?"

"There have been a couple times since I came to Chasen Heights that I could swear I feel like someone is following me. Maybe I'm just jittery or feeble. I never see who it is, just a form, a man, pulling back around a building when I turn to look."

"Sonya, what if Vera saved your letters, like in a safety deposit box and Tony found them after she died? Was there anything in those letters that you would be afraid of Tony finding out about?"

The coffee cup slipped from Sonya's hands and broke on the tiled floor.

* * *

"So, what do you think?" Frank slid into the booth across from Jake at Izzy's.

"I called the baby dicks to check out Gus and Vera, have them go back maybe ten years and peel back some layers of information. There's something Sonya's not telling me. But one thing is for sure, she is terrified that Tony is in town."

"Makes sense. Who else would be causing this much trouble for Murphy?"

"He could have done that from a beach in the Caribbean."

"Yeah, but if Murphy skates because of lack of evidence, that wouldn't satisfy a sociopath like Tony. Remember, he left bread crumbs which we followed to the cabin. So if the authorities didn't nail Murphy for Gina's death, we'd get him for Mickey's. Humiliating Murphy, seeing him lose his job, his wife, maybe get the death penalty. Tony did some long-term planning."

A waitress stopped by and they each ordered a burger, fries, and coffee. "I don't know," Jake admitted. "Murphy could spend twenty years making appeals. I don't think that is soon enough for someone like Tony Barlucci. No, there's a piece of a puzzle we are missing."

* * *

"It's about time. For a minute I thought you went on vacation and forgot all about me." Sam smiled as she spoke with her partner in Phoenix. She walked into Izzy's and was immediately directed to the restaurant side by the owner who was washing glasses behind the bar.

"Well, hey. You never give me anything easy. It's like digging with a spoon rather than a backhoe and I'm still nowhere close to finding out everything," Paul said.

As Sam approached the booth, Jake stood and let her slide in first. She half listened as Jake ordered her an iced tea and a hamburger. "Just don't tell me what your temperatures are while we barely hit sixty. Now tell me what you found out." Sam pulled out a notepad and paper and started jotting down notes.

"When Sonya arrived in Phoenix she immediately had her son admitted to the Mayo Clinic."

"Sonya didn't have a son."

"According to hospital records, she was a bone marrow donor for her son. He made a full recovery."

Sam wasn't sure how many more notes she took. Her head was still trying to wrap around the fact that Gina and Murphy's son was still alive. She hung up and looked at two blank faces staring at her.

"Well?" Frank said.

"Sonya took a nine-year-old boy to the Mayo Clinic in Phoenix. Surprisingly, she was a perfect match for a bone marrow transplant and the boy made a full recovery. Paul said the boy's name was given as John

Doe. Seems a lot of money was spread around to keep his existence a secret, but he did find a retired nurse who worked on the case and might be able to tell him more about the boy."

"We can guess where all that money came from. No wonder Sonya never had to work. She just kept watchful eyes on Gina's son and Gus footed the bill," Jake surmised. "That must be what Sonya was afraid of Tony finding out." Jake filled Sam in on how Sonya had kept in touch with Vera. "She might have sent pictures as the boy was growing up, pictures that Vera was supposed to destroy."

"If she kept them and Tony found out a year ago when going through Vera's things after she died, he would have gone ballistic." Frank grabbed his plate as the waitress passed out their lunches.

"He may be in town to do more than witness the demise of Murphy. After all, Sonya had been pretty vocal about her dislike for Tony and was successful at poisoning his parents against him." Jake poured ketchup on his fries and passed the bottle to Frank. "However, the discovery of Gina's body might flush one more person out whom Tony would like to eliminate."

"Oh my god," Sam gasped. "Murphy's son."

45

"Who wants to be the one to tell him?" Frank said.

Both Frank and Jake looked at Sam. "What? Why should I be the one to break the news?"

"He's your client, sweetheart." Jake pushed his plate toward the waitress who gathered up the empties and placed them on a tray. "Sonya has to know where his son is. Maybe she can warn him to stay away."

"She obviously doesn't trust anyone to know, not even you," Frank pointed out. "Or she would have mentioned it when you spoke to her at the hospital."

"Where is she now?" Sam asked.

"I think she went back to her hotel. It spooked her to know Tony might be in town. She feels strongly that someone has been following her." Jake accepted a refill on his coffee as the waitress filled cups and scooted away.

* * *

Murphy unfolded the note that had been left under the front windshield of his car. Someone knew he spent the night at his house. Someone had been following him. No, not someone—Tony. All he had planned to do was get up this morning and drive to Donna's mother's house in Chicago so he could talk to his wife. Instead, he was going to do a stupid thing. He read the note again:

> *Meet me at the hotel*
> *Come alone*

Murphy parked in the lot behind the hotel. He turned off the engine and stared at the building in front of him. He hadn't stepped inside the hotel in at least thirty years. Had put those memories behind him years ago. How easy it would be to put a bullet in Tony's head but that might be Tony's plan...for Murphy to be caught standing over Tony's body. No, that would be too easy and Tony wouldn't be able to revel in Murphy's misfortune.

Time to go. He pulled the slide back on his Glock, then holstered the gun. The sun was high overhead but temperatures were chilly. He gathered his leather coat around him and approached the back door. The padlock was open and hanging from the chain. How did Tony gain access? Probably took *lock picking 101* in prison. He took one last look over his shoulder at the desolate parking lot and wondered if his Chrysler 300 would still be there if and when he got out.

Once inside the building, Murphy pulled out his gun and cautiously made his way down the corridor. He didn't take time to reminisce on how the lobby looked when his uncle owned the Embers. He knew his aunt would have never let those windows remain filthy.

Lights were on in the mezzanine floors. How thoughtful of Tony to leave the lights on. He climbed the carpeted staircase, keeping an eye on the columns on the mezzanine levels which would make a great place to conceal an ambush. Murphy had a gut feeling Tony would be on the fourth floor, in the room where Gina died.

He smelled a trap but there wasn't much he could do about it. He walked to the stairs leading to the fourth floor. His hand dropped to the pocket of his leather coat where he kept a voice-activated recorder. If he could get Tony talking, he just might hang himself.

Murphy plodded up the stairs, no longer attempting to conceal his presence. "Okay, I'm here. What is it you want?" He stopped at the top of the stairs and listened. The door to his apartment was ajar. He shoved it open with one foot, then waited. Everything he had ever learned during his years on the force was slipping from his memory. He should have called for backup. He should have remained outside of the hotel. Better yet, he should be sitting in a bar drowning his sorrow. Too late now.

The door slowly drifted back at him. With his finger on the trigger, he whipped around the door and pointed the gun at...empty space. He turned toward the bedroom, hearing too late the rapid sound of footsteps coming from the hallway. He was struck from behind and felt himself fall, his fingers releasing their grip on the gun.

The floor smelled like an old cellar and all Murphy could think of was whether his leather coat was getting filthy. He pushed away from the floor and slowly sat up, kneading a knot growing in the back of his head. He blinked the room into focus and saw an old man sitting on the counter, his feet swinging like a five-year-old on a chair too big for him. Tired eyes sagged at the corners. Gray hair was scraggly and his beard might have been hiding remnants of his last meals. Who the hell was this old guy and what did he want? Was he a homeless man who thought Murphy was taking over his turf?

"About time." The man jumped from the counter with unusual strength for an old man. In his hand was Murphy's Glock.

Murphy decided he had to get out on the street more with the guys. He had made a lot of amateur mistakes in the matter of...how long? He checked his watch. He had only been unconscious for ten minutes. The old man swept one hand back and pulled off the gray wig. Next came the beard. Standing before him was a Soprano wannabe. He had the salt and pepper hair greased and combed back, the damn cleats on his shoes, black shirt and pants. The eyes were cold and calculating.

"Life hasn't treated you very well," Murphy said. "You look a little worse for wear, Tony. It is Tony Barlucci, I take it?" He slowly brought his right leg up and felt the ankle.

Tony picked up an object from the counter and held it up. It was Murphy's ankle holster and his Ruger .380. "Looking for this?" He cackled and strutted like a peacock. "Your life is in the shit can about now."

Murphy pushed himself up and dragged his body to sit on the coffee table. "Hate to disappoint you. But we already know you killed Mickey Donovan and Gina, and probably that poor old woman at the homeless shelter. Pretty clever to use my class ring which I gave to Gina. It's amazing what forensics can do these days."

"You mean this ring?" Tony smiled. "They will find it on your finger after you're dead. I've covered all my bases so there isn't anyway to tie me to the other murders."

Murphy didn't understand Gina's fear of Tony. He wasn't a big guy, barely weighed over one-sixty. But how many wife beaters had he arrested in his career who were small and wiry but wielded a large punch? How many women had ended their misery with a gun?

"You have a lot of patience, I have to give you that, Tony. Why now? You killed Gina over twenty-five years ago. Why board up the fourth floor? If her body was found earlier, she could have definitely been tied to me since I was the last person she was with."

"What was the fun in that? You were nothing but a lowly cop back then. I wanted you to fall farther than that and I had a lot of time in and out of prison to do my planning. Here you were running for mayor, of all things. I lost Gina, you're losing your wife. I lost my fortune and my future. You're losing your job, your credibility, your respect. God, how delectable. But I found out something interesting after my mother died." He tapped his head with the tip of the Glock.

"Careful, that gun might go off."

Tony smiled, but it wasn't a friendly smile. It didn't reach his eyes. He pulled the gun from his head and pointed it at Murphy. "Don't you want to know what I found out? What brought me to town? I knew that once Gina's body was discovered and identified, it would bring someone else to your little town."

Murphy wasn't getting it. What the hell was Tony up to? What kind of game was he playing? If only he could distract this guy, he might be able to get to his Ruger. But he needed him alive. Murphy's eyes crawled around the room, looking for something to throw at the idiot.

"What? No guesses?" Tony taunted.

"Not a clue."

Tony laughed, a maniacal laugh of someone slowly losing touch with reality. "Why, I'm waiting for your bastard son."

What?

"I thought that might shock you. Didn't know he was still alive, did you?"

"You're lying."

"My mom kept letters Aunt Sonya wrote. They included pictures of the little bastard as he was growing up. The letters were postmarked from all over the country so no one could trace them back to wherever the hell Sonya was living. But Sonya came into your town alone, maybe to throw me off again. I thought she would feel safe knowing that I was buried in a grave on your property in Wisconsin. But your bastard son must be a chip off the old block."

Murphy said nothing.

"Seems I left you speechless."

Could it be? Why wouldn't Sonya have said anything? Why wouldn't Sam have whipped up some kind of karma knowledge with all of her supposed talents?

"Must have really pissed you off knowing that Gina and I produced a son out of the love we had for each other."

"SHE DID NOT LOVE YOU!"

Now it was Murphy's turn to smile. If he agitated him enough, Tony just might come within arm's reach. "You know the day the bank robbery was to go down, Gina insisted I go back to work. She knew what was going to take place and she wanted to stop it." His wrist brushed the pocket of his trench coat. The tape recorder was still there. Tony didn't do a very good search job. He had only looked for guns.

"SHUT UP!" Tony started pacing in a circle, hands over his ears, the Glock pointed at the ceiling.

Murphy clasped his hands on the edge of the coffee table, ready to launch himself at the idiot. How much of a loose cannon was Tony and exactly how far could he push him? "So your parents must have left you with the family fortune when they died."

Tony stopped pacing. "Fat chance. Dad died before Mom. Besides the bundle given to Aunt Sonya to raise your bastard son, Mom donated the rest to the church. Nothing for me. Do you believe it? All because Aunt Sonya poisoned their minds."

"With Perez dead and Donovan in prison, you had all that money to yourself."

"That meager amount when I could have had a hell of a lot more? Donovan wanted his share when he got out of prison but it was gone."

So that was how he lured Donovan to the cabin. "If you were the black sheep of the family, how did you find out what was in her will?" Murphy slowly moved his feet closer to the table so they were in a better position.

"I still have one or two people who will do my bidding."

"Don't know about that. I'd watch my back if I were you."

Tony laughed and it was at that moment Murphy knew whomever helped Tony in his deception was probably no longer breathing. He was so pleased with himself, Tony was doing a happy dance and it was on his third turn that Murphy charged him. Their bodies collided sending both of them crashing against the counter. Murphy lunged for his Ruger while trying to hold back Tony's gun hand. The Glock went off and Murphy felt a hot blast tear through his chest.

Two seconds later he was staring at the ceiling with Tony standing over him. He did a quick assessment of his injury. The bullet didn't enter the heart, nor the lung. He could still breathe. The injury was lower but not the abdomen. *Shit. Did this crazy ass just blow a hole in my liver?* A tune started playing in his head. Where was it coming from? It was coming from his phone.

"Whatcha got there, Chief?" Tony ripped the side of the coat back and found the cell phone. "Saint Peter must be calling." He read the monitor. "Well, well. Let's see who's sending you a text message. That gorgeous P.I. who has been a royal pain in my ass. Why don't we invite her to the party?"

Murphy dug his nails into Tony's calf but his energy was fading fast. How did things get out of hand so quickly? Tony started to walk away.

Murphy gathered up what energy he could and lunged and Tony. A loud blast exploded from the Glock and Murphy felt another hot searing pain in his chest. This time he knew the bullet did major damage.

46

Sam parked her Jeep behind Murphy's car. She had tried calling Murphy after his text message but he didn't answer. Maybe it was hard to get reception inside the hotel. The back door was unlocked. Lights were on in the hotel but she didn't see Murphy in the lobby. Maybe he found a clue on the fourth floor that the techs missed. On the drive over she had tried to formulate a speech in her head, a gentle way to tell Dennis his son was still alive.

Sam made her way up the staircase to the third floor. Although she wasn't in any rush, there was a certain urgency in the air that propelled her down the hallway to the stairs leading to the fourth floor. Her heartbeat thudded in her ears and a silent voice whispered for her to be careful.

"Murphy?" Sam called out. Why didn't he wait in the lobby and why wasn't he answering now? She dismissed her apprehension as a case of watching too many horror movies. What female in her right mind would enter an abandoned hotel on her own? That was horror movie rule number one. "Murphy? Are you up here?"

The door to the apartment was slightly ajar. Sam reached for her Taurus in the holster on her left, then used it to push open the door. Murphy was lying on the floor, face down, blood pooling around him. Horror movie rule number two: Never enter a room without looking behind the door.

"Murphy!" Sam ran to his side but not before someone shoved her hard. Her gun dropped from her hand as she tried to brace her fall. The side of the coffee table popped into view, but too late. Her head smacked into it with a dull crack and she saw the floor rise up to connect with her head. She tried to close her eyes to stop the room from moving out of focus but her eyelids refused to budge. Feet came into view, shoes a high gloss black, and they made a clicking noise as the man walked across the floor. Who wore cleats on their shoes anymore? Didn't that go out with the demise of *Happy Days*? The room slowly stopped spinning and something else came into view...a wig. It was gray and lying next to several gray tufts that might have been pieces of a beard. Where had she seen someone with long gray hair before? But she didn't remember the person also having a beard.

The shoes moved away and she heard the door close. If Sam thought her eyelids were stubborn, her feet and arms were pure cement. There was a smell permeating the air, subtle at first, then thick.

The man must have returned because she heard a voice above a loud whoosh. "You have to get up." It was a woman's voice, not a man's. Sam's eyelids slowly blinked. It was like seeing through gauze or was it smoke? "Get up," the woman tried again. "He's burning the hotel down."

Fire? Sam got her left elbow under her and pushed herself up. Now she could see there was someone else in the room. But why was it Sam could see through her?

"Here." The woman removed a large painting from the wall. "It's a dumb waiter."

Sam forced her legs to move as flames snaked out from under the door. She got her arm around Murphy's neck and pulled him to a sitting position. "Murphy, you're too heavy. I can't lift you by myself." The smoke was getting thicker as Sam started gasping and coughing.

"Let me help." The woman grabbed Murphy's other arm. Sam struggled to her feet and between the two of them they were able to get Murphy to a somewhat standing position and drag him to the dumb waiter. Sam wiped at something running down her face. She looked at her hand. It was covered with blood.

Flames shot out from under the door and licked up the walls. "Hurry." Sam was glad the dumb waiter was waist high. They were able to sit Murphy on the edge and roll him into the large space. Sam climbed in after and saw the woman reach for the locket Sam wore around her neck. The woman held it up but still her image was opaque. Sam could literally see through her.

"Gina?" Sam asked. But the image faded. Sam watched the door slide shut and swallow them into darkness. As she lost consciousness she felt for her medicine bundle under her shirt and wrapped her hand around it.

* * *

Flames shot out of the windows on all three floors. The roof and whatever was left of the fourth floor was shrouded in flames and dark smoke. Jake leaped from the car before Frank put it in park.

"JAKE, HOLD UP," Frank yelled. They had received a text message from Sam that she was meeting Murphy at the hotel. But when the call came in about a fire at the hotel, Jake's calm, cool facade broke down.

"Whoa, hold it." A fireman in enough gear to resemble the Michelin Man held up his hands. "You can't go in there."

"My wife is in there," Jake shouted.

The fireman, who's badge identified him as Fire Chief Legno, pointed a finger at Frank. "Get control of your friend." Jake and Frank both showed their shields. "Sorry, that doesn't help here. This building might collapse."

"There's a door on the garden side. If you have some heavy equipment you can break it down. It leads to the basement. It looks like the fire started on the top floors," Jake said. "It hasn't reached the basement yet."

"Didn't you hear what I said? The building might collapse." Legno motioned like a traffic cop, directing men and hoses to different sides of the building.

Jake noticed a four-by-four parked at the curb with a brace bar in the front. He also saw that the side gate into the gardens was open. Landscaping trucks used it in the past to gain access into the gardens. "Whose truck is that?" Jake asked.

"Mine. Why?" Legno asked.

"Are the keys in it?"

"Yes." When Jake ran toward the truck, Legno yelled, "HEY! What are you doing?"

Frank ran after Jake. "You aren't going to do what I think, are you?"

Jake slammed the door and burned rubber as he steered the truck down the parking lot and around to the back where the gate was open. There was a straight shot up to the old service door. He just hoped he could get up enough speed to break down the wall.

The truck crashed into the door popping it off of its rusted hinges. He shielded his face as the air bag deployed. Clusters of firemen came running with hoses and pick axes as Jake backed the four-by-four out of the way. He clamored out of the truck as firemen rushed to the opening. The fire chief, beet red, was kicking at the dirt as he looked at the front end of his brand new truck.

Frank held onto Jake's arm. "Just wait. Let them do their job." It took all of five minutes before the call came for two stretchers. Jake sat on the crumpled crash bar, arms wrapped tightly across his chest. He rose from the bumper as the first stretcher emerged. It was Murphy.

"We need flashers on this one," a fireman yelled. "Looks like two bullet wounds."

"That's our chief of police," Frank said.

"We found them in the dumb waiter in the basement," the fireman said.

The second stretcher appeared. For all of his panic, Jake stayed rooted in the same spot. Sam was covered in blood, her clothes, her face. It was hard to tell if it was Murphy's blood or hers.

"Looks like a wound to the head. Both have severe smoke inhalation," one fireman reported. "Neither is conscious."

Jake preferred not to ride in the ambulance. He didn't want to get in the way of the EMTs.

"You don't think Sam shot him, do you?" Frank said, although he couldn't keep the chuckle from erupting. "Sorry. He does have a knack for pissing her off."

"No. I think someone lured Murphy here. No, not someone," Jake corrected himself. "Barlucci. Murphy was probably at the hotel when Sam called him and was forced not to reveal he wasn't alone. Sam was getting a little too close to the truth and Barlucci figured he'd kill two birds with one stone."

"So in case the bullets didn't work, Barlucci set the hotel on fire with them in it. That is one vengeful dude."

Jake pulled out his phone.

"Are you calling Robinson?"

"Yeah. He should hear it from us first rather than the fire chief."

A fireman ran out of the back door and yelled toward the garden. "Got another one, but no need to rush."

* * *

Robinson lumbered into the waiting room on the second floor of the new wing. "I think they should name this wing after our department, we spend so much time here. How are they doing?" He hefted his bulk into an upholstered bench seat and accepted the can of soda from Frank.

Jake said, "Murphy is still in surgery. Sam is resting comfortably but she is still unconscious. They have her on oxygen and are just waiting for a room to open up."

"Did you get an earful from the fire chief?" Frank asked. "We kind of..."

"Acted without thinking?" Robinson leaned against the wall, his gaze crawling over the top-of-the-line decor. "I would have done the same if I knew my wife was in there. Looks like Barlucci did himself in. Either that or the idiot got so much gasoline on himself, he accidentally lit himself up like a torch."

Jake placed a tape recorder and a ring on the table in front of him. "These were found on Murphy. He must have known he was going to meet Barlucci and wired up. I'd place money on Barlucci planting Murphy's class ring on him so as to further implicate him in those two murders."

"Sounds about right." Robinson picked up the tape recorder, rubbing his fingers together to erase the soot. "We'll have to see if forensics can salvage anything."

Jake checked his watch, something he had been doing every ten minutes. Why wasn't a nurse or doctor coming out to update him on Sam's condition? What concerned him most was that she might revert back to a catatonic state, like she did twice before. He didn't know if he could handle it. How many catatonic states does someone have to go through until their body no longer wants to recover?

"Jake?" Frank nudged him. A surgeon was approaching, his grim face not very reassuring. He took a seat near Robinson. He was in green surgical scrubs, a mask hanging below his chin.

"I'm Doctor Browne," he started as he reached out and shook each of their hands. "Chief Murphy is out of surgery but in critical condition. We had to remove the spleen and it was touch-and-go with his right lung. He's lucky the bullet hit low near the armpit. I only had to remove the bottom lobe. He's lost a lot of blood but he's stable for now." He handed Robinson a zip lock bag. "Those are the two bullets. I'll get my written report to you later today."

"Can we speak to him?" Robinson asked.

"He's still in recovery and still unconscious. Once I'm confident he's holding his own, he'll be moved to ICU. I can have a nurse call you when he does wake up."

"What about my wife?" Jake asked. "They were waiting for a room to open up."

"I'll send a nurse out here to update you." With that Doctor Browne patted Robinson's shoulder and left.

"Looks like we need to call out the troops to donate some blood. I'll call the departments and sound the alarm." Robinson hefted his body up. "Hope they have snacks after giving blood."

"What about Murphy's wife?" Jake asked.

"Already called her the minute I heard. She was going to call their daughter in Europe. Donna will head to the hospital. I told her I'd have a car pick up her daughter if she plans to fly in." He motioned for his detectives to follow. "Come on. Let's go bleed for the chief. It will keep our minds off of things."

<h1 style="text-align:center">47</h1>

Sam's eyelids felt glued shut. She wanted to take a deep breath but was afraid she'd unleash a spastic coughing session. What time was it? It looked like daylight streaming through the edges of the closed blinds. How long was she out? Her mind rewound the events at the hotel. Murphy. Where was he and was he still alive? And how had they gotten out? Where did the dumb waiter stop? In the first floor kitchen or the basement storage area?

She saw a figure lying on the cushioned bench under the windows. Jake. Had he slept here all night? She opened her mouth to speak but all that would come out was a raspy "Hey."

Jake woke with a start and sat up. "How are you feeling?" He stood and opened the blinds, letting in a stream of morning light. He pulled a chair over and sat down.

"I feel like I swallowed a carton of cigarettes." It hurt to talk and all she could blurt out next was, "Water."

Jake filled a glass with water and held the straw to her lips. "Not too fast." He set the glass on the serving table, then shoved it out of the way.

"How long have I been here?"

"Almost twenty-four hours."

A large vase of flowers came into focus. She knew Jake wasn't a flower guy but whoever sent them had good taste.

"Jackie dropped those off," Jake explained. "She didn't want to wake you."

"They are beautiful." She could almost detect the floral aroma through her smoke singed nose. "Murphy?"

"Still in ICU. They had to remove his spleen and a bullet almost took out a lung. He's still in critical condition." He brought out a pad of paper and pen. "We think Barlucci got caught in his own fire. Benny is doing the autopsy now. Want to tell me what happened?"

Sam studied her husband. He was surprisingly calm and all businesslike. "Is this the cop asking or the husband?"

"Cop. If I played husband I'd probably throw you over my knee. You keep treating that medicine bundle of yours as though it were a protective amulet. You aren't bulletproof, Sam, and you keep putting yourself in danger."

Sam didn't expect him to understand so she ignored the impending argument for now. It was slow going but Sam relayed everything that had happened since she received Murphy's text message to meet him at the hotel.

"Can you describe Barlucci? Anything different from the prison photos we have?"

Sam thought about that for a second. Then she remembered. "The vet. Remember the vet who sat next to me at Izzy's right after Gina's body was found?"

"Yeah, the guy who claimed to be hard of hearing yet seemed to be eavesdropping?"

"I didn't see his face at the hotel but I did see a wig on the floor."

"So he might have been staying at the shelter while he was in town. Makes sense. Now we know how he met Eleanor." Jake shoved the pad and pen back in his pocket, then sat on the bed and gathered Sam in his arms. He took a whiff of her hair. "You smell like you spent a weekend in a Shanghai smoking den."

"I need to take a shower and wash my hair."

"I brought you a change of clothes and all of your toiletries."

A nurse filled the doorway. She was all one size from her shoulders to the floor, a black woman who could play linebacker for the Chicago Bears. "I trust you have a good reason to sit on that bed."

"She was feeling dizzy."

"Uh huh. In a prone position she was feeling dizzy." She walked over, grabbed Sam's wrist and held it while staring at her watch. Next she popped a thermometer into Sam's mouth. "My name is Gladys as you can see written on the board over your head. Lily is the night nurse so between the two of us we are going to take real good care of you. Your vitals are right where we want them to be."

"Does that mean I can go home?"

"Did you hear me say that?"

"Can I at least take a shower? I need to wash my hair."

Gladys jammed her fists onto beefy hips. "Unfortunately, I have fifteen more patients to look in on so I can't let you shower on your own."

"I'll help her," Jake said.

One penciled eyebrow jutted up. "Oh, really? And I suppose you plan to crawl into that shower with her?"

"Have to keep her from falling over, right?" One corner of Jake's mouth quivered as he refrained from smiling.

"Twenty minutes. I don't want any hanky-panky going on in that bathroom. You hear?"

"Yes, ma'am," Sam replied as they watched Gladys leave.

* * *

Frank found Sonya in the waiting room at the hospital. She stood as he approached. "I'm so sorry to hear about Sam and Chief Murphy. Is it true that Tony was to blame?"

"I'm afraid so."

She twisted her fingers around a hankie. "This is such a nightmare. I'm so glad it's over with."

Frank motioned for her to sit as he took a seat next to her. "Gina's body is being released so our medical examiner needs to know if plans have been made."

"Reverend Tom," she started, then shook her head, still not used to referring to him as a reverend. "Tom has the details as to where she is supposed to be buried and he was to make plans to have her remains flown back to New Jersey. I believe Vera made him the executor of her will since Gus preceded her in death."

Frank thought about that for a minute. "So Tom would have known about Vera's safety deposit box."

"Probably." Sonya started to understand what Frank was getting to. "You think Tom already knew that Gina's son didn't die?" She thought about that for several more seconds. "That would explain why he seemed to be grilling me while he was here."

"I'll send a squad car over to the hotel to check on him."

* * *

Sam felt half human again. She was able to get out of the drab hospital gown and into the flannel lounge suit Jake had brought. As she tied her shoes she wondered what *Nurse Ratchet* would think of her roaming the halls to find Rafe's room. The nurse at the desk had given Jake the items she had on her when she was brought in. Jake had set her medicine bundle and Gina's locket on the side table. Surprisingly, neither had suffered any damage from the smoke and fire. She slipped her medicine bundle over her head. As she opened the locket, she remembered the woman she had seen on the fourth floor, the one who had shown her where the dumb waiter was and had helped her get Murphy to safety. Had she dreamed it all? With a sigh, which brought on a brief coughing spell, Sam shoved the locket into her pocket and left the room.

Rafe's room was down the hall, around the bank of elevators, and down another hall to a side wing. She stopped at the nurse's station and caught the attention of Ellie, Rafe's nurse. "Is it okay for Rafe Bennett to have visitors?"

"He's actually up and around. Here." She went back to her desk and pulled a small brown envelope from the drawer. "He might want to have this back."

Sam opened the envelope and spilled a chain and medal into her hand.

Ellie smiled. "It's Raphael, the Patron Saint of Healing. Raphael was one of my mom's favorite too." With that she clutched her mound of folders and skirted past Sam.

Raphael, the Patron Saint of Healing. Puzzle pieces started dropping into place. Sam had to steady herself before walking into Rafe's room. Seeing Sonya at his bedside now made sense. Rafe was sitting up, dressed in a Tampa Bay Buccaneers jersey and sweat pants. His head was still swathed in bandages.

"Hey, Sam. I'm glad to see you're doing better."

"You gave us a scare for a while," Sonya added.

"Chief Murphy isn't doing so well, though. Jake is visiting him in ICU."

"Sonya was telling me that Tony was behind all of this."

Sam didn't know why she couldn't see the signs earlier. She wondered if she should mention that she saw Gina but decided against it. Few people believed her in her sanest of days. She handed the envelope to Rafe. "The nurse asked me to give this to you."

Rafe emptied the envelope into his hand. "My medal. Thanks."

Sam retrieved Gina's locket from her pocket. "I think you should have this, too. Your mom would have wanted you to."

Sonya gasped. "You know?"

"Have you told anyone else?" Rafe asked.

"No, but I have a feeling Tony found out. Jake feels he was hoping the discovery of Gina's body would bring both Sonya and you into town. I don't know how he found out that Rafe was still alive."

"Tom," Sonya replied. "He had Vera's power of attorney and had access to her safety deposit box. Sergeant Mitchell thought Vera might have kept the letters and pictures I had sent her. I'm sorry I lied to your husband about everything. We have kept Rafe's existence a secret for so long, I couldn't take the chance. I never put in writing to Vera that I had changed little Anthony's name to Raphael Bennett. Gus and Vera were careful when they visited. They'd fly into towns in neighboring states, rent a car and drive to Phoenix. When we moved to Tampa after

Gus died, Vera would come to visit on her own." She reached over and patted Rafe's hand. "When Gus and Vera realized Tony probably killed Gina, they lied and told Tony that the boy had died. They had a private ceremony in a closed casket. The funeral director was a close friend of the family. I left with Rafe the night before the funeral. Drove all the way to Arizona."

"You didn't use Rafe's real name at the Mayo Clinic?"

"I convinced the administrators that, for his safety, I had to use John Doe. Afterward, yes, I thought Raphael was a perfect name."

"Well, Tony won't be able to hurt anyone any more," Sam said. She sat on the edge of Rafe's bed. The strong jaw bone and the clinical way he examined things, Sam should have seen Murphy in Rafe the first day she met him. "Everything makes more sense now. I knew there had to be some underlying reason motivating you to be so passionate about finding missing people. In this case, it was your mother."

* * *

Jake left the ICU and spoke briefly with the cop on guard. He gave him his cell phone number and told him to call if there was any change in the chief's condition. Just as he headed for the stairs, his phone rang. It was Andy Brainard.

"Jake, we're at Reverend Tom's hotel. Tom isn't anywhere around. He hasn't checked out but it looks like there was a struggle here."

* * *

Rafe grabbed the pitcher on the side table, tried pouring but the pitcher was empty. "I'll fill it," Sam said. A clicking sound could be heard in the distance, growing closer. It was a steady sound and one that started to jog her memory. Where had she heard it before? As she stepped into the bathroom, she stayed half hidden behind the bathroom door and watched as a priest walked slowly down the hall. His steps hesitated briefly as he looked into Rafe's room. Sam's gaze dropped to his shoes—shiny patent leather loafers. The clicking sound was made by cleats. Her mind drifted back to the hotel when she was lying on the floor and a man was standing over her. But Tony was dead, caught in his own fire.

She was getting paranoid, had to be. She filled the pitcher, turned off the water, then used a towel to wipe the outside of the pitcher. Her thoughts returned to the face of the priest. He didn't look familiar but it was those damn shoes nudging her memory and her suspicions. If only she had her phone on her she could call Jake. What if she were wrong? Images of Jake kneeling into the back of an innocent, prone priest, sent waves of regret through her. She had been so engrossed in her thoughts that she almost missed the distant clicking of the shoes growing louder, until she heard the door to Rafe's room close and Sonya gasp.

* * *

Jake checked the screen on his phone. "Yeah, Benny."

"Little puzzle here, Jake. This third body pulled from the hotel has a bullet in his head. And he also does not, I repeat, does NOT have a tattoo on his forearm."

Jake waved at Frank who was standing by the nurses station. He no sooner finished telling him about Benny's call when his phone rang again. It was Paul Goddard calling from Phoenix.

"I tried Sam's phone but she isn't answering. I have a name for that boy who was brought to the Mayo Clinic by Sonya Lucci."

* * *

Sam turned the light off in the bathroom and quietly set the pitcher down on the sink. She opened the door a crack and peered out. The priest was standing at the foot of the bed, a gun pointed at Rafe. And here she was unarmed. *Shit! So who was burned in the hotel?*

"Well, Aunt Sonya. Who have we got here?" the priest said. "I bet this is Gina's bastard son," he snarled. "You know how long I've been waiting for this?"

"They said you died." Sonya quickly moved to Rafe's side, sitting on the bed to protect him. But it was Rafe who sat up and placed an arm across Sonya to protect her. Sam knew, in her condition, there wasn't anyway she could attempt to overtake Tony. Her legs were already rubbery from standing on them too long.

Sam exited the bathroom. "Tony Barlucci, I presume. You sure look different from the vet who sat next to me at the bar."

"Damn, don't people in this town ever die?"

"I don't know about that. You obviously didn't die in the fire. So who took your place?" Sam asked. Tony might have been attractive in his youth but there was nothing appealing about him now. His hair was threaded with silver and thinning at the top. Scars mottled what might have once been a flawless face. The black suit was probably hiding a paunch that had been growing over the years. Something he couldn't disguise were the dark, killer eyes. "Someone must have been keeping you in the loop over the years. My guess is it was your cousin, Tom. It looks like you are wearing his clothes. Is it his body in the hotel?"

"What?" Sonya gasped. "You killed Tom?"

Tony waved Sam over with his gun. "He was gutless. He was good for supplying me with cash but nothing more. Now go join them."

"I like it right here." Sam would rather his attention be divided than have all three targets clustered on the bed. "Besides, one shot and this room will be filled with people. You'll have nowhere to go."

"Still the same Tony," Rafe said. "What little I remember of you was never good. I was too sick and too young to stop you from hurting my mom."

"You were a weak, snarling little runt. Should have known you weren't related to me."

"I'm definitely more like my father. I even became a cop."

This shocked Tony. Sam could see the rage building in him, but Rafe didn't let up.

"When you weren't around, Mom would talk about my father, how he was the love of her life. And it certainly wasn't you."

"SHUT UP!" Tony waved the gun around, not sure which person to target.

"She said she never loved anyone more." Rafe smiled and held up her locket. "Bet you didn't know this opened. It was a gift from Murphy and she never took it off." Rafe opened the locket and held it up. "You probably didn't know it contained a picture of them."

"Give it to me," Tony demanded.

"You come and get it."

The door to the room burst open. Sam turned toward the door which was a huge mistake. Tony took a step forward, wrapped an arm around her neck, and dragged her closer to the bed. She felt the gun pressed to her temple.

"Let her go," Jake said.

"Don't think so. I didn't come this far and wait this long not to see Murphy and his bastard son die. Now back away from the door."

"Sweetheart, if you have a shot, take it," Sam said. "Just make sure everything sprays toward the wall. It's hard to wash brain matter out of this fabric." She could see Jake's eyes assessing Tony's exposed body parts. Somewhere in his glare was one meant for her to shut the hell up. There was a staring contest going on bringing with it a silence that was deafening. She could feel Tony repositioning his body parts so they weren't exposed. He had moved his gun hand so the gun was pointed at the back of her head. The silence was soon broken by a sound that couldn't have been any louder if a bomb had gone off in the room. It was the click of a hammer being pulled back.

Both she and Tony slowly turned their heads toward the bed where Rafe was aiming a gun with a cop's steady eye and hand. That was all the diversion Jake needed. She felt the heat from the bullet as it past her head. The first shot sent her diving for the floor. The second shot brought the sound of someone hitting the wall and a woman's scream. She wasn't sure who did the shooting. When she opened her eyes, Jake was kicking the gun away from Tony's body. Rafe was shielding his aunt.

Jake knelt beside her. "You okay?"

"Sure. Would love to go back to bed, though."

"Stick that gun back under your pillow," Jake told Rafe. "As far as I'm concerned, I never saw it."

48

Sam didn't like having to spend another night in the hospital. Jake had wanted to spend the night by her side but she knew he would be beat after filling out all the reports so after his final visit last night to check on Murphy, she shooed Jake, Frank, and Robinson out to dinner and Jake to his own bed.

She pushed her breakfast tray away, took a quick shower, dressed in jeans and a sweater, and waited for the nurse to tell her she could go home. At ten o'clock she had a surprise visitor. Rafe rapped softly on her door. He was decked out in corduroys, a blue turtleneck, and a sportscoat.

"It's amazing," Sam said. "You have your father's dress code, even though you don't know him."

"Sonya and I are going back to Florida today."

Sam didn't hide her disappointment. "You don't want to wait to talk to your father when he wakes up?"

"I don't think I'm ready for that."

Rafe reached into the inside pocket of his sportscoat and handed her an envelope. "Would you give this to him?"

Sam reluctantly took the envelope, then wrapped him in a hug. "You know, Murphy always wanted a son. He will be very proud of the work you do." She released her hold on him.

"If you ever want to change your line of work, I think you and I could really make a good team...work-wise. With your talents and my relentless searching, we could solve a lot of missing person cases."

"Thanks for the offer, but I'm pretty well rooted in Chasen Heights."

Rafe grimaced. "He's standing behind me, isn't he?"

Jake slapped a hand on Rafe's shoulder. "Sorry you are leaving so soon, Rafe."

"This has all been too much stress on my aunt. I want to get her home and back in familiar surroundings."

Minutes after Rafe left, Frank and Robinson joined them in Sam's room. "Murphy's awake and the critical condition has been raised to stable condition. They are moving him to a room later this morning," Robinson reported.

"That's good." Sam fingered the envelope Rafe had left with her.

Robinson lowered his bulk onto one of the chairs. "Got a few details I need cleared up, at least for my own satisfaction."

Frank pulled a chair up while Sam took a seat on the bench where Jake had spent a previous night. Jake preferred to stand, hands jammed in his pockets. She suddenly felt like she was at an inquisition.

"I'm curious how you knew there was a dumb waiter. The crime scene report doesn't mention it, crime scene photos don't show it."

Sam looked at each of their faces. "Why is this coming up now?"

Jake finally took a seat next to Sam and rested his elbows on his knees. "Murphy had a tape recorder on him. It wasn't damaged by the fire and he was able to get Tony to practically admit to everything."

"It's a voice activated tape recorder, Sam," Robinson continued. "It has you talking to someone but there aren't any other voices on the recorder."

Sam reluctantly told them about Gina being in the apartment, removing the large picture from the wall which revealed the dumb waiter. "Murphy was practically dead weight. It was impossible for me to lift him from the floor on my own."

"Adrenaline," Frank said, almost hopefully. "People can lift cars off of loved ones. That had to be it. Plus Murphy used to live there so he knew the dumb waiter was there."

"But Murphy was unconscious," Sam said. "I don't remember much after climbing into the dumb waiter and I didn't wake up until I was in the hospital."

"Won't that tape have to be submitted as evidence?" Frank asked.

Robinson nodded but a slight smile turned up the corners of his mouth. "Strange thing is, I was listening to the tape at home and somehow I accidentally hit the record button right before Sam started talking. Think I was wadding up some aluminum foil at the time so all you hear is static."

Sam was surprised Jake didn't voice any reservations about tampering with evidence. There was hope for him yet.

Nurse Gladys walked in. "Okay, you can get your skinny butt out of here."

Once Nurse Gladys left, Robinson said, "We'll keep this between us, okay?"

* * *

Five days later Sam walked into Murphy's hospital room to find him sitting on the bed playing chess with his uncle, John Kendall.

"Well, well. You do have the most gorgeous visitors," John said. "First your wife, then your daughter. Now Sam."

"Chief, you look like you have a little more color and your wife has forgiven you. Things are looking up."

Murphy gave a shrug which made him grimace and touch the bandage on his chest. "I made the front page, been exonerated, press is parked in my front yard. Donna is in her glory."

John picked up a chess piece and pointed it at Murphy. "You married yourself in a skirt. She's a perfect match." He set the chess piece down and announced, "Checkmate."

Sam bent over his wheelchair and gave him a kiss on the forehead. "I hope you didn't bring your flask with you, John."

"Nah. My nephew is too damn straight-laced. Wouldn't let me spike his orange juice."

Sam reached into her purse and handed Murphy the envelope. Robinson had already informed Murphy of Rafe's true identity. "Your son asked me to give this to you."

Murphy looked at it as though he were staring down the barrel of a gun. He hesitated before taking it from her and spent a full minute just holding it.

"Well, aren't you going to read it?" John asked. A bag of malt balls was on the table next to the chessboard. Jake had been the one to call John after Murphy was brought to the hospital.

How like Murphy to practically have the contents of his desk delivered to the hospital. He reached into a drawer, pulled out a pearl handled letter opener, then carefully ran it under the flap. He pulled out two pieces of typed paper, unfolded them and quickly skimmed through the words.

"Well?" John prodded.

"Maybe it's personal," Sam suggested.

John waved that off as though nothing was personal between uncle and nephew.

Murphy smiled briefly and folded the letter. "I'll read it later. Basically he said I know where to find him."

"Sounds like a road trip to Tampa, me and Dennis," John said with much enthusiasm.

Sam watched as Murphy continued staring at the folded paper. "John, I bet you haven't eaten. Would you like to join me in the cafeteria?"

"Can we order orange juice?"

Sam laughed. "You may but it's a little too early for me."

She wheeled John out of the room. As they reached the hallway, Sam looked over her shoulder to see Murphy unfolding the letter.

From the Author

I grew up in the Calumet City, Illinois area. As a child I sat and listened to stories my elders would share about the colorful Sin Strip days. But at my young age it was impossible to separate fact from fiction. I used the history of that era as the back drop for this book. It gave me a basis for the plot where I used creative freedom to fictionalize the events and characters.

There were a number of people who assisted me in the completion of this book. Since I'm always afraid of forgetting someone, I want to do one collective thank you to all of them. There is one person, however, whom I forgot in two previous books and I had to rely on him again for *What Lies Within*. Doctor David Hunt of the Department of Anthropology at the Smithsonian National Museum of Natural History corrected and clarified all of my forensic questions and concerns. My heartfelt thanks to him.

www.ingramcontent.com/pod-product-compliance
Lightning Source LLC
Chambersburg PA
CBHW032023120726
47898CB00002BB/606